The Architect of Auschwitz

A novel by S.J. Tagliareni

BookLocker
Trenton, Georgia

Copyright © 2021 S.J. Tagliareni

Print ISBN: 978-1-64719-849-7
Ebook ISBN: 978-1-64719-850-3

All rights reserved. No part of this publication may be reproduced, stored in a retrieval system, or transmitted in any form or by any means, electronic, mechanical, recording or otherwise, without the prior written permission of the author.

Published by BookLocker.com, Inc., Trenton, Georgia.

Printed on acid-free paper.

The characters and events in this book are fictitious. Any similarity to real persons, living or dead, is coincidental and not intended by the author.

BookLocker.com, Inc.
2021

First Edition

Library of Congress Cataloguing in Publication Data
Tagliareni, S.J.
The Architect of Auschwitz by S.J. Tagliareni
Library of Congress Control Number: 2021919338

A Dedication

To Viktor and all the survivors who shared their memories with me.

Acknowledgements

Long before the book remotely resembled a novel members of my writing group offered impactful suggestions and insights. They provided encouragement which allowed me to continue the research and write the multiple versions of the book. Ellen Kaplan's insights and Perry Colmore's deft editing suggestions enabled the work to be more focused and readable. Their belief in me and the reason for the work were pillars that kept me energized. I must also say thanks to Sam Catlin for his guidance regarding character development suggestions required to help the reader see the progression of Gerhardt Stark's commitment to the horrors of the Nazis goals.

I am grateful to Viktor Frankl whose presence in my heart and mind has been a constant since the first moment I met him. I wish to also thank my family and friends who consistently support and lovingly encourage my work. Above all, I am most grateful to Elaine my greatest fan as well as my outstanding life coach.

The Architect of Auschwitz

Chapter 1

Early October 1916, Berlin

    The sky was black, gloomy and quite chilly as the north wind blew the "Wir haben Gott bei uns" (We have God with us) banner violently against the façade of the Lehrer station. The Victorian Gothic style railroad station was an imposing wonder supported by a plethora of Doric marble columns and ornamental plastered vaulted ceilings. The ornate building appeared to be more castle than railroad hub. On an ordinary early autumn morning the station would be the site of German citizens and tourists making their way to multiple cities within Germany and Europe. However, it was filled this morning with a massive crowd of military personnel and family members. The occupants and well-wishers were not ordinary citizens. Today was the demarcation of thousands of German troops on their way to the trenches in France. The sounds of the brassy military band reverberated against the steel beams as the notes rose to the heights of the vaulted ceilings. Relatives and soldiers were jammed together like mussels on stone searching for individual platforms. As they jostled and made their way, they removed their hats and joined a choir singing
    Heil dir in Siegenkranz, the unofficial German national anthem.
    The morning had the aura of Oktoberfest without the free-flowing beer and traditional peasant food. The reality of the horrors of war was not even remotely present to this vibrant assembly of warriors. Many of these young men perceived that they were leaving routine jobs to be part of a marvelous adventure. The idea of being killed or maimed had been pushed back to the recesses of their minds. Somehow, they entertained the belief that these tragedies only happened to the other

side. Their fervor for being part of the cause was kindled by the jingoistic speeches of politicians. The soldiers believed they were privileged to wear their uniforms and fight for the Fatherland. Those who would sleep in warm beds tonight had assured them that the war would last but a few months. Politicians promised they would be home by spring bathed in victorious glory.

Captain Wilhelm Stark entered the station through a side door with his wife and 8-year-old son Gerhardt. Captain Stark was a graduate of the prestigious Prussian Military Academy. However, unlike his father and grandfather, he had chosen architecture over the military. At 35 he was one of the most prominent architects in Germany. Tall, with angular features and blond hair streaked with tinsels of grey, he exuded strength and confidence. He was as patriotic as anyone else in this gathering but he did not desire to join this war. Unlike the joyous neophytes shouting their slogans, he understood the consequences that would soon be evident to these soldiers. He understood that weaponry had significantly advanced, canons were larger and there would be flame throwers and gas employed by both sides. He had enormous respect for the German government and did not casually resist the need to defend German soil. However, as an architect he was more disposed to the building of communities and fervently aspired to a united Europe in which countries would live in peace together.

Christina Stark was the eldest daughter of successful industrialist Ludwig Von Furstenberg. A beautiful woman in her late 20s with an infectious personality, she was slender and pale with unblemished milk-white skin and dark chestnut hair. She was stylishly dressed in a tunic-style dress with pleats that allowed graceful movement. Normally gregarious, she was subdued this morning and though trained to be stoic, she was on the verge of tears. Her steel will allowed her to contain her emotions.

Their son, Gerhardt, was a bright, adventurous and clever 8-year-old. Dressed in green lederhosen and a fur cap, he was thrilled by all the hoopla in the station. He had no knowledge of war and was filled with pride at the sight of his father in uniform. The two were bound not merely by blood but also by temperament and interests. Every weekend they spent time building model cities in their basement

In the midst of the thousands of goodbyes a piercing whistle brought the crowd to attention. A sergeant climbed the steps of one of the trains and announced it was time to board in the next five minutes. On hearing the call to leave, Captain Stark opened his duffle bag and withdrew a packet. He knelt in front of Gerhardt and embraced him for what seemed longer than usual. He opened the packet and showed his son new detailed blueprints of an imaginary city. He smiled and said, "Gerhardt this is the most beautiful city that I have created for us. When I return, we will build this together, but while I am gone you can start by yourself." Overwhelmed, Gerhardt thrust himself again into his father's embrace. Captain Stark then kissed his wife and quickly turned toward his destination. He bounded athletically up the three steps and placed his luggage overhead. He secured a seat by the window and waved to his family. He stood smiling as though he did not have a care in the world. As the giant iron engine began to emit massive bolts of steam the train slowly emerged from the station. Gerhardt waved and waved until his father had completely vanished.

Chapter 2

Early November 1916, Perrone, France
The Horrors of Trench warfare

The battle of the Somme had been raging for months when Captain William Stark arrived at the village of Perrone. The town was a strategic high ground and the Germans had thwarted the many attempts of the French and British to capture it and the surrounding area. The conditions in the trenches were light years away from the boisterous celebrations in Berlin that the members of his regiment remembered. The fields surrounding the German trenches were filled with rotting, days-old corpses. The smell of the dead and the overflowing toilets was overpowering. All around were crushed skulls, shattered pelvises and bloody empty eye sockets. These were not merely body parts but the limbs and bodies of friends and comrades. The only consolation of the recent cold and snow was that the stench of the dead, though still pungent, was not as strong had it been warmer. However, daily life was totally depressing. The conditions in the trenches were abysmal. It was impossible to remain warm and dry. Soldiers commonly spent time in the morning prying loose a frozen helmet or leggings from their bodies. The soil inside the trenches was more like a thick slime than mud. Walking, soldiers sank several inches into muck and, owing to suction, it was difficult to withdraw one's feet. Frequently, four or five soldiers had to pull out a soldier who was stuck up to his mid-leg.

In addition to the mud, house flies were a perfect plague. Millions of them swarmed around due to the overflowing latrines. It was difficult to eat. The flies, windblown mud and the constant presence of rats made it difficult to sleep through the night. Complimenting these Kafkaesque issues for soldiers jammed together were infectious diseases such as dysentery and typhoid fever.

The days were a combination of total boredom and terror. Soldiers often spent the afternoon playing cards and writing home fictitious stories about the war. It was rare to be warm or to eat hot food. The destruction of German supply trains meant there was little dry clothing or other adequate supplies. Also devastating was the nightly horror of artillery shelling and constant attempts by the French and British to overtake the German trenches. Trapped in the trenches for long periods of time, under nearly constant bombardment, many soldiers suffered from shell shock.

Captain Stark had lived a privileged life and this military episode felt like sheer madness to him. His patriotism was not blind, and he could not fathom the benefits of this insane venture. Young men on both sides of the barbed wire were fodder for politicians' lust for glory. Of course, politicians, in faraway safe havens, did not live the soldiers' daily nightmares. For politicians, the dead and wounded were merely statistics; sacrifices were necessary to achieve some selfish national gain. Captain Stark would not allow himself to openly state what he felt deeply within his heart, because it would possibly lead to the mutiny of his soldiers. His entire career had been spent developing communities and buildings that would enhance life and now daily he was commanded to kill others. He played the role of confident leader with the rank-and-file but he was not reluctant to share his views with his adjutant. One morning while having a cup of coffee with Lieutenant Boltz he confided, "We will at some point lose this town. We are grossly outnumbered by the French and British and low on supplies. I am sure you know that the morale is close to the breaking point." Initially, Boltz was silent but then asked "May I speak frankly sir?" Captain Stark sighed deeply and said, "First of all drop the sir, my name is Wilhelm"

"Alright I will dispense with your title, Wilhelm. I am tired of the killing and wondering every second whether it will be my last day. No matter how I try I cannot get used to the screams and shattered bodies that are part of each ugly day. I have a wife and two small children. I may never see them again. That thought horrifies me. In addition, the thought of killing others haunts me. I am not a true soldier. There is no way that I was prepared for this; I am a teacher and I was conscripted to this position. Maybe lifelong soldiers get used to the killing but it tears at my conscience. Two days ago, I pierced the stomach of a young French soldier with my bayonet. I will never forget the look in his petrified eyes."

Wilhelm was struck by the innocence and honesty that overflowed from his comrade. "I share your concerns. I am a loyal German officer but I think this war is insane. I read a report yesterday that the French and English dead and wounded are well over 500,000. The general staff freely share those numbers but refuse to give out the numbers of our dead. I have no idea of our number. However, I know that the cost is ghastly on both sides.

Boltz agreed. "But what choice do we have? Chances are high that we will both be killed. However, if we refuse to serve, we will be court-martialed and probably hung. I never share these thoughts with others, but I felt like if I didn't tell you I would explode." Both men continued in silence to drink coffee and ponder the tragedy of their common situation.

The next evening, right after dusk, the nightly barrage of cannon fire began. The ferocity and consistency were more intense than usual.

The thunders of the French guns shattered the ears of the German troops in the trenches. Some of the shells hit trees near the German trenches, the flames gave forth brilliant colors of red and yellow.

Stark walked up and down the trench, encouraging his men to stay calm and prepare themselves to meet the enemy attack when the shelling stopped. He thought about his wife and son for a fleeting moment and wished he was once again back in the warmth of their embrace. The artillery stopped and he could hear sounds of the enemy coming across the fields. He shouted, "Get ready to climb the ladder. When I blow the whistle, we climb out of the trench and counterattack."

Placing the whistle in his mouth, he prayed silently. At that very moment millions of snowflakes were drifting toward the earth in perfect synchronization, the giant flakes gently caressing the earth and lovingly covering the deadly remnants of past encounters. The silence in the trenches was broken only by the beating hearts of those who understood the perils of the next few moments.

The moment came as the sounds of the enemy progressing toward the barbed wire became louder and louder. Captain Stark blew three loud whistles and climbed the ladder, pistol in hand. He raced toward the barbed wire, shouting encouragement to his men. Within minutes he was face-to-face with the enemy climbing over the wire and engaging his men in hand-to-hand combat. He fired point blank into the face of a French soldier but realized his men were being overwhelmed by the sheer number of the French. He paused, and began to shout, "Retreat men, retreat get back to the trenches." A French soldier aimed at him and shot but the bullet just barely grazed his shoulder. He turned and joined his men in retreat when a bullet crashed through his skull. He floated through the air as though he was a gymnast and landed face down in the new snow. Captain Wilhelm Stark was dead.

Chapter 3

November 1916, Munich
An unimaginable loss

Christina hadn't heard from Wilhelm in 10 days. Daily she waited anxiously for one of his letters. Despite Wilhelm's assurances in his letters, she tried to wish away the foreboding thought that he was in constant danger. The late fall had been exceptionally hard and it was almost impossible for her to stop thinking about the peril of the man she so deeply loved. Munich had experienced weeks of freezing rain and snow and she shuddered at the thought that her husband was open daily to terrible weather.

Gerhardt, on the other hand had been encouraged by the few letters that he had received from his father. He especially focused on the parts where his father mentioned the fact that they would build not only the model but the actual city sometime in the future.

This morning, Gerhardt was finishing a model railroad station following the specific directions of his father's blueprints. After sanding the rough edges, he was cutting pieces of balsa wood to begin the process of building the city hall. He gingerly began to glue the front of city hall and smiled because he had accomplished precisely what his father designed. At that very moment, a scream shattered the stillness of the morning, followed by a series of harsh blood curdling sounds that reverberated through the house. Gerhardt was frightened by the sounds and quickly ascended the cellar stairs. He was in such a hurry that he tripped, ripped his trousers and sand papered his knee. He raced through the dining room, and opened the kitchen door to find his mother totally prostrate on the kitchen floor, mumbling. He ran to her side and knelt before her. In a quivering voice he asked, "Mother what is wrong, what is wrong?" He turned and looked up at Aunt Margret whose face was red and blotchy. She had a letter in her hand. "Aunt Margret, why is mother screaming and crying?" Aunt Margret gently knelt down, placed her arms around Gerhardt and said, "Gerhardt I have terrible news." The young boy froze with fear. "We have just received a letter that your father was killed in action." Gerhardt violently pushed her away and yelled, "That cannot be true, it cannot be true. My father is not dead, he's coming home soon and is going to build a model with me. Some day we will build the city, you're wrong, you're wrong." With that he bolted from the room, raced up to his bedroom and slammed the door. He jumped into bed and pulled the covers over his head. He was certain that his father's death was a mistake and soon he would return home from the war. Over the next three days Gerhardt began to realize that his father was truly dead. He could no longer control himself and tears flooded his face. He stayed in the darkness of his room, scrunched up against a wall with his knees tucked under his chin. He only came out when summoned to meals by the servants.

Friends were visiting his home once the news of Wilhelm's death became public and they would invariably speak with Gerhardt. They all tried to assure him that his father was now with God. This assurance, meant to alleviate his grief, did just the opposite. He was confused by these statements and began an anger toward God that would last for the rest of his life.

The morning of the funeral leaves blew like skirts of folk dancers against the stone walls of the burial church. The winds swirled the crystals of snow, coating the stained-glass windows of St. Mark's. Gerhardt's mother, Aunt Margret and Uncle Isidore slowly ascended the steps of the church and waited in the vestibule with Gerhardt. This was a totally new experience for Gerhardt and he had no idea what was happening. Suddenly a hearse appeared, followed by two military cars. Soldiers exited the vehicles and lined up at the rear of the hearse. They lifted the coffin and six pallbearers ascended the steps of the church. The silence was deafening as the pallbearers entered the vestibule. The only sounds were the swishing of the priest's cassock and the squeaking of his shoes on the marble floor as he came forward from the front of the church accompanied by two acolytes with lit candles. The darkness of the interior was gently broken by the flickering candles along the side aisles. It was bitterly cold because the church was unheated and each breath formed a cloud. In a dull monotone the priest began to say prayers and sprinkle water onto the casket. Gerhardt was confused by this; why was this priest-sprinkling the large dark cherry-stained coffin with water? He looked up at Aunt Margret and asked, "Is my father in that coffin?" His words pierced her heart and she gently replied, "Gerhardt your wonderful father is inside."

"Can I see him?" The tenderness of this request made his aunt tear up.
"No Gerhardt it must remained closed."

The organ gently played the *Ave Maria* as the priest turned and headed for the main altar. Once the coffin was blessed the acolyte covered it with a German flag. The ushers placed it on the trolley to be set in the center aisle of the church. The freezing cold church forced clouds of human breath in the air throughout the service. The entire process confused Gerhardt. No one explained the funeral rituals to him. He paid no attention to the Mass and stared at the coffin during the entire service. Gerhardt barely noticed the hymns, pungent smells of incense and musty prayer books. The eulogy, which hardly mentioned his father, did little to alleviate his sorrow and confusion. At Communion time his aunt guided him to the communion rail. He automatically opened his mouth as the priest placed the wafer on his tongue. After the mass, someone led Gerhardt back to the limousine while the coffin was placed in the hearse. The silence in the car was broken only by his mother who was crumpled against the door weeping with soul wrenching sounds. She seemed incapable of speech. The car followed the hearse to the cemetery, just five minutes away. After waiting for the pallbearers to carry the coffin to the grave the family left the car and walked slowly into the cemetery. The only sounds were the rusted iron gate moving back and forth, the biting wind and the crunching of frozen snow and ice under their feet. Gerhardt saw a deep hole in the ground and his father's casket next to a large mound of dirt. The priest mumbled some prayers that the mourners could barely hear because of the howling wind. Gerhardt was cold. His aunt tied a scarf around his neck and wrapped her arms around him. As the prayers ended, he watched his mother thrust herself onto the casket. She was inconsolable. The funeral director and Uncle Isadore kept her from collapsing to the ground. Gerhardt shivered as soldiers fired three shots into the wind. After that, the cemetery caretakers wrapped ropes around the casket and slowly lowered it into the grave. Gerhardt trembled uncontrollably at the sound of the thud when the coffin struck dark, deep bottom. A sob was mired in Gerhardt's throat. He was worried that his father would be cold and alone in the darkness.

Chapter 4

March 1920, Berlin, Germany
A stepfather poses new challenges to Gerhardt

Wilhelm Stark was all that Otto Schoenfeld was not. Born poor, Otto became one of the richest men in Germany. An overweight, short, loud man with a perennial scowl, he evidenced abiding contempt for those born rich. He was at the core a coarse man with a veneer of refinement. He was always railing in his brassy voice against the privileged class. He rose to great wealth by a series of brutal business practices, and fell into the good fortune of being a war profiteer. Despite new, expensive garments he was a bully with no sense of humility or ethics.

Otto married beneath his current financial position but his wife died in the 1918 flu epidemic. Although he adored his two daughters, he'd never thought he'd have to raise them by himself. Three years prior to the death of his wife he attempted to hire Wilhelm Stark to build a massive residence in the most prestigious area of Berlin. However, Wilhelm was called to war before the project started. Aware that Christina, Wilhelm's wife, was a new widow he decided to marry her. Aware from Wilhelm's partner that she had financial issues due to her husband's death he solicitously sought to help in any way possible. A façade of charm and compassion hid the brazen "take no prisoner" personality.

Christina was deeply touched by the kindness and charity of a stranger. She knew little of him, and found his counsel helpful. Wilhelm's business partner, Gustav Radtke, generously continued to pay her for projects that Wilhelm had begun. However, it would not be possible to send payments for the firm's future projects. Financial concerns were real and as she slowly emerged from many months of sadness, she felt adrift. Although bright, she was not privy to their financial matters. She came from wealth and Wilhelm was very successful in the architectural world. All of this ended with his death. The monthly costs of living in a splendid home with servants had almost depleted the family's savings.

Unlike his usual bull-in-a China shop approach to any business issue, Otto's pursuit of Christina was strategically slow. It began with assessing her assets and proposing ways in which the funds could be stretched. He proposed key household decisions and she enthusiastically took his counsel. Making progress with Christina, he introduced her to his daughters and confided that he had concerns about raising them. Christina felt beholden to him so she reciprocated with maternal assistance. Before long they became friends. Otto restrained his impulsive personality but began to invite Christina to the theater and on several occasions boating excursions. Having been in mourning, she welcomed company and felt she had begun to live again.

Initially Gerhardt had no contact with Otto except for one occasion when Christina took him to a picnic with Otto and his daughters. Gerhardt had grown significantly in the past two years and was slightly taller than Otto. This and the appearance of a young blue-blooded child offended his sensibilities but he pretended to portray himself as a kind friend of his mother. Otto had no intention of letting this young man take significant time away from him and his two daughters. His plan worked and eventually Christina agreed to marry him. Early on in the marriage he deliberately began to exclude Gerhardt from select family activities. He often used the pretense that Gerhardt would not enjoy these ventures. In reality they were attempts to move him farther and farther from the presence of his mother. Initially, Gerhardt did not feel excluded and welcomed the opportunities to privately occupy himself with the ever-present objective of completing the model city. He spent hours and hours examining his father's blueprints while continuing to research the current architectural developments in Germany. His late father's partner, Gustav Radtke, periodically invited him to lunch and willingly shared many of the new projects in the planning phases.

Chapter 5

Munich
The growing conflict between Gerhardt and his stepfather

The bedroom was still, quiet. The only sounds were the creaking shutters adjusting to the bitter winter wind and the claps of thunder in the distance. Gerhardt was restless and could not sleep. He was disturbed by his ever-growing negative relationship with his stepfather. After hours of twisting and turning he left his bed, slid into his slippers and grabbed a flashlight off his dresser. Certain that everyone else was asleep he cautiously descended the winding staircase He made his way through the kitchen and opened the cellar door. It opened easily and slowly swung wide but squeaked as Gerhard closed it. Tiptoeing down the steps he turned on the flashlight rather than the overhead light. The model city in progress was a source of great consolation. It was the one place in Gerhardt's life where his father was still present. His stepfather had forbidden him to have any indication of his father's presence in the house. And so, it was more and more difficult to remember what his father looked like. Working on the model city he would imagine the presence of his father, and often he would actually engage him in conversation.

He had been working on the model for about 10 minutes when he heard the squeak of the cellar door opening. The overhead light went on and he could see the feet of his stepfather as he walked down the steps. The footsteps were slow and deliberate. He stopped half way down and glared at Gerhardt. Gerhardt felt panic. He had anticipated a confrontation. Otto's face was red with anger. In a harsh voice he said, "What the hell are you doing down here?"

Gerhardt sheepishly replied "I could not sleep, so I thought I would come down here and work on my model." That response did not satisfy Otto.

"What is all of this?"

"It is the model of the city that my father and I imagined one day we would build as architects."

Otto dismissed this response and charged forward to have every trace of Wilhelm vanish. "I think that you spend too much time in the past. This fantasy in front of me has little value. I believe you are occupied with foolish toys instead of mastering your schoolwork."

Gerhardt felt intense anger at his stepfather's response. "It doesn't interfere at all with my schoolwork and I love working on this model."

Otto walked around the model without an ounce of interest. "You may not think this interferes with your studies, but as your stepfather, I'm saying you should stop working here and take this silly thing down."

The thought of losing his connection with his father shattered Gerhardt, and he could no longer be silent. "You are not my father," he shouted. "This is a gift my father gave to me. I will not take it down."

Otto was incensed. He grabbed Gerhardt by his pajama top. "You will take it down by tomorrow morning."

"I will not!"

Otto slapped him twice and pushed him to the floor. Gerhardt would not give his stepfather the satisfaction of tears. He raced up the cellar stairs.

There was no going back to bed for Gerhardt. He thought perhaps he should tell his mother what had happened. The problem: it might make his relationship with his stepfather even worse. The worst was yet to come. When he returned home from school the next day his entire model had been dismantled and was carelessly placed in the storage area in front of the wine cellar. For Gerhardt this was the most devastating moment since hearing his father was dead. He raced from his home and aimlessly wandered until dusk. Finally, he decided he would go to his aunt's house and confide in her about the ongoing misery of his life. Aunt Margret listened and asked him to stay for dinner. After conferring with her husband, she visited her sister and requested that Gerhardt stay the night. Over the next two weeks Aunt Margret began to offer a plan to have Gerhardt live temporarily with her. She argued that her home was closer to Gerhardt's school and it would provide companionship for her son Micah. Christina, aware of the tension between her son and Otto, thought it would be beneficial for Gerhardt but had no idea that the move would be more than temporary.

Gerhardt enters a new family

Gerhardt was relieved to be out from under the daily verbal barrage and frequent confrontations with his stepfather. Despite this, he was unsure how he would fit into living with his Jewish relatives. Aunt Margret was his mother's sister and a Christian, but she married a Jewish man. Gerhardt had met his cousin Micah on a few family events, but barely knew him. When he arrived at his new home, Micah was at the front door juggling a soccer ball. Micah was dressed in soccer shorts and a team shirt. Slightly shorter than Gerhardt, he had sharp features, chestnut hair and deep brown eyes. He was trim and rather muscular. "You play?" he asked with a charming smile.

"Yes, but I'm not very good at it," said Gerhardt.

Micah spun the ball on his finger tip. "Well, I am a star and I will teach you all I know."

Standing in the doorway, Uncle Isadore smiled and shook his head. "Micah likes to brag about everything. You must get used to his arrogance."

Micah laughed. "Father you always told me to tell the truth. I can't hide the fact that I'm multitalented and a soccer star."

Gerhardt decided he liked his new friend and future buddy. It was refreshing to be in a place where he was not constantly fearful.

The positive relationship between the two young men was almost instantaneous. They were cousins separated by less than a year and connected by family blood. Gerhardt was the more studious of the two. Micah was equally as bright but much more outgoing. Despite their different faiths they found common ground in shared humor and sporting events. On one occasion the two decided to go for swim in the nearby Elbe river. It was an idyllic hot July morning. Birds were chirping and the air was fragrant from the scent of summer flowers. Unknown to both boys, two days prior there was a persistent rainfall in the mountains. The usually calm river's current and undertow was intensified by the rapidly flowing mountain streams. Micah was the stronger swimmer of the two. He dove in immediately. Gerhardt was a little tentative, unsure of diving right in. Micah motioned for him to come into the water. He dove, not as impressively as Micah, who teased about his form. Micah lay on his back, allowing the current to carry him downstream. Gerhardt attempted to copy Micah but he was being carried by the swift current toward the rocks and rapids. Fear began to take over. He frantically tried swimming toward Micah but the current was too strong. Suddenly Micah was aware that Gerhardt was in peril. Immediately he submerged and pointed himself toward Gerhardt. Floundering and taking in large gulps of water, Gerhardt was drowning. He struck one of the submerged rocks that tore a gash into his right leg. Micah was close enough now to go under water and grab

Gerhardt's waist. Gerhardt's pain was intense. He was barely conscious. However, he was pliable and this allowed Micah to more easily embrace his body and swim toward the riverbank. He helped Gerhardt up, tore his shirt and made a tourniquet for the wounded leg. Gerhardt was exhausted and semi-conscious. Micah turned him over and began pounding on his back. Gerhardt moaned and began to throw up his breakfast and gobs of water. Gerhardt's fits of coughing continued. He was exhausted. Micah put pressure on the wound to stop the bleeding. After a brief rest period, he helped Gerhardt get back to the center of town to visit Dr. Schmidt. Ten stiches later the boys returned home closer than ever.

Being active pranksters was part of their repertoire and the two consistently played their favorites on public transportation. One scenario was that one of them dressed in their finest would sit in the front of the trolley with a handkerchief in his suit jacket pocket. The other, when leaving the tram, would sneeze loudly, reach for the handkerchief, blow his nose and give the handkerchief back with a simple thank you and then leave the tram. Another part of their mischief was that one seated in the front of the tram would fall asleep. The other prankster would roll up a newspaper, bang the sleeping person on the head and shout, "Wake up you dumb jerk." Passengers were shocked and perplexed by the sleeping party who would just shrug his shoulders and go back to sleep.

As time went on, the two became inseparable. One event brought them even closer. At the town soccer stadium Micah was teaching Gerhardt how to run downfield and control the soccer ball with a series of athletic moves. One of the local students from Gerhardt's school approached them as they were kicking the soccer ball back and forth. He ignored Micah completely and stood in front of Gerhardt and inquired in a loud, sarcastic voice, "Why are you playing with the Jew boy? Come and join us. We are about to have a game."

Gerhardt attempted to diffuse the situation. "He is my cousin and I live with his family."

The bully scoffed. "Jews don't belong here, now tell him to leave and join us."

"I don't feel like playing right now."

Gerhardt picked up the soccer ball and attempted to leave when the bully grabbed his shirt and pushed him. "Would you rather be with this Jew or with us?"

With that he pushed Gerhardt to the ground while the other six students grabbed Micah. Gerhardt knew there was no choice but to fight. He stood and confronted the bully. The two circled each other. Gerhardt landed a blow to the side of the head and knocked his nemesis to the ground. The blow was so well placed that Gerhardt now turned his attention to freeing Micah from the other villains. With Gerhardt's aid, Micah struggled to free himself and the two cousins were now back-to-back, trying to fight off the six opponents. At the end of the confrontation Gerhardt and Micah were able to flee from their antagonists and head home. Gerhardt's eye was swollen and Micah's nose was bent. Both were covered with each other's blood. Ever the humorist, Micha said, "Well Gerhardt, it appears that we no longer are merely cousins but now blood brothers."

Gerhardt's extended family was kind to him through the years, but as he finished gymnasium and prepared to enter the University, he experienced feelings of sadness, jealousy and depression. Even in the loving environment of his relatives he always felt like an outsider. This despite the fact that Uncle Isadore spent hours with him trying to be a male presence in his life. By age 17 he had experienced the death of his father, the emotional loss of his depressed mother, and exclusion by his stepfather. Also, he dismissed any religious core. All of these feelings were compounded by the reality that even though he had excelled academically, future prospects for employment were relatively dismal. Illusions of building a grand city with his father were now childhood fairytales. He knew after graduation that in all probability he would wind up working as a draftsman in a small firm in either Berlin or Munich. Micah was like a brother to him, but Gerhardt envied him because he had a real mother and father, strong faith and he was beginning his studies to be a medical doctor. Gerhardt was drifting emotionally and without a sense of purpose in his life. He was cared for, but there were enormous gaps of emotional needs and no meaning in his life.

Chapter 6

April 1930, University of Munich
Gerhardt falls in love

The University created not only intellectual challenges and benefits, but also new social options. Gerhardt had mild romantic crushes during his time in high school, but University dating proved to be more intense. Despite his good looks and athletic abilities, he was somewhat shy and clumsy with women. He was utterly mesmerized by a student in his chemistry class. He only knew that her name was Frieda, and that she was often accompanied by one of his soccer teammates. Tall, with golden blond hair and adorable freckles on her cheeks and nose, Gerhardt had memorized every detail of her appearance from afar. Unfortunately, Rolf Niemeyer, a forward on his soccer team and an outgoing charming individual, seemed to be her constant companion. Gerhardt initially made no attempt to speak with Frieda, mostly because he believed she was in a relationship with Rolf. One day he sat next to Rolf at lunch in the dining hall. While they were exchanging the normal pleasantries of two friends who had not seen each other in a while, Frieda entered and waved at Rolf. He beckoned her to come and sit with them. Gerhardt was excited, but also a bit crestfallen that his dream woman was in a relationship with his friend. As she approached the table, Rolf rose and kissed her on both cheeks. He turned to Gerhardt and said, "Gerhardt this is my sister Frieda." Gerhardt was so stunned and overwhelmed that he rose from the table and knocked over his cup of coffee. It spilled down the front of Frieda's dress. Gerhardt was mortified. "What an ox I am," he thought. Frieda graciously wiped up the stain and assured him that the coffee would come out in the wash. It was an incredibly poor beginning, but now there seemed to be exciting possibilities.

For days he could not get her out of his mind but still did nothing to approach her. Finally, after weeks of fantasizing about her, he asked Rolf if there was any possibility that Frieda would go out on a date. Rolf laughed out loud and said, "You clown – she was so disappointed that you did not call after she met you in the cafeteria that she has been sulking ever since. She thought you were incredibly handsome, although rather clumsy."

Gerhardt lost no time in calling Frieda and inviting her for coffee the following Saturday morning. The initial contact was somewhat awkward, but they spent two hours talking and laughing, discovering they had much more than just Rolf in common. When it was time to part, Frieda took his hand in hers and gently kissed his cheek, saying, "I so enjoyed this morning and look forward to our next time together."

In the ensuing six months Rolf and Frieda spent nearly every day together. The friendship blossomed into a deep love. It was a magical time and even their daily goodbyes sometimes lasted for hours. They ended each other's sentences and personal details and subjects were not off limits. With one exception. Gerhardt lived for the moments he spent with Frieda. They held hands and kissed every chance they could. The only unfinished part of their love symphony was that Gerhardt was confused by Frieda's dedication to the University National Democratic Socialist party. But had not questioned her rationale and allegiance to the group. His friendship with Rolf also grew closer, and he began to spend less and less time at home and frequently would sleep over at Rolf's apartment. Finally, after three months of this arrangement, Rolf suggested that Gerhardt share his flat. He said, "You are either here or at my parents' house, so why not simplify your life and move in with me?" Gerhardt decided to move the following weekend.

Gerhardt leaves Micah's home

Packing his suitcase Gerhardt was interrupted by a loud knock on his bedroom door. "Come in," he called as he closed his suitcase. It was Micah standing in the doorway. "I understand you are moving," Micah stated.

"Yes, I am so busy and this cuts down on my travel. I will have more time for my studies."

Micah knew that Gerhardt was seriously involved with a woman. "Does this have anything to do with the person of your romantic dreams?"

Gerhardt feigned shock at Micah's question. "I could tell you that I am devoted solely to my studies, and have no time for love, but that would be a complete falsehood."

Micah smiled and asked, "What's her name?"

"Frieda."

"Can I meet her?"

"Hopefully some day you will, but only after she falls hopelessly in love with me. If she meets a clown like you, she might abandon me. When we are truly a couple, I will introduce you as my mysterious, weird cousin."

Micah laughed. "I wish you all the best and I hope you won't forget your family." The two men who had shared so many moments hugged as Gerhardt picked up his suitcase and began the next phase of his life.

Gerhardt is introduced to the Nazi world

Rolf Niemeyer was actively involved with an emerging political party -- National Socialism. It seemed to Gerhardt that he was rarely home in the evening. One night, as Rolf was leaving for another meeting, dressed in a brown shirt and matching cap, he stopped at the front door and asked Gerhardt what he was doing. "I'm working on my architectural project."

"When is it due?"

"In another three weeks, but I hope to get a head start so it will be really simple to finish it early."

Rolf took this as an opening to invite Gerhardt to accompany him to a meeting. "My sister is going to my grandparents this week so you will have extra time to study then. Come with me tonight."

"Where are you going?"

"To a rally that I believe will change your life completely."

Gerhardt smiled. "Who says I want my life to be changed?"

Rolf laughed and replied, "As a student of architecture I believe you should be genuinely interested in the future of Germany."

"In what way will your meeting be connected to architecture?"

With enthusiasm, Rolf said, "Just join me this evening and you will see."

"Ok but can you give me some inkling of where we're going? If this is a political rally, I'm really not interested in politics."

Rolf replied, "That is nonsense, everyone's interested in politics. I am about to introduce you to a movement that is so dynamic it will change not only your life but also the lives of everyone in Germany. I've tried to be gentle but now I am insisting that you accompany me."

Gerhardt grabbed his sweater and reluctantly accompanied Rolf to the meeting.

When they arrived at the downtown Municipal Cultural Center Gerhardt was amazed at the size of the crowd waiting to enter the building. Most of the visitors were dressed in the same brown shirt and cap as Rolf. Huge banners bearing the symbol of the Nationalist Socialist party were positioned on the entrance walls and in the main auditorium. The noise level was deafening, and all of the brown shirt attendees were greeting each other with the same greeting, "Heil Hitler."

Once the room was filled, all of the attendees stood and sang "Deutschland, Deutschland," followed by a song that Gerhardt had never heard before. Gerhardt thought to himself that this group had a religious fervor that appeared to mesmerize the members. After the singing, the evening was filled with one speaker after another shouting a series of similar platitudes. Gerhardt's reaction was somewhat negative. He felt uncomfortable, especially with the anti-Semitic rhetoric. At one-point Rolf leaned over to him and said, "Some of these people are rough around the edges, but do not throw out the baby with the wash."

"What do you mean?"

"Listen to the core message," Rolf said. "This is all about our rising from the ashes and establishing the role of Germany as a political force in Europe." Gerhardt asked "Why is that important to you?"

"Because it focuses on what is possible for every German in the areas of work and daily life."

"I can understand that but I'm really uncomfortable with the anti-Jewish rhetoric in this room. My uncle and cousin are Jews and I have been close to them for years." Rolf paused before answering, realizing this was a vital concern of Gerhardt's. "That may be true, but there is danger in that; because once you start making exceptions, you lose sight of the fact that it is the Jews that have brought down Germany."

Chapter 7

July 1930, Munich
The Nazi Seduction of Gerhardt

Rolf saw in Gerhardt the perfect candidate for the growing Nazi party. He knew that Gerhardt was exceptionally bright, had excellent organizational skills, and was already an accomplished student of architecture. There were many brutish thugs in the Nazi party, but few intellectuals who could assume leadership positions. It was not pure love of party that motivated Rolf, because he knew that he could attach himself to Gerhardt's coattails. Gerhardt had been, up to this point, very resistant to take National Socialism seriously. Rolf decided on a multifaceted strategy to convince Gebhardt to become involved.

He would begin by soliciting the support of his sister Frieda who was an avid member of the University National Socialists. He had observed that Gerhardt was totally smitten with her. The once casual dating had blossomed into a genuine romance. If he could convince her to share her reasons for participating in the party it would certainly enhance the possibility that Gerhardt would take the party more seriously.

Rolf also decided to share this challenge with Hans Becker, his National Socialist group leader, who was a key recruiter for the party. One evening after a leadership session Rolf asked Hans to have coffee at a local pastry shop. After stirring his coffee and taking a sip Hans said, "Rolf I have the feeling that you wish to discuss something personal with me."
"I do, and it is about someone I believe would be a perfect candidate for the party." "Tell me about him."

"His name is Gerhardt Stark, age 21. He is finishing his architectural degree at the Blenheim Institute and takes some classes at the University. He is an exceptional student and an obvious leader with significant speaking and organizational skills."

"What do you know about his personal history? Is he a full-blooded German?"

"I believe he is because his grandfathers were both officers in the German army. However, I know little about his immediate family. He occasionally mentions his mother but I cannot recall one time that he referred to his father."

Hans lit a cigarette and blew a smoke ring. "That is where you must start. The way to convert any candidate is to begin with the family history. Once that is known you can build the key concepts of opportunity, the new Germany and the traitors that are in the way of our glorious future."

Rolf made mental notes of this counsel and decided to take direct action with Gerhardt.

After a few beers at the local biergarten one night, Rolf began to execute his strategy. "Gerhardt, I know something about your mother, but I literally know nothing about your father."

Gerhardt thought for a moment. "I have only vague recollections of my father because he died when I was eight years old."

"How did he die?"

"He was killed in the first world war. He was an accomplished architect, but was drafted into the military. I know he went to military school, but chose architecture over becoming a career officer."

"Was he a foot soldier?"

"Yes, I have a document that states he was a captain in the Army and was killed in France in 1917."

Rolf saw this as an opportunity to explore. "Do you know where he was killed?"

"Yes, the document states that he was killed in the battle of the Somme."

Rolf thought to himself, this is critical! This was an opportunity to score some points for his beliefs. "The battle of the Somme was an important battle in the war. Do you know anything about that battle?"

Gerhardt responded, "Very little."

Rolf sensed that the facts blended with the personal might have some positive influence on Gerhardt. He decided to start with historical data. "Gerhardt it was the most critical battle of the great war! The German military initially overwhelmed the French and the British, despite their advantage in numbers and materials. Thousands of the enemy were killed and the German army retained the advantage of holding the high ground when the betrayal came."

Gerhardt asked, "What betrayal?"

"The Jewish industrialists working worldwide despised Germany and controlled all of the necessary resources that were vital to Germany's ultimate victory."

Gerhardt seemed confused. "I'm not sure what you are referring to."

"I'm talking about the railroads, supply chains and all the things that the Jews completely controlled. It was their intention to cripple Germany and make sure that we would lose the war. They destroyed Germany economically by the vicious anti-German treaty, known as the Treaty of Versailles. Are you aware of what that treaty has done to the people of Germany?"

"I have only a vague awareness," Gerhardt said.

Rolf replied sharply, "The Jews not only tilted the war against Germany, the treaty insisted that Germany pay all of the war's cost. That alone has caused the depression in our country."

Rolf now moved to the personal. "Were you close your father as a child?"

"I was, but I only have vague recollections of him now."

Gerhardt recounted the story of the model city and shared the discomfort of living with the man who married his mother after his father's death. Rolf instinctively understood that this was key to his best strategy. "I believe your life would be very different if your father had lived."

That deeply touched Gerhardt. "I'm sure it would be. I know that I am studying architecture because my father was an architect."

The question about his father opened the floodgates and Gerhardt poured forth the pride he had in his father's accomplishments. "Many of the buildings that are notable in Munich and Berlin were designed by my father. His partner once told me that if he had lived, he would be the premier architect in Germany today."

Rolf shook his head and replied yes. "And to think that he died so that the Jews could profit financially from his death."

Gerhardt initially felt unconnected to that statement, but Rolf pursued the insidious logic of his argument. "We never explore the personal pain that the global conspiracy has punished a German family like yours. You grew up without a father because rich Jews sitting around a table decided that money was more important than morality." Gerhardt had never attached his father's death to a conspiracy. At least for the moment he reflected on this view of history that Rolf was sharing. He began to explore the possibility that his father died because of the greed of a Jewish conspiracy. That evening while seated on his bed he wept for a long time. He never stopped missing his father and this evening was a sharp reminder of what he had lost.

Chapter 8

April 1931, Munich
Gerhardt searches to understand National Socialism

Gerhardt's life had changed dramatically in the last year. He completed his architectural studies at the Blenheim Institute and began employment as a draftsman in a small architectural firm. He desperately wanted to ask Frieda to marry him, but there were significant impediments. He had barely enough money to pay the rent, and he lived in a small one-room apartment in a not-so-desirable section of Munich. But that was not the primary hurdle. During the year he was daily bombarded with information about the Nationalist Social Party. It appeared to him that the Nazi movement was becoming more and more significant, and he could no longer just dismiss it as a temporary phenomenon that would evaporate. Initially his thoughts were that Nazis were a cult-like group of thugs that could find no root in polite German society. This conviction was not held by people like his friend Rolf who embraced the party. More importantly, Frieda, the woman he adored, was intimately involved in the party. There were no secrets between him and Frieda. He felt comfortable exposing every portion of himself even at times revealing his fears and financial insecurities. She in turn had been just as open, and yet there was never any significant conversation about the Nazi party. Gerhardt had experienced the kindness and social graces of her university acquaintances, which seemed vastly different from the meetings he attended with Rolf. Why was she and other bright, caring individuals so taken with the Nazi party? He needed to understand why this was so important to her. He understood that the law and politics provided a necessary bridge to the future, but he could not fathom why this woman he so loved was committed to a movement that at times made him uncomfortable. He decided that it was critical for them to understand and accept each other on this important topic.

One evening after class, Gerhardt met Frieda before dinner and invited her to take a walk through Schutzen Park. As they walked, Gerhardt was unusually quiet, and Frieda became uncomfortable with his silence. She knew him well and recognized that there was something on his mind. When they arrived at the Fairytale fountain, Gerhardt motioned to a bench and invited Freda to be seated. His serious demeanor was unusual for Gerhardt. Often when he was with Frieda the relationship brought out the playful boy in him. At times he would act silly by breaking into song or quote a poem or even spontaneously dance. This was one of the reasons Freida so adored him. He was different from any other young man she had dated and often daydreamed of spending the rest of her life with him. There were so many positive aspects to their relationship that it seemed almost too good to be true. But at this moment, Frieda was anxious. She decided to speak up. "Gerhardt, you are acting rather strangely and I don't remember a time when you have been this quiet for so long. Is there anything that you want to discuss with me?"

Gerhardt took her hand and said, "I'm sure you know Frieda that I love you deeply. You are constantly on my mind and in my heart. However, there is one question that I have never asked that has been somewhat confusing for me. I would really like to explore this issue with you."
Though uncomfortable, Frieda responded without hesitation, "Gerhardt, I may not have said it has openly as this, but I love you with my whole heart. There is nothing I could not honestly discuss with you. Whatever is on your mind, please tell me what it is."

With this assurance, Gerhardt began his search for understanding. "Frieda, I know that Rolf is committed to the Nazi party, and I totally respect that, but I do not understand your loyalty to the University version of National Socialism. What has attracted you to becoming a member of the party?"

Frieda did not immediately answer and seemed to be building a response in her mind. Finally, after moments of stark silence she began to present her answer. "I don't know that there is a one- or two-line response to your question. My first exposure to the Nazi party was through my parents and brother. My father was a soldier during the Great War and was wounded. For my entire youth he told stories about his anger at Germany's losing the Great War. Even as a little girl I remember hearing conversations about how Germany had been betrayed. I didn't understand this at the time, but I'm sure those words had some effect on my current beliefs." Gerhardt asked, "Is that the primary reason for your joining the University group?" "I don't think so, but it may have been the foundation. Rolf, being so active politically, also had some influence. I dearly love my brother and we have always been close. But I think that the teaching at the University has had the most influence on my beliefs. I have had two courses in History and both raised facts that were new and vibrant for me."

"What were those?"

"Well, Professor Schmidt spent days teaching us about the Holy Roman Empire and how Germany was a part of that period of conquest and world rule. He emphasized that the German heritage had been seriously denigrated by Jewish influences throughout the centuries."

Gerhardt winced at the common Jewish refrain but remained silent.

"Also," Frieda continued, "I was totally unaware of the treaty of Versailles, the harm it has done to our economy, and the betrayal of the German military in the First World War. All of this, plus the companionship of my classmates, has had a strong influence on me. However, the most important influence is the vision of the new Germany."

Frieda paused and blushed before making her next statement. "Gerhardt, someday I hope to have children and it is in the new Germany, where opportunity grows, that I want to raise them."

Gerhardt was deeply moved by Frieda's words but especially by the statement about the future and children. They embraced and Gerhardt now had a deeper understanding of his beloved and why National Socialism was so important in her life. The prism of a new Germany had an immediate emotional impact on him and he vowed to more deeply understand her political beliefs. This evening was another experience that enhanced his love for Frieda and he believed that they would soon find a way to marry.

Rolf was emotionally warmed at the news that Gerhardt had inquired about Frieda's commitment to the Nazi party. For months he had strategically tried to influence Gerhardt but now he knew it was time to play his ace in the hole. He had access to Albert Speer, an architect who was becoming a confidant of Hitler. He thought exposure to Speer might lead Gerhardt to becoming a member of the party. Through his group leader, Hans Becker, he received word that Speer would be happy to have coffee with Gerhardt sometime in the next two weeks. Rolf pursued the offer and arranged for Gerhardt to meet Speer at the Café Landauer in Berlin on the following Monday at 10. Gerhardt had mixed feelings about this arrangement because he was a mere draftsman and could not fathom why a successful architect would spend time with him. He thought perhaps it was a gracious gesture because of his father's influence on German architecture. Apprehensive, but also excited to have the opportunity to speak with one who was actually building new edifices in Germany, he agreed to meet Speer.

Albert Speer rose from being unemployed to becoming an influential member of the expanding Nazi party. His father had arranged for him to have a low-level position in Berlin but he soon caught the eye of Adolf Hitler. The two had a bourgeoning desire to imprint central Berlin with new audacious designs and Hitler positioned Speer as one of the architects that would redesign the German chancellery. In addition, as symbols and signs became more prominent in Nazi propaganda, Speer was to create the format for future massive rallies that would be held in Nuremberg.

Unlike most prominent high echelon Nazis, Speer was not a boisterous blow hard. He was a tall, elegantly dressed, charming professional who was highly educated and well mannered. He had been a sickly child, frequently experiencing fainting spells and convulsive episodes. Because of his physical ailments he was to some degree initially shy and socially distant. His home life, though financially comfortable, was in an emotionally cold atmosphere. His mother was physically distant and his father expected perfection in his academic pursuits. Recently, before he joined the Nazi party, he had few prospects and was barely making a living, and yet today he was riding one of the most formidable German waves in history. He had exceptional organizational talents and was an advocate for the growth of German industry.

Gerhardt's train arrived in Berlin precisely at 8:45. He had adequate time to meet Speer at 10. He left the trolley and walked briskly on this crisp morning to the Café Landauer. He had no idea what Speer looked like but felt confident they would find each other.

Speer sat at the front of the café. He thought to himself: this young man is probably where I was a few years ago. He had few prospects and was barely making a living, and yet today he was one of Hitler's most trusted colleagues. Speer, like most members of the party, believed that the German Jews had become too powerful and in essence, he was an anti-Semite. He was enamored with Hitler and was convinced that he was the natural person to oppose Communism, which Speer believed was the greatest threat to contemporary German society. Periodically glancing at the patrons opening the door to the café his eyes focused on the image of the perfect Aryan man. A tall, blond, physically fit man was scouring the café.

Are you Herr Stark?"

The young man smiled and made his way to Speer's table. They exchanged greetings and Speer offered the young man a cup of coffee and a piece of fruitcake. Gerhardt sat and said, "Just coffee please."

Speer poured the cup and as Gerhardt put two spoonfuls of sugar into the cup began the conversation. "May I call you Gerhardt?"

"Yes, please do."

"I know that you are the son of Wilhelm Stark."

Gerhardt was surprised. "Do you know of my father's work?"

"Gerhardt, every architect in Germany knows of your father. If he had lived, he would be a legend in the architectural world. I am very familiar with the work he did in Berlin and I must say he was one of the forces that paved the way for contemporary design."

Gerhardt said, "I was just eight years old when he was killed in the great war."

"Is he the reason you became an architect?"

"Probably because when I was just a little boy, he would spend hours with me building models of a city that someday we would actually build. I vaguely remember him, but have always been drawn to the idea of architecture."

"What are you currently working on?" Speer asked.

Gerhardt was embarrassed by the question. "Nothing significant. I am merely a draftsman because there are few opportunities for young architects in Munich." Speer smiled. That, my friend, is about to change."

Speer then shared that a few years ago he was mired in believing that there was almost no future for him but things have changed dramatically for the better. He explained in great detail some of the projects he was now working on.

He then inquired, "Are you a member of the party?"

"No, I am not though people I admire are members. I have some reservations about the Nazi party."

"What are some of those?"

"Well, it appears to restrict civil liberties."

Speer asked him to give some examples and Gerhardt said that free expression seems to be stifled by those who follow the Nazis.

Quickly, Speer responded, "Every great social movement requires pain through the first phases of the transition. Many are conflicted because of personal loyalties. For example, every German has a Jewish friend and wants to preserve that relationship.

However, we must look at the greater good and these relationships must be severed. I would venture that much of what you have learned about moral principles has little relevance in Germany today. It is critical that we examine our values based on the day to day needs of the German people. Gerhardt, we are on the brink of a new and glorious German period. Temporary civil disruptions may seem unjust but they are vital and will be corrected once the total vision has been achieved."

Speer hesitated but then realizing it was a critical component to the young man's future, he offered, "I believe you should join the party because if you do, I might be able to secure some work for you on a project I have been commissioned to design -- the entire process for meetings at Nuremberg. These will be attended by hundreds of thousands and must be in concert with Nazi beliefs. Much will be done at night because torches and candles add a solemnity that cannot be achieved in daylight. Also, Gerhardt, many of the participants do not have your Aryan appearance. You are the perfect image. Unlike you, many are short, overweight and must not be the focal point of the message. If you join the party, I will see if there is a possibility that you are temporarily assigned to my staff. Also, there will be no need for you to move to Berlin. You may stay in Munich until further opportunities arise."

The multifaceted stream of persons that Gerhardt respected created a combination of emotional feelings that forged the personal and historical into his believing. He now began to see National Socialism through the prism of his love for Frieda, the historical reasons for his father's death and the potential mentorship of Albert Speer. Gerhardt was overwhelmed by this meeting and informed Frieda and Rolf that he would join the party that week. This was the moment of his psychic birth as a Nazi.

Chapter 9

June 1933, Munich and Passau
Gerhardt totally rejects his family ties

Frieda's family was originally from Kassel but because of her grandparents' advanced age, the family decided that the wedding would take place in Passau. The date was set for early May, but establishing the wedding list presented a significant problem for Gerhardt. He would love for his mother to be present, but under no circumstances would he invite his stepfather, Otto. He realized that by excluding his stepfather there was a high probability his mother would not attend. This issue was relatively insignificant to the one that disturbed him the most. His newfound Nazi membership made it impossible to have any relationship with any person of the Jewish faith. He knew that his future in-laws were staunch Nazis, and would under no circumstances allow a Jew to participate in Frieda's wedding. Gerhardt had no contact with Aunt Margret, Uncle Isadore and Micah for the past 16 months. Despite his recent conversion to the core of the Nazi propaganda regarding the Jews, there was still that remnant of loyalty he felt to them. He decided he would pen a note to Micah, explaining that the wedding was to be held on short notice and limited to immediate family members. After writing the note, he thought that any contact with Micah regardless of past loyalty would be foolish, and therefore it would be best not to contact him. Perhaps his mother would mention it to him, but upon further reflection he came to the conclusion that part of his former personal life was closed, and not open to any consideration. Like all of his pursuits in life, Gerhardt opted for a complete submersion into his new world. The past was the past, but the future for him, Frieda and Germany was in the views of Hitler and Goebbels.

My Dearest Gerhardt,

Yesterday when I received the invitation to your wedding, I had feelings of joy and sadness. My joy is that my son will be with someone who will love and care for him for the rest of his life. I do not know Frieda but I am sure that she is truly a wonderful woman who will be your partner and the mother of your children. Although I have not seen you in years, you are, and will always be my cherished son. I wish that all the blessings of life will be showered on you and Frieda.

However, your wedding invitation also created feelings of deep sadness. I cannot attend your wedding without Otto because it would be most painful for him as well as me. I understand that in the past there was a falling out between you, but that was years ago. Otto has been a loving, caring husband, and I wish you could find it in your heart to invite him to your wedding.

What pains me more is that you have chosen not to invite Aunt Margret, Uncle Isadore and Micah. In many respects, they raised you and your exclusion of them, for whatever reasons, is difficult to understand. Micah, in particular, is hurt by this because he believed that he would be part of your wedding party.

Despite all of this pain, I end by wishing you and your beloved Frieda a wonderful wedding day and years of happiness.

Love,
Mother

In the past he would have responded to his mother's letter but he realized he had made a choice about his life and she and the rest of the family were no longer a part of his present or future.

The day before his wedding Gerhardt arrived in Passau. This was his first visit to this enchanting place, dubbed the Venice of Bavaria. Passau was a small town located in the lower Bavarian region of Germany where the tributaries of the three rivers Danubio, Liz and Ills meet and flow as one. The city was also called the "City of Three Rivers." As he walked near the river he was mesmerized by the beauty of the waterfront and the baroque architecture. The town had the aura of a fairy tale. Frieda had not been yet arrived in Passau so he walked leisurely through the town for hours. Because he was an architectural student, certain buildings became the focus of his attention. Framed by Oberhaus fortress to the north and Our Lady of Mercy pilgrimage church to the south, this beautiful town was dominated by the buildings of Italian architects. A thriving center of trade, the town had long been a hotbed for creative expression. Towering majestically above Passau was St. Stephen's Cathedral, the mother church of the eastern Danube region and of St. Stephen's Church in Vienna. This imposing baroque edifice contained the largest cathedral organ in the world.

All of the beauty, architecture and history were interesting but there was something more important happening within Gerhardt. He felt an exhilaration that not only would he be joined with Frieda in marriage but also that he was experiencing a whole new life. He had been a nobody with limited opportunities as an architect but was now immersed in an exciting period of growth and opportunity. He was dealing with issues and opportunities beyond his imagination. In addition, he was becoming part of a family and hopefully in the future would have children of his own. The hole in his heart caused by his father's death would be healed by all that was in his present and future. He could finally put away the bitter memories of his childhood and concentrate on the bright future that was unfolding. As he gazed at the three rivers coming together and flowing as one, he realized that there were forces flowing together in his life that had healed his pain and offered him a life full of meaning and purpose.

Two days later:

In full crescendo the organ hushed the conversations of the guests as the bride slowly walked down the aisle. Frieda's father, dressed in the uniform of the Nazi party, smiled broadly as he nodded to the rows of well-wishers.

Arriving at the altar, father gently uncovered daughter's veil and then placed the hand of his daughter in Gerhardt's hand. Frieda smiled as she felt the warmth of Gerhardt's skin on hers. They ascended the two steps to the altar and were warmly greeted by Bishop Freund. The celebrant of the Mass was a personal friend of the Niemeyer's. He was joined at the altar by five other clerics. Bishop Freund was a patron of National Socialism and had publicly supported the plans to force all of the local Jews to emigrate. He held the abiding view of many clerics -- the Jews had willfully rejected the Messiah and were responsible for many of Bavaria's economic woes.

It was a traditional Mass. The vows the couple exchanged were simple ones, spoken before by millions. Gerhardt looked into the eyes of his beloved and with all of his being loudly said, "I do."

After the traditional Bavarian wedding celebration Frieda and Gerhardt were able to avoid the common Bavarian pranks of kidnapping the bride and the placing of all sorts of booby traps in the bridal suite. They had kept their honeymoon site a total secret and all of the usual suspects had failed to discover their hotel, which was located just outside of Regensburg.

The ride to their honeymoon destination was full of anticipation for the two, but both were somewhat fearful. Frieda and Gerhardt were virgins. They had never seen each other naked and almost all sexual activities would be new to them. The decision to remain virgins while courting was religious. Frieda, in particular, felt that God wanted them to be as pure as possible on their wedding night.

After they checked into their hotel room there was a period of awkwardness. Frieda excused herself and went into the bathroom for a prolonged period of time. She wondered how the entire act of consummating their love should begin. Gerhardt was equally nervous and smoked one cigarette after another while pacing back and forth in the living room. Finally, Frieda returned and sat on a love seat. Gerhardt joined her and said, "I cannot believe that we are finally married." Frieda smiled, caressed his hand and kissed him gently on the cheek. He placed his arm around her and kissed her, first gently and then with more passion. He felt physically excited and realized he had a full erection. With trembling hands Gerhardt slowly opened her blouse. When it finally fell open, he admired her beauty, and caressed her breasts. Though excited, he reminded himself to be gentle with Frieda. Holding her hand, he led her to the bed. He quickly undressed and helped her remove her undergarments. After more touching and kissing Gerhardt slowly entered her and after she wrapped herself around him, they made love. Surprisingly, Frieda experienced no pain, and loved that Gerhardt was so gentle. These moments were beyond her imagination and it was tender loving. They spent hours cuddling before they fell asleep.

Chapter 10

May 1933, Munich
Gerhardt is now a true believer

The changes in Gerhardt's character were slow and initially imperceptible but each new concession of conscience was creating a different person. Even his mother would not recognize the person that he had become since he joined the Nazi party.

Gerhardt had by this time become fully acclimated to his new way of life. He had moved from being a draftsman with a limited future, to being one of the core leaders in the Nazi Munich headquarters. His responsibilities centered on developing and designing all signs, symbols and materials for the party's journals and newsletters. In addition, he was given select assignments by Albert Speer in preparation for massive meetings to be held in September at Nuremberg.

He rose early on this momentous day in May, and after a brief breakfast went into the attic and opened a steamer chest that contained some of his father's architectural books. Most of them were standard texts, and to a large degree were no longer in tune with the contemporary architectural movements in Germany. However, one book in particular caught his eye -- "The Foundations of German Architecture in the 19th Century." The author was Professor Solomon Frieberg. Dusting off the cover he opened the book to the inscription page. It read:

To Wilhelm Stark.

You are destined to make significant contributions to the future of German architecture. It has been a pleasure to have you as a student and assistant.

With regards,
Professor Frieburg.

As he turned the pages, he wondered whether his father would have embraced the current political movement in Germany. Now, there was tremendous potential architecturally and Wilhelm probably would be one of the leaders in creating the new Berlin. He supported this belief by falling back on the fact that his father had made the supreme sacrifice. He died for Germany and had he known that his death was to occur because of a betrayal by a Jewish conspiracy he would certainly have joined the party. This book was part of the fraud that deceived his father and now was the opportunity to symbolize that his death would not be in vain. The lingering doubts of his involvement in National Socialism had withered to occasional moral glances and tomorrow would be another step toward enthusiastic belief in the movement.

He closed the chest, placed the book under his arms and returned to the kitchen. Frieda, who was six months pregnant, was having a cup of coffee. Gerhardt bent down, kissed her and affectionately stroked her stomach. "How are you feeling on this glorious May morning my wonderful wife?"

Frieda blushed and patted Gerhardt's hand. "I am well but our child has decided to have an early morning kicking episode. I hope that the baby will be less active for today's trip."

As they chatted over breakfast the front door opened and Rolf entered the room carrying a duffle bag and a box of breakfast cakes.

He offered his travel companions some strudel and enthusiastically asked, "Are you ready? I thought we could catch the early train and roam around Berlin before the festivities begin tomorrow. I made arrangements for us to stay with a member of the party whose father owns a small hotel near tomorrow's event. Have each of you selected a book that will be part of the program?"

Frieda and Gerhardt nodded ascent and prepared to leave for the train station.

The following morning was clear and sunny as the trio walked to the State Opera square where they were joined by thousands of University students. It resembled the first day of class by the level of chatter and excitement, which included live music, singing, "fire oaths," and incantations. The square had a platform and, in the center, there was a massive pile of books formed into a pyramid. Once the throng of 40,000 students and party members assembled there was a series of whistles and one of the organizers of the event asked for silence and attention. At precisely 10 a.m. official government cars roared into the parking area near the square. In the lead car was minister Josef Goebbels who was greeted with shouts of joy and the common salutation of "Heil Hitler". He and his entourage plunged into the mob of students and the festive occasion was off to a roaring start. Goebbels ascended the steps of the platform and after a few minutes of cheering he motioned for the crowd to be quiet. He began with the usual statements about how thrilled he was to be here to take part in this momentous ceremony. With energy and a booming voice, he said, "The era of extreme Jewish intellectualism is now at an end. The breakthrough of the German revolution has again cleared the way on the German path. The future German man will not just be a man of books, but a man of character. It is to this end that we want to educate you. As a young person, to already have the courage to face the pitiless glare, to overcome the fear of death, and to regain respect for death -- this is the task of this young generation. And thus, you do well in this midnight hour to commit to the flames the evil spirit of the past. This is a strong, great and symbolic deed -- a deed which should document the following for the world to know -- Here the intellectual foundation of the November Republic is sinking to the ground, but from this wreckage the phoenix of a new spirit will triumphantly rise."

When he finished speaking an assistant handed Goebbels a book. He held it up for the cheering crowd to see and triumphantly strode down the steps to the pyramid of books. A member of his staff lit a torch and threw it into the center of the books. As the flames began to consume the books Goebbels hurled his book into the inferno. The crowd cheered and followed his example. Hordes of books were flying through the air like geese in formation as the students followed Goebbels' example. Rolf sped through the crowd but Gerhardt and Frieda waited because of her current physical condition. Gerhardt opened the book and again glanced at the inscription and wondered whether his father would participate in this historical movement if he were alive. He focused again on the belief that his father gave his all to the Fatherland and would be immersed in restoring what had been lost. It was another moment of accommodation and rationalization to quell any lingering beliefs of yesterday.

The dancing, shrieking crowd dwindled and Gerhardt led Frieda to the edge of the blazing fire. As tiny fragments of parchment and sparks filled the sky, they both hurled the last of the forbidden works into the middle of the inferno. Gerhardt momentarily hesitated but quickly reminded himself that he was the son of one who made the supreme sacrifice for the Fatherland. The ashes of pages at this point in his conversion would one day lead to the ashes of persons.

Chapter 11

Berlin, June, 1934
Creating symbols for the Nazi Messiah

It was sweltering. The humidity created streaks of water on the conference room's windows. The whirring fans merely churned around the warm air that penetrated the room from outside. The office was like an oven and complimenting the fans was the droning buzzing of the myriad house flies on this early June morning. Albert Speer and Gerhardt Stark were examining preliminary plans and drawings for the September Nuremberg Rally. In January Hitler gave Speer his first major commission: to build a permanent reviewing stand for the Nuremberg Rally. Speer engaged his young associate Gerhardt to come up with preliminary ideas and drawings for the event. After two weeks of investigating historical settings for mass meetings, Gerhardt presented the Pergamon Altar of ancient Greeks as inspiration. He suggested they build a massive stone structure some 400 meters long and 24 meters high on the Zeppelin Field at Nuremberg. This was to be the focal point of the rally and the place where Hitler would give his addresses to adoring crowds over four days and nights. Speer was delighted with this proposal and believed that it would create a magnetic religious overlay to the ceremonies. Neither he nor Gerhardt had any deep religious convictions but assumed that it would create a messianic setting for Hitler. In addition to the two architects, Leni Riefenstahl joined them this morning for a planning session. Gerhardt had not met Leni and was not aware of how she would be involved in the project.

Leni was a stunningly beautiful woman, an outstanding dancer. However, a significant knee injury ended her career. She became a prominent actress as well as a film maker. She was small in stature with jet black hair and piercing brown eyes. Speer introduced Leni to Gerhardt and said, "Leni why don't you bring Gerhardt up to date of how you will be involved in the September meetings at Nuremberg."

Leni began to give some background. "Gerhardt, I spent most of my professional life as a dancer and actress but have been dabbling in movie films as a director for the past few years. It is impossible not to be aware of what is happening in Germany politically but I had only a casual awareness of Hitler and the Nationalist Socialist party. I have a certain amount of public notoriety but was shocked that somehow Hitler was aware of my acting background and current involvement as a filmmaker. I received a call a month ago requesting that I meet with him. Of course, I was flattered but had not the slightest idea why he would meet with me.

Gerhardt was impressed. "So, you actually have met the Fuhrer?"

"I met with him several weeks ago and he requested that I contact Albert to discuss a film that would focus on the September Nuremberg meeting. I was shocked that he would want me to be involved and also very anxious. I am relatively new to the world of films and I was uncomfortable thinking about taking on such a project. I tactfully shared with the Fuhrer that I did not have an in-depth understanding of the movement and certainly others would be more qualified to make such a film. I clearly indicated that a documentary would be vastly different than anything I had directed.

Intently listening Gerhardt asked, "How did the Fuhrer react to your comment?"

"He summarily dismissed my lack of experience and told me that he was familiar with my work and that he wanted something that would be new and bold. He felt that my approach to film making was closer to his concept than any of the long-time film directors. He wanted a film using spectacle that would capture the feelings and desires of the average German. At the end of our conversation, I believed he wanted a film that would appeal to the hearts and minds of those who wished to create the new Germany. He suggested that I work with Albert so that the symbols and purpose of the four-day meetings would be seamless. I concurred with his view. It would be helpful if I could understand some of the architectural and symbolic components you wish to employ during the four days."

Speer said, "Gerhardt I believe it would be worthwhile to give Leni an overview of the preliminary structures and symbols we have identified."

Gerhardt moved to the large wooden table in the center of the room and unfolded a series of documents with architectural drawings and specific visuals for the event. His initial explanations focused on the large altar-type structure.

"We wish the meeting to promote the idea that the entire German nation is in the hands of a charismatic leader. The images are to be captivating with an aura of religious fervor. I have no official dogmatic, religious convictions but am impressed by the power religious symbols and images can have on the masses."

Speer interjected, "Also, we believe that the most powerful moments of imagery take place at night. I have access to floodlights that will lend a mysterious backdrop to the events. We will borrow them from the Luftwaffe, which may cause problems with Goring, because they are from Germany's strategic reserve. However, I have discussed this with the Fuhrer and he has overruled Goring's concerns. He thinks the floodlights will serve two purposes, first as a marvelous backdrop and, second, if we use them in such large numbers for events like this, other countries will think we're swimming in searchlights."

Speer continued, "The feeling created will be one of being in a vast room with the beams serving as mighty pillars of sparkling outer walls."

The initial meeting of the three planners was the first of many. After multiple days of intense give and take, Leni proposed the filming process and outlined each section of the meeting. She also requested that Gerhardt agree to be part of the filming process because he was the perfect image of the Nordic warrior that the Fuhrer wished to portray. In late July the architectural plans and symbols were finalized by Speer and Gerhardt. Leni approved of all the designs and presented her plan for filming.

"I think that the scenes have to begin away from Nuremberg and lead the viewers to the meetings."

"I am not sure I follow you," said Gerhardt.

"Well, my initial thought is that we would begin the film with Hitler flying in a plane toward the event. And then after he landed at the airport, he'll be followed by his auto taking him along the route to Nuremberg while adoring crowds are cheering on the side of the road."

Speer said, "I like that image."

Continuing, Leni said, "I would envision opening with shots of clouds above the city, and then move through the clouds to float above the assembling masses below, with the intention of portraying the beauty and majesty of the scene."

Gerhardt asked, "Will this part be silent or will there be an overlay of music?" "That is an excellent question," she said, " I intend to use the stirring arrangement of the Horst-Wessel-Lied."

Now, Leni had their undivided attention. They were captivated by her ability to graphically frame the beginning of the film.

Leni continued, "The second day I would like to begin with images of the charming countryside of Nuremberg as the sun comes up."

Speer was intrigued and suggested that the music that accompanies the scene be from Hitler's favorite composer.

Leni concurred. "I am happy that I have such musical enthusiasts on this project. I also thought of Wagner and an extract from the Act III Prelude (Wach Auf!) of Die Meistersinger von Nuremberg would be perfect. Following this I would identify the key members of the party and attendees preparing for the opening of the Reich Party Congress, and footage of the top Nazi officials arriving at the Leopold Arena. I have to admit, Gerhardt, that none of them portray the Aryan warrior as well as you."

With a twinkle in her eye she said, "Not to be mentioned outside of this room but some are short and bald while others are fat, and, God forgive me, homely."

Albert and Gerhardt laughed at this physical assessment of the Nazi inner circle.

Gerhardt asked, "Are we now at the actual meeting?"

"Yes, and Rudolf Hess will actually open the event. After he introduces Hitler, I plan to transfer the scene to an outdoor rally, which is primarily a series of quasi-military drills by men carrying spades. This will be brief as a backdrop to Hitler's first speech focusing on the merits of the Labor Service and praising them for their work in rebuilding Germany.

Speer said, "I think the imagery is powerful. How long will the speech be?"

"I would envision four or five minutes of highlights and then end this day with a torchlight parade in which Viktor Lutze speaks to the crowds. "

Speer said, "I am duly impressed with your imagery and the scene with thousands with spades is powerful for a population that has experienced a depression and is hungering for work."

Gerhardt added, "Also, it glorifies common work and has the effect that everyone has a vital part to play in the cause."

Leni was thrilled that her format so far met with total approval and support.

"On the next day I would love to have a focus on thousands of German youths pledging their allegiance to Hitler. I intend to have an aerial view of the Hitler youth assembled on the parade ground before Hitler is introduced by Baldur von Schirach. I then envision, after thunderous applause, Hitler will talk about how they must harden themselves and prepare for sacrifice. That night Hitler will deliver another speech by torchlight, commemorating the first year since the Nazis took power and declaring that the party and state are one entity. Does it make sense so far?

Speer and Gerhardt gave Leni enthusiastic approvals.

Speer said, "It is so well thought out and persuasive that I don't know how you can improve it on the fourth day."

Leni smiled. "Actually, that may be the easiest part of the meeting. I have spent hours trying to birth an explosive end to the film, building it around Hitler walking through a long, wide expanse with more than 150,000 troops standing at attention, as he lays a wreath at a First World War memorial. Hitler then will review the parading SA and SS men, following which Hitler and Lutze deliver speeches. New party flags will be consecrated by letting them touch the Blutfahne (you know, the same cloth flag said to have been carried by the fallen Nazis during the Beer Hall Putsch) and, following a final parade in front of the Nuremberg Frauenkirche, Hitler will deliver his closing speech in which he reaffirms the primacy of the Nazi Party in Germany. I have previewed the speech in which he will state, 'All loyal Germans will become National Socialists.' Hess will then lead the assembled crowd in a final Seig Heil salute for Hitler, marking the close of the party congress. The entire crowd will then sing the Horst-Wessel-Lied as the camera focuses on the giant Swastika banner, which fades into a line of silhouetted men in Nazi party uniforms, marching in formation as the lyrics 'Comrades shot by the Red Front and the Reactionaries march in spirit together in our columns' are sung."

Speer reached to shake Leni's hand. "I have grown to agree with the Fuhrer's instincts even before I clearly understood his rationale. It is obvious to me why he chose you, Leni, to make this film."

Leni was slightly embarrassed but after a brief pause responded, "Albert your work and Gerhardt's portrayal of the settings and symbols were enormously helpful in my plotting out the four days. Had I not spent this much time with both of you the film would lack the vigor and meaning required"

The Closing Ceremony.

Gerhardt was emotionally overwhelmed as the spotlights created a cathedral setting for one of the key moments of the event. It was not important that anyone know that he was one of the architects of this magnificent night. Gerhardt Stark had grown from disbelief to devotion. There were no longer anguished moments of conscience forcing him to look at required accommodations. Rationales were no longer necessary. He had arrived at the solid ground of meaning in every quarter of his life and now gave joyful consent to the Nazi way of life. He had embraced the vision of the 1000-year Reich but in reality, there were gifts that were more personal and resident in the now. He had compartmentalized his emotions, suppressed his conscience, sold his soul for the opportunity to work on the grand projects that Speer was involved in.

He had drifted in pain from early losses in his life for years. Before his Nazi life he was going nowhere personally or professionally. That all changed when he embraced the mantle of National Socialism. A wife, family, children all tore away the scabs of his pain and he was no longer a nobody standing on the sidelines of life. He was a leader who was helping to change the world and rectify the perceived crimes of yesteryear. He had imbibed the belief that his actions were paybacks for the tragedy of his father's death and the loss of his mother's emotional presence. The bitterness of his feelings toward his step father, Otto, was replaced by a new family and children of his own. He had no regrets in his behavior and this glorious night in Nuremberg enabled him to pledge even his life to the Fuhrer. At this point, for Gerhardt there were no longer questions of ethics or morality. The trappings of meaningless rules and religious beliefs were severed from his mind and soul. He had been given the gift of genuine purpose that would enable complete total responses to all the cause would require in the future.

Chapter 12

November 1938, Munich
Gerhardt is completely transformed

If she met her son today, Gerhardt Stark's mother would be completely amazed at how he had changed in the last few years. He once was a total skeptic of the National Socialist movement. Presently he was intimately involved in the key significant events in the Nazi rise to power. He, with Albert Speer, had prepared the architectural plans and symbols for the 1934 Nuremberg festivities. In 1936 He assumed responsibility for the maintenance of the Olympic village after the principal Jewish architect was fired and committed suicide. Selected personally by Reichsfuhrer Reinhardt Heydrich he accompanied Hitler on his triumphant entrance into Austria after the Anschluss and was instrumental in setting up the Zentralstelle fuer Juedische Auswanderung in Vienna. This organization was to be responsible for the "solution of the Jewish problem" in Austria. The main objectives of this function were to relieve the Jewish community of all financial assets and force them to emigrate.

Businesses as well as homes and other private property were transferred to the German government or influential non-Jews.

Gerhardt was given clear instructions on his role from the first day on the job in Vienna. He had written guidance that stated the goals were to relieve Austrian Jews of all of their money and valuable possessions, all confiscated assets were to be to be sent to the SS main office in Berlin. However, his superior, in a private conversation, stated, "Our job is to steal assets but if some falls to the floor and is swept up by you and me that is only fair." This counsel was the beginning of Gerhardt amassing a fortune of art, jewelry and money as well as an apartment near St. Stephens that had been owned by a Jewish business man who committed suicide after the Anschluss.

Gerhardt was rewarded handsomely for his other accomplishments. He, Frieda, and their three children were awarded a nine-room apartment on Prinzegetontemmplatz, the most fashionable street in Munich. The apartment was stolen from a local Jewish industrialist and was filled with antiques and elegant furnishings. In the foyer there was an original bust created by Rodin and the walls were adorned with paintings by famous French impressionists The owner was an avid art collector and the paintings and sculptures in the apartment were worth millions of German marks.

As he played with his youngest son, Wolfgang, on this overcast November afternoon in Munich, Gerhardt was mentally thinking of his next assignment. He had been transferred to the SS. After months of intensive training, he was on a 10- day pass to spend time with his family. Fortunately, this coincided with an invitation to represent the SS at a commemorative dinner honoring the memory of the Putsch event in 1923. He was excited because Hitler was to be the main speaker and there was a strong possibility, he would actually meet him. Caught up in the thought of this dinner, his three-year-old son, Wolfgang, brought him back to the practical world of fatherhood. Wolfgang was insisting that his teddy bear was hungry and was forcing lingenberry jelly into his mouth. Some wound up on Gerhardt's pants. He was glad he had not yet formally dressed for the evening's dinner. Frieda, watching the feeding of the Teddy bear jokingly chastised Gerhardt, "You are spoiling our little darling and when you leave, he will be impossible to discipline." Gerhardt smiled at her remark. He was so deeply invested in being a father that he would do anything for his children. He had painfully felt, to this day, the loss of fatherly love and attention and though he was absent for long periods of time he was devoted to his children. However, this love of his children did not transmit to the children of others. During his official duties in Vienna, he had seen many incidents where Jewish families were harassed and even tortured by German soldiers and members of the SS. He never reflected on the horror of Jewish children who witnessed the pain and fear that accompanied their daily existence. His children were living in a fairy tale world where all of their needs were met in a splendid community and the joys of childhood were never threatened by the misery of persecution. Somehow, he had separated his role with his own children from caring about other people's children. He had that deep commitment to his children that made their health and safety always foremost in his mind. Yet he had not the slightest semblance of concern for the psyches of Jewish children. He never even wondered for a moment whether they could be damaged for life because of what they were experiencing daily. He did not pause to reflect that the anxiety of Jewish parents would penetrate the hearts and souls of their children. As he walked past innocent Jewish parents forced to clean with toothbrushes sidewalks stained with human waste -- while their children wept as bullies tormented them -- he ignored their pain. All Jews were invisible to him and he was now immune and barely noticed the ugliness of such behavior. He did not inquire about the family that had been evicted from his splendid apartment. Were there children in his stolen residence? What was it like overnight to be thrown out of your home and cast into the daily pain of homelessness and hunger? His mental world had no room for those outside the party and his Jekyll and Hyde posture was serving him well. Witnessing brutality toward the Jews did not deter him from the work he was to undertake and accommodations of conscience created a new moral code for him. The vision of a thousand-year Reich obliterated much of what he believed initially to be ethical. Compromised by privilege, power, and the lure of personal career gain, he was totally seduced. His conversion was analogous to water dripping on stone that eventually penetrates. Gerhardt shed layers of early ethical guideposts and embraced the current vision of Nazi world dominance. In spite of his total conversion, he would not share any of this with his wife, Frieda. She was a devout believer, but had no real knowledge of what he was charged to accomplish. She, like many other Germans, was an anti-Semite, but had no direct blood on her hands. She supported migration and exclusion, but torture and murder were not something she could currently entertain. Gerhardt knew that he could never share his true work with her because she would be horrified that he was involved directly in killing innocent persons.

Gerhardt's star was on the rise and it appeared there was no limit to how far he could rise in the Nazi party. Josef Goebbels, on the other hand, was now only on the periphery of the inner circle. Once the first among equals, he had lost his premier status in the party. His open sexual affair with the Czech actress Lida Berova forced his wife to meet with Hitler to ask permission for a divorce. Hitler adamantly refused and in a furious rage ordered Goebbels to immediately sever any relationship with the actress. Not only did Goebbels lose his position as the key adviser to Hitler, but also there was the possibility he would wind up dead in an alley like so many people who displeased Hitler.

Suddenly there was an opportunity for Goebbels to restore his relationship with Hitler.

Ernst Van Rath, a low-level diplomat at the embassy in Berlin, was shot by a Jewish teenager. It was unclear whether the teenager knew him but that was insignificant to Goebbels. Van Rath lingered for a short period before succumbing. While attending a dinner in Munich,

Goebbels kept in constant contact with the hospital where Van Rath had been taken after the shooting. Before Hitler could address the group at the dinner, Goebbels was notified that Van Rath had died. He seized this news to immediately reposition himself with Hitler. Goebbels knew that Hitler was displeased with the pace of removing the Jews from Europe. Once Hitler learned of the incident, he immediately dispatched two of his physicians to Van Rath's hospital. Goebbels seized on Hitler's response and understood that Anti-Semitism had been his way of influencing Hitler in the past and this was a moment to get back in Hitler's good graces. Goebbels conferred with Hitler and informed him of Van Rath's death. Hitler counseled that there should be swift retaliation and the Jews should feel the pain from the German people but it must be done anonymously. Hitler then left the dinner party without giving his address and the role was taken over by Goebbels. After his speech Goebbels put in motion an immediate plan to make the Jews all over Germany pay for Van Rath's death. He understood clearly that this fortuitous opportunity had restored his relationship with his master. His mandate was clear. He was to find ways to punish the Jews. As usual, Hitler did not want his fingerprints on the ensuing violence but he did concur with Goebbels' view that the Jews must pay for this murder. Goebbels sought out Gerhardt and four other party attendees and instructed them to change their uniforms and have members of the SS contribute to the violence. However, it was critical that they not be identified as members of the SS. The word of Van Rath's death quickly spread throughout Germany. By the time Gerhardt appeared on the street the carnage had begun. He joined the mobs that were burning the significant synagogue on Herzog-Rudolf Strasse. In an instant the entire building was an inferno. Gerhard understood Goebbels' counsel and ordered his colleagues to blend with civilian mobs. Gerhardt encouraged them to create a fervor for destruction in the massive crowds that were assembling all over Munich. Jewish taunts reverberated through the crackling sounds of fire as Gerhardt and growing numbers of SS members appeared on the streets smashing the windows of Jewish establishments. Nazi chants for revenge for the death of someone they did not even know took foothold in the simple minded.

All over Munich streets were filled with shattered glass and Jewish men were beaten and being rounded up. The fire department did nothing to protect Jewish buildings from being burned and were only on standby to prevent damage to German-owned properties. Hundreds of Jews were arrested, beaten and tortured. There was a rash of suicides during this barbarous night. The horrors of that night were not the only tragedy committed against the Jews. The following week the official policy announced by the German government was that Jewry was to be totally responsible for the damages done throughout the country. It was decreed that 24% of all Jewish property was to be confiscated to pay for the damages. This period was a foretaste of what the European Jews would experience during the next seven years.

Unknown to Gerhardt at this time was the fact that his Uncle Isadore was arrested with many other Jewish men and sent to Dachau.

Two mornings after Kristallnacht;

Aunt Margret and Micah showed up at the SS headquarters in Munich at precisely 8 a.m. They had not been in contact with Gerhardt for years but hoped he would use his influence to free Uncle Isadore. Gerhardt knew they were waiting to see him but made them wait for more than two hours in the lobby. He was signaling his superiority over them. Finally, he sent word to the main desk that he would see them. When they entered his office, he made no gesture of the fact that they were once a vital part of his life. He did not greet them with words of affection and did not even rise from his sitting position. He sat behind his desk and showed no level of personal feeling or emotion. There was no warm greeting, no hug. He merely assumed an efficient Nazi posture as if they were total strangers. Micah's mother had cautioned him to restrain himself, because she knew that he harbored a high degree of anger toward Gerhardt, his cousin and friend. Now Gerhardt was a person that he barely recognized. The memories of yesterday and all they had meant to Gerhardt were buried and barren. Micah was repulsed by the fact that Gerhardt was now a full-blown Nazi. Aunt Margret took the lead in the conversation,

"Gerhardt two nights ago Uncle Isadore was arrested and sent to some sort of camp called Dachau. We are most concerned, because as you remember, he is a diabetic and we fear that he may have run out of insulin. Please, Gerhardt, use your influence to see that he receives the necessary proper medical care and if possible, arrange his release. He is innocent of any wrongdoing and is not involved in politics."

Gerhardt felt uncomfortable and for a brief moment realized that he owed a great deal to Uncle Isadore and Aunt Margret. However, the realization was brief and almost immediately removed from his consciousness.

Coldly he responded, "If he has not broken any laws, I'm sure he will be released."

At this my point Micah lost complete control of his emotions.

He stood up and shouted, "What is wrong with you? My father loves you and took you under his roof. How can you not immediately have him released?"

Coldly, Gerhardt answered, "One more word out of you and you will join him." Aunt Margret restrained Micah and forced him to be seated. She pleaded again with Gerhardt to intervene for his uncle's welfare.

"Gerhardt you are our only hope. I am sure you know in your heart that Uncle Isadore has done nothing wrong. Please remember all that he has done for you when you most needed love and kindness."

Even though Aunt Margret was a vital part of Gerhard's past life, her words did not move Gerhardt.

He began to shuffle papers and without even looking up at his family he said, "All right, now leave because I have a busy schedule this morning."

Gerhardt chose to contact the administration at Dachau and stated that he wished to interrogate a prisoner. He gave Uncle Isadore's name and announced that he would be there the following morning. Upon arrival a guard ushered him to a conference room and advised him that the prisoner would summarily be brought to him. Gerhardt lit a cigarette and began to pace back and forth. The memories of his past childhood flooded his mind and he was being confronted with a growing uncomfortable situation. He hoped that when his uncle arrived, he would not respond as if he knew him. After a brief period, the door to the conference room opened and a guard entered with a prisoner who was barely recognizable to Gerhardt. The guard roughly threw Uncle Isadore on to a wooden bench. "sit down on that bench you Jew swine." Gerhardt was stunned by the sight of a frail, unshaven image of the robust vigorous man that had once been a father figure to him. He dismissed the guard and with gentle tone began to speak with his Uncle. The memories of his past childhood flooded his mind and he was being confronted with a growing uncomfortable situation. A voice in his head overrode the memories and reminded him that caring for his uncle could create career issues. He gazed again at this once important figure in his life and rationalized that he is apparently going to die soon and my intervention will have no lasting effect. He summoned the guard and left the room without even a parting farewell.

Uncle Isadore died the following weekend. The official statement to his family was that he died of medical complications in his sleep.

Chapter 13

June 1939, Wiegrovwicz, Poland
Threat of war with Poland

Dr. Abraham Slawinski was a thoughtful, gracious physician with strong ethnic features, a lot of very soft white hair, and ocean blue-green eyes. Recently he had a look of wariness, because of the difficult political days in Europe. An elder in his Temple, he also was a senior member of the medical faculty at the University of Warsaw. On a Sunday morning he sat deep in thought about the evolving situation for the Jews in Germany and wondered about the implications for Polish Jews. He was somewhat unaware that his wife was voicing concerns about their youngest child.

"That child of yours is going to be the death of me yet," Esther's mother confided to her husband in a moment of sheer exasperation. Her husband smiled as he drank his coffee at the breakfast table.

With annoyance she barked, "Sure, smile, most of her brazen behavior is your fault. Unlike the boys, you spoil Esther."

Her husband paused and said, "It is true that I treat her differently and that is because she is exceptionally bright and has such an inquisitive mind."

This annoyed his wife who was not looking for insight but rather understanding and acceptance of her position. "She should be focused on becoming a responsible Jewish woman in the community, not dreaming about being someone she can never be."

"What do you mean by that?" her husband asked. "She plays doctor and you shouldn't support it"

"Instead of nurturing her fantasy you should be telling her to listen to me and do the things that your mother requires. Stop filling her head with dreams of the city and medicine."

Dr. Abraham Slawinski knew in his heart that Esther was different. Although she was remarkably beautiful, she wasn't focused on being pretty. At age 14, besides her physical beauty, she was athletic, an excellent soccer player and she could hold her own with her older brothers. At times she was even more athletically capable than they. She climbed trees, ran races and wasn't afraid to play with the boys and get messy. She was spontaneous and insatiably curious. In any circumstance at home or school she was calm, self-assured and endearingly charming.

Often reading medical journals in her father's office she had a vivid imagination and career dreams that were forbidden in her community. Her dreams of the future were focused on medicine and she adored spending her time in the university medical labs peppering her father with questions about anatomy and medicine. She was never disrespectful toward the traditional roles of Jewish women in her community but saw beyond those.

Despite his wife's reservations. Abraham secretly took his daughter to the University one Sunday morning in late June. His wife was visiting her sister and would not be home until late in the afternoon.

As Abraham and his daughter Esther arrived at the medical building at the University of Warsaw Abraham made his daughter promise that she would not tell her mother that she spent time at the university. Upon entering his office, he informed Esther that he would be busy with paperwork for the next two hours and that she could spend time using the microscope in the laboratory. He cautioned her not to touch any of the medical supplies and vials but allowed her to explore a box of anatomical slides that he took from one of the closets. He gave her a preliminary explanation of what the slides were and told her to write down her reactions in a notebook. Privately, he was thrilled by her insatiable curiosity and was somewhat saddened that because she was a female the world of medicine was closed to her.

It should have been a time of celebration for Dr. Abraham Slawinski because he and his colleague Dr. Kristopher Hobbs recently received the Shyer award for outstanding medical contributions in the field of cardiology. Their two most recent medical papers proved that high blood cholesterol levels created early heart disease in over-age-40 overweight men. However, praise from the outside world had little effect on the reality of their experiences as members of the medical faculty at the University of Warsaw. They were never fully accepted as members of the medical staff by their Polish colleagues. The issue with Abraham was that he was Jewish, living in a community that almost overwhelmingly had no use for Jews. Also, there was a high degree of resentment that he had been appointed a full professor over some of his Polish colleagues. The ill feelings for Dr. Hobbs were no less apparent, but they had different roots. His father was at one time a German ambassador, and despite his English name his ancestry was deeply German. He and Abraham were more than colleagues, they were friends and had on multiple occasions spent social time together with their families.

Abraham had not shared his anxiety about the potential political dangers in Europe with anyone but he was greatly pained by the fact that his sister and her family were leaving Germany for a permanent trip to America. Upon pouring himself a cup of coffee he reached into the top drawer of this desk and pulled out a letter written by his sister in January.

He opened the letter and reread it for the 10th time. The letter had been smuggled to Warsaw by a business associate of his sister's husband.

Dear Abraham,

It is with great pain I inform you that Isaac, the children and I will be leaving Germany as soon as possible. Isaac's factories have been confiscated by the Nazis and there is the strong possibility that our home will soon be the next loss that we will incur. Life here has become impossible and since that awful night in November, life for all Jews in Germany has been terrifying. We are verbal targets on the streets and some of our non-Jewish friends and associates have become openly hostile to us. We thought in the beginning that this wave of terror would be temporary and that the German people would never succumb to such barbarous behavior. We were wrong. Fortunately, Isaac has strong business associates in America, and though leaving our home is painful, we have chosen to start over in a new land.

My fear is that the movement will not end in Germany and it obviously may spread to all parts of Europe. The Nazis lust for new lands and I fear that Poland at some point may be occupied. I worry that you and your family may become targets. It would please us if you would consider joining us in America. I know little about the medical community but your outstanding achievements would be sought after there or in England. Please give serious thought to leaving before it is too late.

For now, my dear brother, I miss you deeply and long for the day when we once again will be reunited.

Love,
Miriam.

Caught up in the letter Abraham did not realize that someone was knocking on his door.

Entering, Dr. Hobbs said, "I gather I'm not the only workaholic who comes to the office on Sunday. You obviously were so caught up in something that you didn't even hear me knocking."

Devilishly handsome and almost 50, Hobbs looked much younger. He was short but had a lean physical dexterity to his walk and presence. His chestnut brown hair was long and he was the epitome of an English gentleman. He was a gifted teacher with a great sense of humor.

Abraham rose and shook his friend's hand. "I was deep in thought about a nonmedical function."

"Can you share that with me?"

Abraham was not sure that he should but Kristopher was such a dear friend. He thought he could understand some of the anxiety that any Jew would feel at this time.

"I was just re-reading a letter from my sister who is leaving Germany because of the current political situation in Berlin."

Kristopher said, "I don't mean to be nosey, nor do I wish to make you uncomfortable, but is she leaving because of what is happening to her and her family because of the Nazi administration?"

"Yes, they have suffered many losses already."

Kristopher winced because he too was somewhat aghast at what was happening in Germany. "As you know my last name is somewhat misleading. I am more German than English. In studying my family history, I learned that years ago, members of my family moved from Germany to London. I gather my German grandmother married my British grandfather and that is how I would up with the name Hobbs. Despite growing up in London my initial language was German and German culture was part of my daily experience. However, I share your concern about what is happening. On our most recent visit to Bavaria my wife and I were shocked to realize that the Nazi party controls the entire nation. My parents and relatives are aghast with the cultural and political changes that have already occurred."

This peaked Abraham's curiosity. "What are the changes that you observed?"

"You can't go anywhere in Bavaria without seeing people in uniform and the swastika, which seems to be ubiquitous, is in every public and private building. My wife, Selma, and I found even in cafés and restaurants there are Nazi flags everywhere. The Nazi party seems to have completely overtaken the government. Like some Germans, I thought it would never take root in polite German society, but after speaking with my parents, I'm aware that this is not a phenomenon that is likely to pass soon."

"What does your father think of Hitler and the Nazi party?" asked Abraham.

"He often keeps his opinions privately to himself, but over dinner one evening he confided to us that he believed that in the not-too-distant future Europe would once again be engulfed in world war. He said the accommodations that the French and British made regarding Hitler's usurpation of the Sudetenland, Czechoslovakia and Austria makes him believe there is no power that will resist his desire to create a German continent."

The openness of Kristopher's comments pushed Abraham to ask a question that was most important for his understanding. "What about the treatment of the Jews?"

"That question came up in our conversation. My father indicated that Hitler and the German government are focused on driving the Jewish community not only out of Germany but also out of Europe."

Disturbed by this assessment Abraham asked, "Do you see any possibility that Hitler will invade Poland?"

"I have no way of answering your question, but at this stage of the game. I would not dismiss it. Do you have concerns about that possibility?"

"I do, and it has created a tremendous amount of personal internal conflict. In one sense, I am obviously Jewish but I am also a patriotic Polish citizen. Poland is my home and where I have lived my whole life. As you know, I have deep roots here. My family has lived near Warsaw for generations. I am an elder in my synagogue and this is where I met my wife and the village where my children were born. I am concerned that at some point my family will be in peril."

Kristofer took Abraham's assessment seriously. "I can understand that. What do you think your alternatives are?"

"While it is obvious even here at the University, I am an outsider. I'm certain that most if not all of the members of the faculty would be happy if I left."

Kristopher laughed and said, "Well my standing may not be as precarious as yours, however, they don't exactly love my presence because I am German."

Abraham smiled and said, "Well I'm sure that's true but as a German you would not be at risk."

"I agree but if your fears were to become reality, I would still have influence because of my father. I would do everything in my power to see that you and your family are protected."

Abraham was deeply touched by Kristopher's words. He said, "Thank you. I know that your words are spoken from your heart and I deeply appreciate them."

Chapter 14

July 1939, Berlin
Gerhardt joins the killing squads

Gerhardt and 80 other members of the SS were invited by Reichsfuhrer Reinhardt Heydrich to become leaders of the newly formed Einsatzgruppen. Their primary function in collaboration with local officials was to annihilate all members of resistance to the Nazi regime in Poland. Special attention would be given to the liquidation of all Jewish populations before the establishment of the ghettos in the large cities. The responsibility of this group was to immediately follow the invasion of Poland by the Wehrmacht and quell any local resistance. On July 24 at the German Chancellery in Berlin the candidates were assembled to meet with Heydrich at 8 a.m. in the main auditorium. The group was composed of members whose function would be to follow the Wehrmacht and terminate anyone considered to be an enemy of the Reich. Heydrich's staff had prepared documents and folders that identified all those who must be liquidated once the country was occupied. This included not only Jews but priests, journalists and the wealthy aristocracy.

Gerhardt had never worked with Heydrich but understood from Albert Speer that he was devoutly Catholic and despised the entire Jewish community. Heydrich was a rising star in the party and had immediate access to Hitler. He had an exceptional gift for organization and could manage an entire supplier network designed to address the goal of a Jew-free Europe. The past few months Heydrich had become intoxicated with power and was feared not only by the Jewish community but also by those closest to Hitler.

Wandering through the assembled crowd, Gerhardt was pleased that he was part of an elite, cultured, refined group of loyalists. The group was considered to be the intellectual cream of the crop in the SS. They were intellectuals and many had already established outstanding reputations in their own professions.

At precisely 8, Heydrich entered the conference room. He walked to the front, took off his leather overcoat and handed it and what appeared to be a riding crop to one of his attendants. He did not have to call for attention because his presence alone put a stop to all conversation. As he walked up to the platform all attendees said, "Heil Hitler" and then were seated. Heydrich was a striking figure that fit the desired look – a tall, lean Aryan leader. Gerhardt was surprised at the falsetto voice as Heydrich began to address the group and from the podium began his conversation with the attendees.

"I come to you after having spent the last few days with the Führer. Negotiations with the Polish Government have not led to acceptable conclusions despite the olive branch offered by Germany. We are aware that in Danzig thousands of Germans are being punished by the Poles. It appears that despite the Fuhrer's good will it will be necessary to wage war. We are on the brink of war with Poland, which will probably occur in the next five weeks. Once this has actually happened your task will be to focus on the removal of Polish intellectuals, Jews and anyone deemed to be an enemy of National Socialism. In many of these small towns you will be assisted by Germans living in Poland as well as the local police. The task is mammoth and the goal, besides the final removal of these enemies of the state, will be to create a level of fear that will make the processing of Jews to their assigned cities and ghettos run smoothly and without resistance.

Your work is top-secret and is not to be shared with anyone. This is critical work and I hope you understand that it is directly connected to the Führer's ultimate plan for Jew-free Europe. He paused for a brief moment and then in a high piercing voice said "this is the moment when you will become part of the glorious history of the Fatherland. Seize it with every ounce of energy and will."

The last statement was wildly accepted by all of those who stood up and applauded'

Heydrich waved his hand and gestured for the assembly to be seated.

"I need your absolute understanding and acceptance of this goal. To ensure that there is no misunderstanding or confusion of your tasks I will now entertain your questions or concerns. I would welcome any questions you have."

One SS member raised his hand and asked, "Who will have jurisdiction in the villages that we are to occupy -- us or the Wehrmacht?"

Heydrich replied, "The tasks and functions are totally separate; the Wehrmacht is to do the fighting and you are to clean up the populations after they have secured the village or city. Your functions will be to terminate enemies of the Reich and acquire items that have financial value. Money, valuable art and jewelry are to be turned in to the central SS administration. Members of this office will accompany your group as you make your way through Poland."

Another question was raised, one that had serious implications for who would live and who would die in the villages. "Will our focus be only on military aged men or does the task also require that we target, women, children and the elderly?"

Heydrich paused. "It is our desire to exterminate primarily men but on certain occasions, especially with regard to small villages, it may be impossible to exterminate just the men. I would leave that up to your judgment if you feel that an entire community must be liquidated, then I think there should be no exception with regard to any of the inhabitants. The reality is that ultimately, we have to face this one vital consideration whether a Jew is a baby or child or teenager or an adult or elderly; a Jew is a Jew, male or female. I remind you that the ultimate goal is a totally Jew-free Europe not a partially Jew-free Europe. Eventually it does not allow provisions to spare children, women or the elderly. The mission is to rid Europe of the entire Jewish race. The other thing I would offer to you is that we use the word evacuation in any of our official communications or correspondence. There is to be no bourgeois concern for this work. The rules of the Geneva convention do not apply to you. The Führer has granted you total immunity for any actions that you perceive to be necessary."

Gerhardt. was pleased by this assignment and assured by his immediate superior that this work would be temporary and when the process was accomplished, he would be reassigned to Speer's immediate staff. Gerhardt was impressed with the intellectual level of his new colleagues. These were not merely police officers; many had already achieved a degree of success in a professional field. There were lawyers, accountants, professors, doctors, and in his case, an architect.

At the conclusion of the morning Heydrich, referring to his notebook, asked that Gerhardt Stark stay after the meeting ended. Gerhardt was somewhat surprised to hear his name. As his colleagues were leaving the conference room, he approached Heydrich. "Good morning Reichsfuhrer I am Gerhardt Stark." Heydrich gave him the once over and asked him to be seated. Heydrich assembled his papers and put them into a briefcase before he sat down and faced Gerhardt.

"The reason I asked you to stay is that I have had glowing reports of your abilities from Albert Speer and I wish to give you an initial assignment."

Gerhardt was thrilled. In the past every position offered him more and more exposure to the Nazi inner circle.

Heydrich continued, "Once we enter Poland the task of mobilizing multiple Jewish communities will be difficult and complex. Our goal is to herd them from their villages to major cities like Warsaw and Krakow. In order to facilitate this, it will be essential that the tasks are carried out without any Jewish resistance. We will not have enough manpower to achieve this if they do not willingly accept our authority and orders. I believe that creating an additional element of fear will serve the process."

Gerhardt was attentive to every word that Heydrich uttered. and said. "I understand that Reichsfuhrer. Is there a role for me in your plans?"

"Yes, I do not want you to share this with any of your comrades but I wish you to select a village, preferably near a major Polish city, filled with a significant Jewish community and once the war starts terminate the Jewish population. This event will spread like wildfire through other Jewish communities and will be an implied threat if they do not comply with evacuation to the city centers. Do you understand what I am asking from you?"

"I do Reichsfuhrer but I only have one question. If the invasion happens where will my initial location be in Poland. I ask this because I would like to do research and identify a community in that area that has a large Jewish community."

Heydrich smiled and took out a map of Poland from his briefcase and said, "I see why Speer recommended you so highly. You are probably an excellent chess player who is two moves ahead of his opponent.

You will be in Zone One which is the closest to Warsaw. Heydrich rose, closed his briefcase, shook Gerhardt's hand and left the room.

Chapter 15

October 27, Wiegrowicz, Poland
The Village massacre

 The night before the intended mission in the Polish countryside Gerhardt had difficulty sleeping. His role in the Jewish question was not new but this assignment was at a higher level of commitment. He was not someone who lusted for the opportunity to terminate civilians. However, it was important for him to establish in his mind a clear rationale for why he was enthusiastic and willing to carry our such an order. The rationale for believing had been reinforced by the success of the German government internationally as well as the prestige and power he had received in the past few years. He was grateful that he would not directly kill anyone and deluded himself with all of the mental moral adjustments that allowed him to accommodate behaviors that would have been forbidden in the past. It was important that he remain calm and solicitous during the event in order to perform the task in a humane manner. Gerhardt had sanitized mass murder by years of mental and emotional deceptions. Tomorrow would not be in his mind an act of savagery toward innocent civilians. It would rather be a necessary event that would eventually create a world of peace and justice in the new Germany.

The Village Massacre:

 It was a clear, crisp late October Sunday morning, in the village of Wiegrowicz. The village was comprised of one third Jews and by and large they had been assimilated, though not fully accepted, by the majority Christian community. The marketplace was filled with merchants and despite the beginning of the war between Germany and

Poland the villagers seemed relatively unconcerned. There was even a sense of festivity in the air. Off in the distance from the town the sound of mechanized vehicles rolling through the Polish hills created echoes that were coming closer and closer to the village. The people in the marketplace suddenly became aware of thunderous sounds of cars and trucks. There were shrieks of horror as through the gates of the village came hordes of German soldiers, trucks and armored cars. Villagers were fearful, stunned and aware that their village was about to be occupied. Many of the residents began to scurry around and attempted to flee toward their homes. Almost immediately the entire marketplace in the central part of the village was entirely surrounded by German troops. A German officer left his vehicle and walked to the steps of the synagogue and began to address the frightened population.

"I am Captain Gerhardt Stark."He deliberately gave his full name and conveyed a warm posture by the tone of his voice. "There is nothing to fear from us. If you comply absolutely with every directive I give, life will soon return to normal. This village and the entire nation of Poland are now under the jurisdiction of the German government. In order that we may have discipline and order I am about to give you specific instructions. All of the members of the Jewish community must remain in the square. The non-Jews are required to go to their homes and remain there until further notice. I want the Jewish persons to form three separate groups. The first group will be men, regardless of age, over 15 years."

There was confusion as to where they should form and the officer pointed to the area that was closest to the fountain in the middle of the square. Once this was achieved, he informed them that they would be escorted into the woods and were to gather kindling and to chop down trees for firewood. He told them that this would be used by the German military in the coming evenings to provide heat while they camped outside the village.

Once this group started toward the woods the officer issued the directives for the next group.

"The second group will be adult women and we ask that they be accompanied by all children and infants under the age of 14. The third group will be young women between the ages of 14 and 18."

Initially, there was mass confusion and a tremendous amount of anxiety because many of the children and infants were crying. One of the participants, Esther, stood literally in front of the German officer. She could not believe what was happening and tried to glance over her shoulder at her father and two brothers who were being marched into the woods. Her father seemed calm. He waved to her.

Unknown to the community, the area in the forest had been scouted out by German spies the previous week and the ridge overlooking the Sun river had a machine gun nest. The German soldiers forced the men to stand facing the river at the edge of a deep precipice. After a period of about 15 minutes, there were muffled sounds that emanated from the woods, creating greater anxiety among those who were waiting to go into the wooded area. The German captain then told the soldiers to take the next group into the woods

"The second group will be adult women and we would ask that they be accompanied by all children and infants under the age of 14. The third group will be young women between the ages of 14 and 18."

Once this was accomplished, Stark and the soldiers stood in front of the young women -- about 50 in number. The soldiers escorted them to their individual homes. They were ordered to gather anything of value and warned not to resist or try to hide any money, jewelry or anything of value. Stark said, "If you do these simple tasks, you will be unharmed and at the end of the day be reunited with your families."

The terrified young women were now escorted to all of the Jewish homes. Esther, age 14 was accompanied by a young man who was barely four or five years older than her. However, looting was only part of the motive to visit their homes. Once they had searched her parents' home, the young soldier ordered her to take off her clothes. Horrified, Esther refused. In a loud voice he repeated, "Take your clothes off now." Again, she refused. The soldier slapped her face twice and grabbed her by the hair and dragged her to her parents' bedroom. He threw her on the bed and began to tear off her clothes. She kicked and screamed and he punched her in the face with such force that he broke her jaw. She was to lose her virginity to this monster on her parents' bed. She experienced great pain as he roughly penetrated her. This was only the beginning of the nightmare because in the next few hours five other soldiers raped her. Barely conscious at the end of the carnage she was dragged outside and forced to march with all the other women into the woods where prior murders occurred. As before, the victims were lined up at the edge of the cliff over the river. Shivering from the cold, Esther was in great pain from her bruised, broken and raped body. She looked up and saw a flash of the machine gun fire. One bullet grazed her head and she fell backward, rolling down the hillside. However, she did not fall completely into the water. There were so many bodies falling off the hill that she was pinned between those that had been shot before her.

Unconscious for hours, Esther was only partially submerged in water. On regaining consciousness, she crawled off the bodies to land at the edge of the water, fighting nausea as she understood the scene around her. Shivering and in a daze, she found a path that led up the incline and through the woods. Willing herself to keep walking, she entered the village. She heard a voice calling her name. It was her father's friend and colleague Dr. Hobbs. He raced toward her and she collapsed in his arms. She awoke to darkness in a bed. She had no idea where she was. Totally disoriented, she attempted to sit up but a gentle arm forced her to stay in bed. Terrified, she saw the face of Dr. Hobbs.

"Do not be afraid my dear, you are safe. You are in my home. You have been through a terrible ordeal and I will make sure that you are protected."

Esther blurted out, "Where is my family? Are they all alive ?"

"We can talk later my dear but right now you must rest and in a little while I will need to change the dressing on your head. Now close your eyes and try to sleep."

Dr. Hobbs walked from the bedside to the door where his wife, Selma, was standing.

"Poor child," Selma said, tears running down her cheeks. "How can we tell her what happened to her entire family?"

"I'm not sure, Selma, but right now the most important thing for Esther is sleep. The sedatives will help. The wound is not life-threatening, but the one thing we must try to do is prevent infection. In her state of mind, I'm not sure she can survive her own trauma and the death of her family."

When they finally told Esther, what happened to her family and the rest of the village she was catatonic for days. Eventually, she slowly began to speak. The Hobbs were gentle and patient with her. Dr. Hobbs knew from Esther's father that she had an avid interest in medicine so he began to leave journals and basic medical text books outside the door to her bedroom. In the following months Dr. Hobbs asked her to assist him with clinical preparations and slowly involved her in keeping his private patient schedule and clinical notes. Hobbs contacted his father, a former German ambassador and arranged to have a passport sent secretly that allowed Esther to go under the name of Luise Hobbs. Dr. Hobbs' brother and sister-in-law had been killed in an accident a few months previously and they would pass Esther off as their niece. Selma dyed Esther's hair blond and they began to teach her German and English. In six months, she was fluent in both languages.

Chapter 16

Early October 1941, Berlin
The plan to systemize the Genocide

There was no paper trail but everyone at the highest level of the Nazi party knew Hitler's goal with regard to the Jews. Himmler was tasked with the mammoth responsibility of resolving the Jewish question. It sounded simple because the German government had encapsulated and trapped all of the Jews of Europe. In essence that was the easy part. However, the intention was complex, without simple remedies. Himmler had mixed feelings about this task. It was first and foremost in Hitler's mind so there would be a tremendous advantage of delivering the desired results. However, there were so many resource questions to be answered that Himmler initially floundered regarding the intended Jew-free Europe. In searching for solutions, he learned that a ranking member of the Einsatzgruppen had an extensive background in architecture and organizational design. His name was Gerhardt Stark and he was currently assigned to the liquidation program in Russia. Himmler summoned Stark to a meeting with him in Berlin.

Gerhardt left Russia just before dawn. It was pitch black as he entered the squad car that was to take him to the airfield where he would hitch a ride on a transport to Berlin. The first rays of sunlight were breaking through the grey overcast clouds. There was an eerie silence to the ride, broken only by the Russian wind that was signaling the beginning of the cold that was increasing each day. Whenever one is summoned to a meeting with an official at the top of the organization, there are pangs of fear and worry. In Gerhardt's case, this would not be the issue because his rise had been meteoric and he had received plaudits, not only from Heydrich, but also from many members of the Nazi hierarchy. He was in tiptop physical condition and, unlike so many of his cohorts he had weathered the emotional and physical challenges that surfaced doing the work of eliminating large sections of the Jewish community in Poland and Russia.

Before he left Russia, he had gone to the administration building and borrowed a two-volume work that listed the inner circle of the Nazi party and their individual biographies. Despite the bumpy air ride, he was able to get specific background material on Himmler's career. In addition, two of his immediate superiors had been on Himmler's staff and the evening before he left for Berlin, he interviewed them. He was struck by their insights. On the plane he reviewed his notes from those meetings.

"Himmler is a trusted and skilled organizer and a capable manager who understands how to obtain and use power. The Fuhrer has given him complete control over solving 'The Jewish Question.' Himmler is the ideological and organizational driving force behind the rise of the SS. Moreover, he understands his SS men and knows how to secure their loyalty to the Fuhrer and his own person and to the concept of the Nazi elite to which they belong. His ability to give his subordinates leeway to exercise initiative to implement Nazi policy is a significant factor in the success of many SS operations. When he took over the SS, Himmler recognized the importance of internal security and determination of racial purity for the Nazi movement and successfully expanded the functions of the SS to meet these ideological and practical needs. Himmler understands the importance of police power separated from legal constraint and state supervision; he persuaded Hitler -- over the arguments of powerful rivals in the party

and the state -- that fusion of SS and police would forge the instrument for the Nazi regime to achieve its core, long-term ideological goals.

Gerhardt was excited that one so close and trusted by the Fuhrer possibly had meaningful work for him. Whatever the assignment that Himmler had in mind, he was certain it would allow him further access to the inner circle and perhaps even direct contact with Hitler.

At Berlin airport there was an official government limousine that transported Gerhardt to the main Gestapo headquarters in Berlin. Upon arrival, a uniformed officer greeted him and he was summarily passed through security and led to Reichsfuhrer Himmler's quarters.

The room was more like an apartment in an exquisite castle than an office. The furniture and selected photos of the Nazi world were intentional. The room was filled with German antiques, warrior paintings portraying the gallant historic images of the Aryan past. Heavy brocaded black and red fabrics adorned the opposite sofas and the tinted colored windows introduced a rainbow of colors against the mahogany walls. The room was more bold than gracious. In its center was a massive marble fireplace that was in full glare on this chilly morning. Himmler entered the room moments later and motioned for Gerhardt to be seated. Gerhardt had only seen him from a distance at Nuremberg so had no idea that he was short and not a man of dominating presence. Somehow because of the significance of his position Gerhardt imagined that he would be taller and more physically fit. He was really just average size, somewhat overweight, with pale milk-white skin, a rather large nose, and a short-cropped haircut.

Remembering the critical comments that were made at the Nuremberg meetings by Riefenstahl about the Nazi hierarchy, Gerhardt smiled.

Himmler sat behind a massive oak desk and opened what appeared to be a folder. He quickly turned the pages of the folder before speaking.

"Gerhardt, I see by your record that you have been promoted four times in the last two years."

Not wishing to appear arrogant Gerhardt said, "Yes, that is true, and I have been very blessed to serve such a forward-thinking organization."

Himmler continued, "You probably are wondering why I have summoned you to Berlin."

"Reichsfuhrer, I have learned to be patient when I am requested to appear before my superiors because I know that in due time the purpose of this meeting will be made eminently clear to me."

"I like your attitude and will begin by telling you that the conversation that we are about to have must remain absolutely secret. There will be no written communications and you must pledge absolute secrecy to what we will discuss. You are not to share any of our conversations with other colleagues or anyone else outside these four walls."

"I completely understand that and pledge my secrecy to whatever it is that you wish to convey to me this morning."

"Gerhardt it is the expressed desire of the Führer that we deal directly with the Jews. As you may realize, the Jewish question is a code for total annihilation. Initially we had hoped that all of the Jews would freely emigrate to other parts of the world. At one-point Madagascar was a possibility. However, the goal has changed in the past year. The Führer has never put this in writing, but has discussed his desires directly with me and others, including Goebbels. It is manifestly clear for all of those who serve the Führer that his intention is a Jew-free Europe. This is an admirable goal, but as you well know, the logistics of such a goal are complex and what makes it even more difficult is the short timeline. One of the reasons I have asked you to come this morning is because your background and current assignment may help me solve some of the challenges. First let me ask you what is the status and morale of the Einsatzgruppen?"

Gerhardt realized that this was not a moment to be timid, that he should convey clearly some of the issues he encountered leading his group of assassins.

"In my experience there are three groups within the Einsatzgruppen. The first group enjoys the killing and are ready to kill any and all perceived enemies of the Reich. The second group does not enjoy the killing but they are rule followers and will perform their duties regardless of their feelings. The third group is the most problematic because they are unwilling to directly kill civilians. I would say that one of the big concerns now especially in this third group is problematic drinking. Also, there have been some psychological problems and growing sick bay requests."

"What do you attribute this to?"

"I believe that some men do not have the emotional and psychological makeup to deal with direct killing and they do not have the necessary background to understand the ultimate goals."

Himmler responded to this information with a personal question. "what group are you in."?

"I personally am not in any of those categories and have resolved that issue because if you think that you are killing human beings -- men, women and children -- it becomes a huge obstacle. Rather, if you see this as a requirement to purify the German race in order to develop a superior Aryan future, liquidation becomes simply part of one's duty. I am not an anti-Semite but after months of studying the rationales underlying the Fuhrer's plans, I completely support his goals."

"That is well said and insightful. I would like you to document your observations and give me a written report on the current status and some ways that we can deal directly with the challenges. Also, do not keep a copy of this request. I wish there to be only a single version of your impressions."

Gerhardt agreed and said, "I will attend to your request immediately after this meeting."

"Good. Now the second issue is much more complex. I am sure that you are aware that our success in the Russian campaign has left us with thousands of prisoners. We will have to deal with them and currently we have neither the manpower nor the resources to house them permanently. There is an urgent need to develop a methodology, other than direct shooting, to terminate them. This is compounded by the reality of our current plans for the Jews. In a short period of time, we will begin to herd them into ghettos. In addition, we have to come up with a way in which we can maximize our ability to terminate all the Jews in Europe. The past methods are filled with problems. Unlike in the east where the populations openly assisted in the terminations, the German public will not support such overt behavior. I am confronted with a lack of solutions to how we kill them and hide the process and where this can occur. In addition to these mammoth questions there can be no direct relationship to the Führer."

Gerhardt asked, "Can you give me some approximate numbers for the coming year?"

"Gerhardt, I am talking about hundreds of thousands of prisoners, Jews and enemies of the state in the next year. Where can we house them, how can we terminate them and how will we dispose of them? Also, it is critical to do this in secret and last but not least how will we pay for this? Currently the only place that has potential is the camp at Auschwitz because it is so isolated. I would suggest that you begin there and visit Commandant Hoss. I have made him aware that you might be visiting him and I am sure that he can give you a vivid appraisal about the capability of the camp to solve the problems."

Gerhardt asked, "Is it possible for you to give me a specific time period in which to answer your concerns?"

"Yesterday," Himmler answered sarcastically. "Realistically I would need recommendations in a few weeks with a rudimentary road map for how we proceed. You have carte blanch resource-wise. Call on me or my office for any help you require. I suggest that your first step will be to contact Commandant Hoss at Auschwitz. He has had some success using gas to terminate prisoners but I fear that the location cannot handle the future numbers."

Gerhardt summed up the meeting by feeding back to Himmler the questions that must be addressed in the coming weeks. Himmler concurred with Gerhardt's summation and rose, indicating the meeting had come to a close.

Gerhard left Himmler's office with the realization that this could be a tremendous opportunity for him. For a brief moment he experienced some trepidation in the realization that he would be directly responsible for establishing plans for mass killing. There was a dryness in his throat and temporarily some feelings of discomfort. However, he dismissed these thoughts because this request provided great visibility at the top of the organization and even the possibly that he would be recognized by Hitler. He also made the decision that he would stay in Berlin and not return to Munich until he had completed this assignment. Himmler's office made a reservation for him at the Hotel Adlon in Berlin for a two-week period.

Chapter 17

1941, Berlin
Gerhardt outlines the tasks that must be addressed

After being led to his hotel room Gerhardt ordered a pot of black coffee. He could feel his level of excitement and pulse rise with each swallow. As he identified the challenges that Himmler had laid before him, he ran a hand through his blonde hair trying to segment the questions to be answered. Where do I start? he asked himself. Obviously the first part of his assignment was to visit Auschwitz. What is the current capability of housing the numbers? Are the rail facilities adequate to handle the perceived future numbers? What is the current process of selection? Is the intent to kill all the prisoners or can there be some use for retaining those with skills? Can the camp be expanded and still be isolated? How will the new building program be financed? Are there any personnel and family issues of staff that need to be addressed? Is there any possibility that the German industrial complex can be involved in the process? In addition to all of these questions he once again delved into the biographical background of Hoss' career.

He skimmed over much of the biography but wrote the following in his journal:

Born in the Black Forest in 1900 to Catholic parents.
He served in World War 1 as the youngest NCO in the German Army, experiencing a desperate sense of betrayal at the subsequent loss of the war. In the early 1920s, Hoss joined the paramilitary Freikorps to help counter the perceived communist threat on the boundaries of Germany, before his involvement in violent right-wing politics led to his imprisonment in 1923.

The Architect of Auschwitz

For Hitler, Hoss and others on the Nationalist Right, the most urgent need was to understand why Germany had lost the war and agreed to such a humiliating peace. And in the immediate post war years they believed they had found the answer.

Hoss believed that the Jews -- with their alleged communist sympathies -- had stabbed Germany in the back.

Hoss joined the Nazi party in November 1922, shortly after it was founded. Heinrich Himmler, an ardent Nazi talent spotter who knew Hoss from the early days, invited him to become an active member of the SS. Hoss accepted and in November 1934 arrived at Dachau concentration camp in Bavaria to start his service as a guard.

Hoss is a model SS man and rose through the ranks, eventually being promoted to Rapportfuhrer, chief assistant to the commander of Dachau. In September 1936 he was made a lieutenant and transferred to Sachsenhausen concentration camp, where he remained until his elevation to commandant of the new concentration camp at Auschwitz.

The next morning Gerhardt took a train from the main station in Berlin to the closest station near Auschwitz.

The buildings were in serious need of repair. Many had parts of their roofs missing and were leaking into the main areas. The straw mattresses were damp and the interiors of the buildings wreaked with the odor of diarrhea. The barracks were filled with rats and other vermin and the sanitary facilities were primitive and overflowing.

He was used to perfectly attired soldiers who took pride in their appearance. That was sorely lacking here. Himmler had given him a dossier on the commandant Hoss. He read the biography on the train. Once through security he was taken to the commandant's office. Hoss greeted him and said, "I have been contacted by Reichsfuhrer Himmler and instructed to spend the day with you. Would you like some breakfast before we chat?"

"Thank you no but I would like some coffee."

Hoss went into the hallway and gave instructions to bring coffee to his office. He motioned for Gerhardt to be seated. "I am not fully aware of the purpose of this meeting so please let me know how I can be helpful."

Gerhardt took a notebook out of his briefcase. "Would it be all right if I took some notes?"

Hoss reassured him, "It would be fine with me."

"I know little about the operation of the camp and Reischsfuhrer Himmler requested that I seek advice from you and others regarding the possibility of expanding your facilities. Before I try to construct what the future might look like, it would be really helpful for me to understand your current situation."

Hoss replied, "This is a difficult place not only for the German soldiers but also for their families. Is it a camp basically that we inherited, and from the beginning we have not had all the resources we need. I am sure even at a casual glance you perceive that there are major areas of repair required. This once was a Polish military garrison and had been abandoned for years. The need to have an isolated post that in secret could terminate enemies of the state is what made it so desirable. However, my recent talks with Himmler make it literally impossible to meet his future forecasts. We are already behind the modest schedule of terminations that I set for the fall."

"How have you handled the terminations so far?"

"The most successful attempt has been with Russian soldiers. We put them in a particular barracks, sealed it and then used Zyklon B gas to terminate them. Are you familiar with Zyklon B?"

Jotting down the name of the gas in his notebook Gerhardt replied, "Not really."

"It was finally successful in killing the Russians, but it took 15 hours and with the kind of numbers I envision coming from Russia and occupied countries, I'm not sure we will be able to actually meet the challenge."

"Is it fair for you to say that your camp as currently constructed cannot handle future growth?"

"Not with the numbers I perceive you are going to reveal to me. The other consideration is that we are close to the town and mammoth expansion will certainly be observed by local citizens. I'm afraid that would become a problem because information transmitted would become available in other parts of Germany and even Europe."

Gerhardt stopped writing. "One thing I understand is that you have excellent train lines."

"Yes, that is the least of our problems. We have almost unlimited train lines that can transfer prisoners from Russia as well as all the central points in Europe."

"Could those lines be extended to a proximate area outside the current camp?"

"I suppose. What number of new prisoners are you talking about?"

"I would think the minimal number would be 100,000."

Hoss sighed and shook his head. "That number leaves me speechless."

Gerhardt agreed. "That is staggering and could possibly be even larger than that."

"Gerhardt, there is no possible way you can extend this camp to meet those numbers. You would have to literally build an entirely new camp."

Gerhardt accepted at face value Hoss's assessment. "To your knowledge, is there any land proximate to this camp where we could extend rail lines and build a completely new camp that would house the numbers that we are talking about?" Hoss thought for a moment. 'There is extensive land on the other side of the camp, literally a few kilometers away but the real considerations are who would build it? How would you pay for it?"

"Those are excellent questions. Partial resources would come from those who are imprisoned and the rest from corporations that will hire those who survive the initial selections. I think part of the solution is various mammoth German companies that are interested in employing many of the prisoners, so there would be a daily fee paid to the SS which would defray some of the cost. Secondarily, I perceive that many of those who pass through here in transit have either liquid funds or hidden jewelry. We have already taken their properties"

"Gerhardt, you have not addressed the key issues of how would you terminate the astronomical new numbers? In addition, how will you dispose of their bodies?" Gerhardt furrowed his brow and did not immediately respond. "Those questions are part of the puzzle we must solve. In the next 10 days I will seek the counsel of the medical community regarding termination strategies."

"Gerhardt, in your research I would ask that you also consider the German soldiers and the families stationed at the camp. I can tell you that the camp is not a delightful place for assignment. This area has dismal weather and limited access to cultural forms of entertainment. Months of duty here wear down a lot of people and additionally they are overworked because we are understaffed. The numbers continue to grow and I don't have the facilities nor the financial ability to radically change the place."

Never in the hours of conversation were there any words spoken about the victims who would arrive here and be murdered. Both Hoss and Stark acted as though they were merely expanding a manufacturing plant. After lunch Gerhardt asked, "Would it be possible for you to give me a little bit of a tour the facility?"

"I would be glad to do that. In addition, I would be honored to be a resource in your ongoing plans."

The visit to Auschwitz was successful in many respects because it clearly ruled out the possibility of expanding the existing site. However, there was clear evidence that in the area merely kilometers away there would be massive land available that would have rail access and be private. The key issues that needed attention were: was Zyklon B the answer to termination? And if so, how could the period of termination be shortened?

The day after his visit to Auschwitz, through Himmler's office Gerhardt made an appointment to spend time with doctors at the Schoenberg institute. He told them in strict confidence what the issue was with Zyklon B and he asked how could the timeline could be shortened.

Dr Schreiber the Director of the institute said, "First consideration is that the system must be humane. The prisoners must not be frightened and clearly, they must believe that this is only a shower. You must reassure them that they have a role in the future work force. It would seem to me that the reason it takes so long is that you do not have a perfectly sealed system. The gas should take no more than 20 minutes to be effective."

Dr Sheide the associate director added, "There will be serious contamination in the chamber and it should be thoroughly cleansed after each use. For hours the physicians of the institute briefed Gerhardt on the necessary requirements for the gassing.

The day-long visit with the physicians was helpful. Next in the need to answer was how will this expansion be resourced? Again, through Himmler's office, Gerhardt. had appointments for the next three days with the heads of the largest industrial-military giants in Germany. He wished to explore the possibility of using a select number of prisoners, not only to build the camp, but also to serve the industrial corporations that needed to add to their workforce. If this was feasible, the companies would pay worker fees to the SS, which would go toward the costs of construction.

In addition, he visited the crematorium plant and engaged officials in conversations about creating at least three crematoria on the new site. They said if the order was placed within the next month the ovens could be manufactured in a three-month period. He instructed them to explore a process that would not only burn the bodies but also would be automated with conveyor belts that would transport the corpses. He wanted to solve the question of the bodies but also to keep German military personnel away from the actual killing and disposal.

After two weeks of research, meetings and developing a strategic plan for Reichsfuhrer Himmler, Gerhardt was exhausted. He had barely slept for days and had consumed little food while constantly drinking coffee and smoking one cigarette after another. The morning before he was to meet with Himmler, he looked awful. His hair was uncombed and he had not shaved for two days. The spacious, elegant hotel room was in disarray. There were note pads and typed papers strewn on the furniture and bed. Gerhardt hoped he would finish the final draft by noon and then pull himself together physically. Despite the impossible task in such a minimal amount of time he was encouraged by all the data he had assembled.

Gerhardt presents his report to Himmler

October 21st Berlin, Gestapo Headquarters; the Extermination Strategic Plan

It was difficult to ascertain who was more nervous about the report Gerhardt was to deliver to Himmler. The Reichsfuhrer was experiencing increasing pressure not only from Hitler but also from the others in the inner circle who would use delays in the process against him.

Gerhardt had requested a large flip chart. He began his remarks with a question.

"Would you prefer to go through my presentation line by line or have me make the presentation and then go over some of the considerations you have?"

Himmler glanced at the document, which was seven pages long. "I would prefer that you give me an overview and then I will see what questions I have."

"Fine, thank you."

With that, Gerhardt began to frame the key considerations he had discovered during his two weeks of research. "I believe the best way to address the concerns you have about the massive numbers of prisoners that you will have to deal with in the coming year is to break the considerations into two areas. The first I will refer to as the need to systematize. You have clearly said the past methodologies when dealing with large numbers of extermination are woefully inadequate. They are haphazard, expensive and have serious deficits as well as the potential to create public havoc. I concur with your assessment that the German people would not tolerate or support mass terminations in their local communities. And so, my conclusion is that we must create a system that is capable of handling extraordinary numbers, that is cost-effective and feasible within a relatively short period of time. Prime consideration here is the method for extermination. I have consulted with physicians at the Manheim and Schoenberg Institutes and they all concur with the following methodology. They agree that Zyklon B is the preferred choice. They believe the current use at Auschwitz is ineffective because of a filtration flaw. The initial attempts done at Auschwitz were rather crude. The physicians stated that what is required is a complete loop system that would recirculate the air within the chamber. It would be airtight and greatly speed up the process. With their guidance, I have contacted 2 engineering firms and they are in the process of designing a system that would literally keep all of the particles of air recycled in the chamber. Once this is implemented the physicians believe that death will occur between 15 and 20 minutes. In addition to the selection process of who would be terminated upon arrival, they made other suggestions about how we could shorten the lives of those who are retained to work. One of the ways that this can be achieved is for us to provide a minimal number of daily calories to sustain life. While they are employed, they will be fed somewhere between 700 and 900 calories a day. This number of calories will, in essence, be incapable of prolonging life for more than a few months.

Himmler leaned forward. Gerhardt sensed he was enthusiastic about the presentation.

"In order to create a successful system, it is essential that we look at the current facilities. Commandant Hoss was most helpful when I visited Auschwitz. He candidly explained to me why the current location could not possibly handle the numbers that you and I have discussed. The facility is in dire need of repair and has very limited space in which to expand. However, he informed me that on the other side of the camp, merely kilometers away, there is a vast amount of farmland that could be utilized to develop the construction of the new camp. He also assessed the possibility of extending current train lines to the new site and believes that would be fairly simple. An overview of the new camp would require a vastly different approach to construction. Initial construction would develop a series of barracks that would be made of prefabricated wood. That would be vastly cheaper, faster to construct and forced labor would shorten the life of those who survived the initial selection process. My initial thoughts are that these barracks would house a minimum of 700 prisoners. An additional bonus of the site is that it would still provide complete secrecy and be far enough away from the town. There would be no ability for townspeople to completely understand what was happening at the camp.

In order for the site to be effective, we must deal with the questions of not only how we kill, but also how we dispose of the bodies after the gassing process. The current Auschwitz site has one crematorium and that would be woefully inadequate for the numbers we are discussing. I have contacted the crematorium company that constructed the oven at Auschwitz, and they have assured me that within a four-month period they could deliver between three and four crematoria that would certainly serve the initial construction phase. I have adhered to your need for absolute silence, but I'm sure you are aware that the executives are fully cognizant of how the crematorium at the current site is being used. The senior executives of the company are also fully aware of our future intentions. I'm sure you're wondering how we intend to finance this massive project."

Himmler nodded in agreement. "I am with you so far, but that is the key question for me."

"I will try to address that under the heading of systematize. In my research I learned there are major German industrialists who are directly connected to war production. There are too many to examine in such a short period of time, but I have identified four companies that I believe could be involved in the process of developing the new site. Each of these companies is in dire need of additional personnel because so many of their workers have been drafted into the military or are performing other functions that are directly connected to the war efforts. It is my plan that those who survived the initial selection would be employed as workers and that the companies would contribute in a twofold manner. One is that they would establish on-site manufacturing facilities on the property and they would subsidize the SS on a daily rate for workers who are employed in their business. All the executives I have spoken with in these companies agree they would enthusiastically participate in this program. Again, there is no fear of their involvement leading to the outside communities because they already are aware of what happens on the current site. In addition to this financial foundation, I would develop a plan whereby all properties that are owned by the new prisoners, as well as any valuables they have retained and brought with them on site will go to the cost to defray construction and maintenance of the new site. It has been my experience in both Poland and Russia that many of the communities that we have visited have substantial amounts of jewelry, currency and art. The daily industrial fees and the valuables will sustain the building and maintenance of the new site.

"Before I go on to the second aspect, which I will refer to as the sanitize issues of the project, do you have any questions?"

Himmler enthusiastically responded, "I don't have anything specific and so far, I completely understand the basis for your analysis."

"Thank you. Then I will proceed to the question of sanitizing the process. I would envision that from the inception, when the prisoners leave the transportation by either rail or truck, that you will maintain the current process in which physicians will decide who will immediately be terminated and who will be retained for short-term labor. In order to keep German military from having any psychological issues with the process of termination, I believe we should sanitize the entire system. After selections, when the guards move them to the waiting area where they will disrobe and be prepared for what they believe is a cleansing process, German military should be totally absent. I believe that we can utilize other prisoners to perform the process of preparing them for what they believe to be the next stage before they are housed. In other words, I would envision that prisoners already there would herd them through the process, disrobing, gathering any valuables they have taken with them, and identifying their property with a number to further the belief that they will gather their belongings later. We can have them talk to the new arrivals about food and beverages that will be given to them after the shower. It will help create a humane aspect to the process. The prisoners will be easier to handle if they are not frightened. We need them to believe that we have further use for them. The other reality is that the physicians at the Institutes told me there will be an exceptional amount of human waste in the room after the process has been finished. Again, we must keep German military away from the process. We would have prisoners clean the chamber to sanitize it. Then they would take the bodies manually and transport them to the various crematoria. In addition, I believe we need to provide more of a normal life for the German military and their families. We must provide certain cultural and educational events that would make being part of this complex more desirable. I gather the climate itself is very difficult so providing a better quality of life is imperative."

When Gerhardt finished his presentation, he could tell by the expression on Himmler's face that he was exceptionally pleased and relieved. "This is an excellent overview, Gerhardt. I have specific questions but overall, I totally concur with the dual concepts of systematize and sanitize. I believe that you have answered the major challenges. I have no illusion that this will be simple. However, I have a higher degree of confidence than I had previously. Before you return to Munich, I would like you to meet Hans Stosberg who will be the primary architect of the expansion. I would imagine that he would insist that you be involved in the ongoing work. I will see that you have absolute clearance to be available to him and me for further counsel."

Chapter 18

May 1942, Hitler's Retreat House
Gerhardt's reward for role in the genocide

Along with Reinhard Heydrich and Adolph Eichmann, Gerhardt was invited to attend a celebration with Hitler at Berchtesgaden. The purpose of the invitation was their involvement and planning in the Final Solution to the Jewish question. Gerhardt had spent most of the last seven months working on the expansion of the concentration camp at Birkenau and the facility increasingly was meeting the growing numbers of prisoners. Frieda could not contain herself knowing that her husband would personally be in the company of the Fuhrer. When she asked about the purpose of the meeting Gerhardt lied and said it was a reward for the work that he had done in the past with Albert Speer at Nuremberg. It was interesting that he had not the slightest twinge of conscience about his role in the ongoing genocide and yet found ways in which to hide his involvement from his wife.

The ride to the Berghof was breathtaking. When they passed through security Gerhardt was stunned by the edifice on the mountaintop. He saw the Berghof off in the distance perched on the top of the mountain.

In 1933, Hitler had purchased the property with funds he received from the sale of his political manifesto Mein Kampf. His rise to power needed a more elegant residence so Hitler hired famous architect Alois Degano to enhance and expand the building. When the work was completed, Hitler renamed it the Berghof. The residence had been greatly expanded and the sloping wings of the roof gave it the appearance of a bird in flight as the sun gleamed off the side of the building.

After Gerhardt and the rest of the honored guests were led to their rooms, they changed clothes and were invited to a large terrace that was filled with colorful, resort-style canvas umbrellas. In formal attire, Hitler greeted his guests and paid particular attention to Gerhardt. "So, this is the brilliant young architect that Albert Speer has praised."

He reached out his hand. Trembling, Gerhardt shook his hand. Asking his guests if they would mind if could be alone for a brief period, Hitler invited Gerhardt to join him for a short walk and led him to his private studio. Gerhardt was somewhat aware of Hitler's interest in architecture but was amazed that the studio was filled with blueprints and models of Berlin. Hitler pointed to one of the table tops and said, "This is what Speer and I imagine Berlin will look like in the next decade. I know from the work you have done at Nuremberg that you have the talents to be part of this transformation."

At that moment Hitler's personal photographer entered the studio, clicked a photo of the two of them examining a blueprint. Gerhardt was informed that the picture would be developed and framed as soon as possible. When he left the Berghof the next day, he was given the framed photo inscribed, "To Gerhardt Stark from Adolph Hitler with gratitude"

Chapter 19

Milan 1908
A child genius is discovered

Noah Contini had been the primary caretaker of the De Genova estate on the outskirts of Milan for more than 20 years. He was married and the father of six children. His youngest, Svi, was three years old and on this bright summer morning he accompanied his father to work. Noah had concerns about Svi because, unlike the rest of his children, he was relatively passive. All of Svi's older brothers and sisters were quite verbal at this age but Svi was yet to speak. Unlocking the huge wooden doors, Noah held Svi's hand and led him through the massive foyer through the living room and into the formal music room. He placed Svi on one of the sofas in the room and gave him a wooden sail boat to play with and counseled him to stay on the sofa. He said he would return in a few minutes. He left the music room and entered the small office off the kitchen. He took out the scheduling book and began to fill in the week's work assignments.

Noah had finished the first part of the monthly landscape maintenance tasks when he heard the sound of a piano. He was startled because Count de Genova and his family were at their summer residence on Lake Como and no one else should have been in the music room. He put down his schedule book and made his way back to the music room. When he opened the door, he was amazed to find his son seated on a large pillow on the piano stool playing. Svi was not merely pounding away at the keys as any three-year-old would, given the opportunity to make sounds. He was actually playing the piano and the sounds had a pattern and harmony. Noah realized Svi was unaware he was in the room so he sat down and watched in sheer amazement.

The little boy's fingers glided over the keys as though he had been musically trained. After what felt like 15 minutes Noah tapped Svi on the shoulder. The little boy turned around with a cherubic smile on his face. He actually began to speak. "Do you like it Daddy?" Noah was overcome with emotion. All of his fears about his son vanished. He was not slow nor was he a child with some sort of disabling condition. He did not completely understand what was happening but realized there was something special he needed to address.

Svi was bright and only 3. He'd had no formal education. Noah was thrilled to return home to tell his wife, Maria, about the miracle. She was pleased that something special had occurred but thought perhaps Noah was embellishing the story. Noah would not accept Maria's doubts. He insisted they learn how this was possible. Noah knew that the De Genova's were very close to the local priest, Father Antonio Padovano, and that he had on numerous occasions given piano recitals at the castle. Although he was not a Catholic, he thought that Father Padovano could help him understand what happened that morning.

The next day Noah, accompanied by Svi and Maria, visited the church of Santa Lucia in the hope that Father Padovano would be available to discuss Svi's performance. As they approached the church, they saw Father Padovano reading a book seated in the garden beside the rectory. Noah approached the priest and before he could speak the priest rose, closed his book and greeted them. Noah responded, "Good morning Father. I am the caretaker of the De Genova estate. I hope we are not bothering you."
Smiling, Father Padovano said, "One is never bothered by a family being in his presence."

The warmth of the priest's smile and the kind words helped Noah tell the priest what happened in the music room. Father Padovano listened intently. Being an accomplished musician, he thought perhaps the father was exaggerating.

"Before I became a priest, I was actually a concert pianist. I have tried to keep up my skills but I do not have the time to practice every day because of my parish duties. Why don't we go into the rectory and see what the little boy can do on my piano. By the way, what is his name?"

"His name is Svi, father."

Father Padovano knelt down and said, "Svi would you like to see my piano?" The little boy did not know the word "piano" so he did not respond. Father Padovano said, "Let's go inside and show Svi my piano."

At this moment the priest believed that the father had exaggerated and Svi was just a normal child, not a musical genius. Once inside the rectory Father Padovano led them to what was again a music room and in the corner was a large upright piano. Father Padovano took Svi's hand and led him to the piano. As he lifted him up to the bench he realized the little boy was too short to reach the keys. He left the room for a minute, returning with two large sofa pillows. He placed the pillows and lifted Svi onto the bench. He opened the keyboard, smiled, and said, "All right Svi, now show Papa and me how you play."

Svi seemed pensive. Father Padovano was not surprised. He decided that in a few minutes he would take them to the kitchen and offer the child some refreshments. Suddenly Svi placed his fingers on the keys and began to play. The priest did not know the tune but it was a harmonious, balanced tune that was pleasing. The tiny fingers swept over the keys with such precision that it was almost impossible to believe that the child had not been trained. Svi played seamlessly for more than 10 minutes and it was not simply hitting the same keys. He had the ability to move his tiny body on the bench so that he could hit notes on both ends of the keyboard. Father Padovano was so stunned he was speechless. He felt like he was witnessing a miracle. Father Padovano sat next to Svi and played a simple tune. When he finished Svi played the same tune perfectly. Then the priest played a melody that was a little more difficult. He repeated this process six times and each time the three-year-old who had never had a lesson replicated each tune perfectly.

When Svi was finished the priest invited them for refreshments but the conversation was vastly different than earlier imagined.

"Noah, I am amazed at what I have just seen. It is too early to determine but I have the distinct impression that your child is a genius."

Noah and Maria were shocked. They were full of questions. They had no idea how to proceed in dealing with their son's talent.

"Father, I am a simple man and I had no idea. What should we do now?"

"Maria and Noah, I believe we may be witnessing a special gift from God and we must find a way to nurture this talent."

Maria was confused by the situation and spoke

"But father we do not have any idea what to do. We do not even have a piano in our home."

"I understand that but this is something that we must think through and plan. My thought now is to contact one of my professors at the conservatory in Milan and seek his advice. Please do not be worried about how we should proceed. Once I have some information, I will contact you. Is it best to visit you at your home or the De Genova estate?"

Noah responded, "Yes. Father, please contact me there. We are so grateful to you because we had no idea what we should do for Svi."

Leonardo Biancamano was a crusty old piano maestro who reveled in shattering the opinions of parents who brought so-called piano prodigies to his attention. This morning as he had his third cup of espresso, he reminded himself to be a little more respectful at the 10 a.m. audition. Father Anthony Padovano, one of his former students, was bringing a child who he believed had genuine talent. He realized that at least it wouldn't be some parent who knows nothing about music fawning over some mediocre player. When he arrived at the audition room he was greeted enthusiastically by his former student. No one had told him that the performer was a three-year-old.

"Father, have you chosen to play a joke on me by bringing a child?"

"Maestro I would never waste your time. The reason I am here is that I totally trust your opinion. I will say nothing further but ask you to play a simple piece and ask Svi to play it after you."

"I did not bring any music for a child."

"He does not read music and will not need it."

Leonardo took this with a grain of salt. Smiling, he sat on the two bench pillows. He played a three-minute minuet and then pointed for Svi to perform. Svi did not immediately understand. His father stepped forward and spoke to him. Despite the time elapse Svi played the piece perfectly. Leonardo was still not ready to accept that he had a wunderkind in his presence. And so he played a slightly more complex piece. Again, without missing a note Svi played it perfectly. Leonardo selected a piece that required more dexterity and certainly more memory. He was amazed by the perfection and perfect timing of Svi -- a three-year-old who could not read music. This was no ordinary talented child. This was, perhaps, a once in a lifetime opportunity to develop a musical genius.

Life changed for the entire Contini family from that day forward. Once Count De Genova was made aware of the little boy's talent, he offered to finance the schooling at the conservatory and allowed his employee, Noah, to have a flexible schedule in order to take Svi back and forth to the conservatory.

Maestro Biancamano devoted hours and days to teach Svi how to read music. There were no gaps in the child's ability to immediately learn the key musical concepts. The original melodies that he had mastered on his own were now replaced by piano concertos. In a two-year period, the skill level of this child surpassed all of the adult students at the conservatory. By age six he had performed formal recitals at the De Genova castle and maestro Biancamano was preparing a tour for Svi in Milan, Lucca and Bologna. The concerts were exceptional achievements and the local Italian newspapers began to compare Svi to Mozart.

It is not uncommon for a child pianist to hit the wall of limited performance at some point but this was not the case for Svi Contini. His skills as a pianist appeared to be without limit. In addition, as an adolescent he was composing and had performed three piano concertos at La Scala that were written by him.
By age 20 Svi Contini had performed in every major concert hall in Europe and in 1937 he made a voyage to the United States where he performed At Carnegie Hall. The New York Times did a feature article on him. In it, Arturo Toscanini was quoted saying, "It has been more than a privilege to conduct an orchestra where such a talent as

Contini is featured. He will go down as one of the greatest pianists who ever lived."

In 1939 just before he turned 22, Svi married Lisa Barone and the following year they became the proud parents of twin boys, Carlo and Davide. Life appeared to be on a wonderful path for the Continis but the social and political changes in Europe would soon affect their lives.

Svi did not believe that the Italian people would ever be influenced by the negative policies toward Jews in Germany. However, just two months after the formation of the Rome-Berlin Axis the Italian government published a series of anonymous pronouncements in a fascist newspaper, *Il Popolo d'Italia*, that set the tone for the dictatorship's new attitude toward Italian Jews. The core of the articles explained that "anti-Semitism is inevitable wherever there is exaggerated Semitic visibility, interference and arrogance. It is preferable to eradicate Jews entirely from society than to coerce changes in those Jewish behaviors and customs that had long frustrated Italians and Catholics."

Fascism had taken hold in Italy and to some degree the rise of anti-Semitism had become common place. Slowly but surely the war on the Jews was spreading. Svi had no use for politics and refused to support the Mussolini regime. Naively, he believed that being a known musician would protect him and his family from the persecution that was about to penetrate the Italian way of life. There were incidents in rehearsals where other musicians made derogatory remarks about Svi being a Jew and on more than one occasion his patriotism was challenged. He and Lisa had their family roots in Italy and although his fame would have allowed him to go to America as a visiting artist they chose to remain in Italy. Things began to change when Svi refused to play Giovinezza, the unofficial Italian national anthem, before a concert. Thugs rushed the stage and physically beat Svi. The intervention of his manager and a few musicians literally saved his life. This incident frightened Svi and Lisa. They realized they could not remain in Italy. The "Manifesto of Racial Scientists," which appeared in the fascist press on Bastille Day 1938, signaled the start of the official anti-Semitic campaign. Written by Mussolini in collaboration with a group of scholars, the manifesto established an irremediable divide between Jews and Italians. It legitimized anti-Semitic prejudice by inviting Italians to "proclaim themselves openly racist."

The belief that Svi and Lisa could escape the coming deluge ended in 1943 when the Italian government surrendered to the allies. The German persecution of the Jews in Italy was far more virulent than in prior years.

Milan 1906
Another brilliant Jew is caught in the Nazi net

As an adolescent Lorenzo Kaplan was interested in psychiatry. His initial attraction to the field was Sigmund Freud. However, at the same time, he began to explore the intriguing concept of existentialism. By nature, and the foundation of his family, he rejected those who were extremely negative about the human experience. On the other hand, he was attracted to those whose philosophy was more positive and even at times religious. This was confusing at times for a young man who was trying to put together a philosophy of life. He was willing to deal with some of the contradictions of most of the schools of thought. By age 17 Lorenzo had assembled a theory of life that was eclectic and centered on the concepts of purpose and personal legacy.

After completing his high school studies and entering the University of Milan he decided to study medicine. While in medical school he became deeply attracted to the study of psychiatry. Initially, Sigmund Freud was one who had a major influence on his thinking but as his studies progressed, he developed theories that began to separate him from a mechanistic view of human behavior. He began to see persons as beings not exclusively guided by internal unconscious tensions and drives. After endless hours of study, he arrived at a theory based on the belief that human behavior is characterized by purpose. He viewed Freud, Jung and Adler as giants but believed that their views were too limited. He began to grapple with the concepts of love and meaning, which he believed were at the core of a meaningful life. Although he had kept a lot of his convictions private, he was encountering a serious conflict with his mentor, Arturo Montalbano, a devotee of the Adlerian school. Among the many young clinicians who were constantly following Montalbano, Lorenzo was selected as the heir apparent. In daily gatherings at the Café San Eustachio in Milan, Montalbano would often leave the role of teacher to Lorenzo. It was clear to all that Lorenzo had been chosen as the Benjamin to carry on his work.

The complete separation of Lorenzo from Montalbano came one cold February night in Milan. Lorenzo had been chosen to represent the Adlerian school of thought at a major seminar held for all of the psychiatrists and psychologists in Italy. The plan was for Lorenzo on stage to be asked three questions and then expound on what he believed was the most effective school of psychiatric therapy. His mentor, Montalbano, was seated in the front row of the auditorium and was proud that Lorenzo would select his school, which focused on the concept of power. Lorenzo was nervous before his appearance. Up to this point he had kept his eclectic beliefs private. The auditorium was filled beyond capacity as he climbed the four steps and stood in the center of the stage. The master of ceremonies introduced the format and then turned to Lorenzo. He asked the first question. "Is a person's primary drive sexual?"

This was the cornerstone of Freud's platform. Lorenzo crisply answered, "No."

The second question was "Is the drive Archetypal?" It was the foundation of Jungian theory. Again, he answered a strong no.

Montalbano beamed at what he thought would be the answer to the third question. "Is power the drive that is most important?"

Lorenzo hesitated before answering, "No, it is purpose."

Feeling betrayed, Montalbano bolted from his seat, followed by his loyalists. He never spoke to Lorenzo again.

In 1927 Lorenzo finished his medical studies and became a physician at the Gargiulo clinic in Milan. In the course of six months, he began to establish a program to minimize the possibility of suicide by university students. He published a series of papers on the subject and began to teach at the University of Milan.

By 1935 he had established a new theory of psychiatry and was in contact with an American, George Vlahos, whose conclusions about human deprivations connected perfectly to Lorenzo's thoughts on purpose. They authored a paper together entitled "Deprivations that prevent Purpose." Lorenzo was fascinated by the theories of Vlahos, which primarily attributed much of psychic trauma to early deprivations. His theory was based on the clinical evidence that basic human needs were frustrated early in life and persons lacking care and unconditional love were vulnerable to believing they were unlovable nobodies. Vlahos made a clear distinction between self-worth and worthiness. He put forth the concept that self-worth was emotional and fluctuated, whereas worthiness was a constant. The foundation was that the value of every person is unchangeable and has a rational base. This move away from the strong deterministic schools of thought melded with Lorenzo's evolving theories. In a similar manner Vlahos had fully accepted the premise that the search for meaning was a drive that could alleviate much of the harm done by early deprivations.

By 1937 Lorenzo had become the director of Psychiatry and Neurology at the Ospedale San Marco

He had a thriving private practice as well as teaching assignments at the university. All this changed after the Italian government surrendered to the allies and he was forbidden to practice on non-Jewish patients. The Nazi's employed restrictions that forbid Jews from professional and business dealings with non-Jews. Lorenzo maintained the director's title and did all that was possible to prevent the Nazis from killing Jewish patients. In the midst of the Jewish persecution Lorenzo was contacted by Vlahos who urged him to emigrate to America. Lorenzo had married Ella Schwartz by this time and was convinced that he could secure two letters of transit and accept Vlahos' invitation. However, there was no possibility that he could secure two transit visas for his aging parents. After weeks of reflection, he and Ella decided they would stay in Italy.

Lorenzo continued to perform minimal surgeries on patients with mental issues and sedate them heavily when German authorities showed up at the clinic for spontaneous investigations. Lorenzo knew that most of the experienced physicians were attached to military units and the visitors had limited medical knowledge. He also created a fictitious highly contagious ward in which he housed 14 psychiatric patients. Whenever he had guests he would put on protective gear and invite the German authorities to do the same. He cautioned them that the virus was highly contagious and there was no cure. No German authority chose to enter the unit.

The subterfuge and freedom ended in 1943 when Lorenzo, Ella and their families were arrested and transported to Auschwitz.

March 11, 1943, Milan
Jews transported to Auschwitz-Birkenau

Hundreds of Jews crammed together on this chilly March morning at the Stazione Ferrovia in Milan. German soldiers as well as Italian police forced them into cattle cars. They were packed like mussels on stone and it was difficult to breathe in the boxcar. There were about 100 people in the car with no ability to move or sit. They were without food or water and the only air came from four little windows at the top of the cattle car. There was no bathroom facility, just a bucket against one wall that was used as a toilet. The level of anxiety was palpable and children were crying. They had been told on the platform before entering the cattle car that they were going to a labor camp. They had no idea where the final destination would be.

The train moved rapidly and some of the occupants became dizzy and vomited. After 10 or 11 hours of motion sickness plus the overflow toilet bucket, the odor was nauseating.

Every six or seven hours the train would stop at a station. The car was guarded by a soldier with a machine gun. The persons in the car would beg him for water. He agreed but the price for water was diamond rings and gold watches. Some of the elderly members passed the rings and watches through the barbed wired windows. The guard would fling from a bucket a wave of water through the barbed wire.

The ride seemed endless but at the end of the third day the train arrived at its destination.

Panic again spread through the car. People were shouting and crying. As the doors opened everyone was forced from the car. There were barking dogs and German soldiers shouting orders. As the car emptied it was apparent that four persons had died during the trip. Families were split up. Someone in a long white coat ordered people to one of two lines. Svi was told to go to the right while Lisa and the boys were to go to the left.

At the rear of the line Lorenzo was ordered to the right and Ella was pushed into the other line. Lorenzo turned to blow his beloved wife a kiss. It was the last time Lorenzo and Svi would see their loved ones. Both men were unaware that in the future their lives would be bound together forever.

Chapter 20

March 1944, Theresienstadt
The fictitious humane concentration camp

The last few years were difficult for Micah Goldstein. His father died at Dachau after being arrested on the evening of Kristallnacht. Micah, a Jewish physician, was forced to leave his position at the Mendelssohn clinic in Munich and eventually, he and his mother were incarcerated and transported to Theresienstadt. When they were arrested, he pleaded with the arresting officers not to take his mother because she was not Jewish. This plea fell on deaf ears.

The German government was under increasing pressure worldwide because of the rumors of the murders of Jews in the concentration camps. Himmler ordered the creation of a camp that would portray Jews being treated humanely and with respect.

In February 1944,[the SS embarked on a "beautification" German: *Verschönerung*) campaign to prepare the ghetto for a Red Cross visit. Many "prominent" prisoners and Danish Jews were re-housed in private, superior quarters. The goal was to portray life in the camp as relatively normal. The streets were given Jewish names and they were spotless. Business shops were open and the feeling of a small town. There was to be a school and playgrounds. The SS encouraged the camp leaders to create a series of cultural and musical events.

The Nazis' attempts to use the former military fortress Terezín to cover up their actual plans and what they were really doing to Europe's Jews reached their height in June 1944, when a delegation from the International Committee of the Red Cross visited Terezín for a day.

The Nazi government was under increasing pressure regarding their treatment of the Jews in Europe. The International Committee of the Red Cross as well as the Danish government had been trying unsuccessfully for some time to gain permission to visit one of the Nazis' main concentration camps. In June 1943 the head office for Reich Security granted the Red Cross permission to visit the Terezín ghetto. It was the Nazi strategy to persuade the world that there was no truth in the growing number of reports that Jews were being murdered.

Prisoners were ordered to wear their best clothes for the day of the visit.

The three-member delegation visited the ghetto on June 23, 1944. It consisted of two Danes -- Frants Hvass from the Foreign Ministry, and the plenipotentiary of the Danish Red Cross, Juel Hennigsen, and a functionary from the International Committee of the Red Cross, Maurice Rossel from Switzerland. The delegation was accompanied by a number of high-ranking Nazi delegates. They were allowed to talk with the Danish prisoners, but prevented from making contact with other Jews. The eight-hour tour was rigidly constructed so the report of the visit would be favorable and used by Himmler as propaganda. One of the visitors, Maurice Rossel, wrote a report that was totally supportive of the belief that no Jews were being mistreated. The report stated that no resident of the camp is sent elsewhere. The Nazis were successful in fooling the delegation.

Micah Goldstein had spent his whole life living under the guidance of compassionate Judaism. However, in the last four years he experienced hatred toward those who had done such great harm to his family and the Jews

Micah's world was turned upside down. He currently was incarcerated at Theresienstadt. He had no illusion that the camp the Nazis were building would last for the duration of the war. It was plain and simple, a ruse to camouflage the killings that were happening in concentration camps all over Europe. It was a difficult position for him to be in because as a physician, especially as a pediatrician, he wanted to remove the children in the camp from the dreaded future that he knew would probably occur. Once the charade was over, the grapevine within the camp had nurtured the reality that all would be sent to their demise at Auschwitz. He vowed that despite the teaching of forgiveness, if he survived, he would hunt down his cousin and kill him. Daily the vivid thoughts of that possibility sustained him.

He was preparing the prescriptions for the morning when he heard a tap on his office door. A thin, short woman with a suitcase stood in the doorway and inquired, "Are you Dr. Goldstein?"
"Yes, I am."
"I was told to report here. I am to be your assistant in the clinic. My name is Inge Rystock."
Micah shook her hand. "Where are you coming from?"
"Copenhagen. I was a physician in the Children's hospital. By training I am a pediatrician but that seemed to mean nothing to the Nazi who interviewed me. He said one Jew doctor is the same as the next."
Micah gestured for Inge to be seated. "Like you I am a pediatrician. I was the director of a clinic in Munich but was transported with my mother to this place. Inge, were you sent here alone?"
"No. My husband, two children and my parents are also here. What do you make of this place?"

"This is the Nazi fairy land that they hope will convince the rest of the world that they are loving and kind to the Jews. This will be temporary, and eventually they will get rid of all of us."

Inge was shocked by the bluntness of this remark. "I hope you are wrong about that because we have heard that the war will soon end."

"I don't believe that because I have been hearing that for years. I lost my father after Kristallnacht and last week my mother was taken and sent somewhere else. I would like to believe that she is safe but I realize she may be in Auschwitz."

"What is Auschwitz?"

"It is the final destination for those they wish to kill. The news has leaked out that they gas thousands of Jews there and so that is the reason for this camp. First you come here. Then to Auschwitz."

Inge needed to shield herself from the picture Micah was painting. "Maybe it is just a rumor."

"I would like to believe that but it is the reality."

Inge was horrified. "Why do they hate us so much?"

"I don't know. I have given up trying to find the answer to that question. The Nazis have the ability to totally change human beings into killers with no memories or conscience. I grew up with a German cousin who was like a brother to me. My parents took him in when his stepfather treated him poorly. He was then my best friend and now he is a Nazi monster. When my father was arrested, he as a member of the SS could have saved him but he would not lift one finger to help. My mother and father loved him like a son and yet he completely turned his back on them. I never knew I could hate someone who I once loved like a brother but I truly despise him."

Inge acknowledged Micah's feelings. "I can understand that but I don't want to have hate take over my life."

"I admire you if you can maintain that but at this point I don't even want to achieve that. In the meantime, while the Nazis are playing out this fantasy for the Red Cross it is important that we do everything we can to keep the children here healthy."

PART TWO

Chapter 21

February 1944, Munich
Gerhardt the hunter was soon to become the hunted.

Gerhardt Stark realized his life was now in peril. He clearly saw the handwriting on the wall. As he stood in his steam-filled bathroom his life of plunder and murder was soon to end. For years he had been a key instrument in the hands of Heinrich Himmler, wiping Jews from the face of Austria, Poland and Russia. As one of the architects to create a Jew-free Europe, his commitment to the elimination of the Jewish race started slowly when he joined the SS Waffen in 1934. Before he became a Nazi, he was a man of letters, music and architecture. His dreams centered around the teachings of world-famous architect Constantine Doxiadis. He was enthralled with Doxiadis' concept of a parabolic city, a place where all citizens would live close to the center. The city would expand on both sides of the center and no one would be farther than a 10-minute walk to all of the key civic activities. His professional passion was to design cities that enhanced the concept of community access to all the joys of a metropolis. He admired renaissance architecture, but desired to create buildings that were functional as well as physically beautiful. This goal died when it was replaced by the idea of creating a world filled only with pure German blood. He jettisoned the beauty of architecture for the power of personal gain. Once a nominal Christian, he found in the Nazi vision of the world something more compelling than Matthew, Mark, Luke and John. His new bible was Mein Kampf. He was baptized into a cult that was going to last for a thousand years.

The transition of his character was not immediate but slowly he began to compromise all he had learned in the first 20 years of life. It did not happen overnight, but attracted to the transforming power of Hitler and the Nazi party he began to justify the evolution of the punishment of the Jews. He traded his formal years of belief that one should love thy neighbor as thy self in order to justify the means because of the potential ends. Initially he engrossed himself in the delusions that measures against the Jews were essential but transitory. Beliefs overcame conscience and he immersed himself in the conviction that the immediate goal was to force Jews to emigrate. When that became impossible, he moved his rationale to stronger measures that were critical to alleviate the plight of the ordinary German citizen who was suffering pain and deprivation. Blinded by ambition and seduced by propaganda, he traded the gentle sounds of Mozart for the shrieks of murdered women and children. They were no longer human beings but rather viruses that must be prevented from spreading. He literally imbibed the teaching of the Fuhrer that no act toward any Jew was abominable and he transferred this cancer to all those in the SS who served under him.

He entered his shower and forced the temperature to the highest possible setting and stayed motionless without soaping his body. As the water scalded him, he felt the anxiety of the coming reality. There were no longer illusions and shadowy premonitions about a glorious 1,000-year Reich. At one point he was so fearful about his situation that he almost collapsed. He leaned his head against the tile wall in the shower. There was no shame in his thoughts, only the desire for self-preservation. On the brink of mental decomposition, he finally left the shower. As he stood motionless in front of his bathroom mirror the sounds and visions of some of his atrocities paraded through his brain. There were so many moments when he could have refused to cooperate but he rationalized the first few acts that seemed relatively harmless. Slapping a rabbi who resisted arrest was not in his mind horrendous. Daily forcing young men to work beyond exhaustion for the Reich had meaning and purpose. However, the slope became slippery and those initial acts led to unimaginable horrors. There were moments when he could have halted his complete adherence to the growing tragedy. Some regular German army members refused to shoot unarmed women and children while they stood helpless in a ravine. Momentarily he paused before joining the carnage but dismissed the choice and fired at will. There were other occasions when the residue of his humanity would rise but over and over, he resisted any choice that was not in concert with the desire to rid the Jews from the Nazi brave new world. In spite of these momentary cracks in his murderous passion he was not tormented by images of young SS soldiers spearing infants with bayonets as he laughingly gave the order for them to be hurled from a hospital nursery window in Lodz, Poland. He remembered the smells of burning corpses in the Polish village Zadgroski where not a single soul remained after he gave the order to kill every living Jew while having dinner next to the bodies stacked upon each other.

These atrocities were once part of a regimen without thought or conscious guilt and even now he did not regret his past. The faces of Jewish women pleading for the lives of their children still had no effect. Pangs of conscience had more than occasionally confronted his behavior but they were dismissed by rationales of glory and the restoration of a nation. He had ignored the challenges to a moral code that once guided his life. He deceived himself with pledges of fidelity to his wife and never took part in the sexual exploitation of his captives. This veneer of morality never allowed him to feel the pain of destroying the lives of entire Jewish families. He was still proud of his architectural and organizational insights that contributed to the building of Birkenau. He despised others who allowed the killing to drain them from the ultimate goal. Unlike him, his master Himmler understood the damage done to the psyches of some SS officers. He had employed Gerhardt to launch a new sanitized way of killing. Auschwitz and the other extermination camps were the answer to fulfilling Hitler's dream while at the same time saving the sanity of his SS henchmen.

Gerhardt's only regret had nothing to do with the extermination of the Jews but rather the unintended consequences of this war. His wife, Frieda, and three children were incinerated in the firebombing of Kassel. The only guilt he experienced was that he should have known the military industrial complex would be bombed. He had been informed by his brother-in-law, Rolf, that his family sought safety and had gone to an air raid shelter. After the bombings the only thing that remained in the shelter were pools of green liquid and bones. His wife and children had literally been vaporized by the fire. His grief shattered him but he could not for one second feel guilt for the atrocities he had committed. Sluggishly trying to shave he thought to himself, did those British and American pilots tuck their children in bed before they left to bomb and kill innocent families? Did they think they were doing something honorable by attempting to wipe women and children from the face of the earth? The sounds of his children's laughter as he played with them on the grounds of his summer home in Passau rang in his ears. He remembered the smile of his wife caressing his hair as she walked past him in the library. Days long gone of falling in love with her at the University of Munich and their life together sprung to his conscious mind. He remembered the births of his three children and the moments of love and joy they shared. All these flashbacks of love and memory never crossed to the arena of those he had massacred.

His personal losses were compounded by the reality that the war was already lost. The exhilarating and glorious days of parades and rallies at Nuremberg were over. No longer were there masses of smiling young faces exhilarated by waving flags and the stirring sounds of trumpets and drums. The total willingness of his verbal allegiance to be loyal to Hitler, even at the cost of his own death, on a bright September morning still made sense. He had pledged himself for personal and national gain to a life of murder and torture and to this moment he had no doubts about his involvement. The daily bombings of German cities had replaced the pomp and circumstance of days gone by. The Third Reich was crumbling and his fate would soon be altered by the downfall.

What were his choices facing the ever-present reality of what he had done? He would certainly be defined as a war criminal and justice and retribution would be demanded. His name was on all the drawings and plans for the Birkenau development. The best he could hope for was that he would be captured by the Americans to spend the rest of his days in prison. If he was captured by the Russians, he would certainly be tortured and executed. In light of this future, he opened the medicine cabinet, stared at four cyanide capsules and contemplated suicide. The pain could end this very morning, but somehow that choice, despite putting an end to his psychic misery, was not compelling.

Leaving the bathroom and making his way to the kitchen this once tall image of Aryan supremacy seemed frail and despondent. The golden locks of hair had hordes of gray and his taut muscular body had become soft and paunchy. The stillness of a room that once was filled with the tones of Bach and Mozart was eerily silent as he sat mindlessly gazing out at the bleak rainy day. Flight from Germany perhaps could offer some way to at least exist. He rose and as he donned his SS officer's uniform, he decided that he would no longer actively participate in the ongoing slaughter. Going AWOL became more and more appealing but he sensed that no matter where he fled the Allies, fueled by Jewish thirst for revenge, would never cease their search for him.

Chapter 22

Trip to Rome
Gerhardt's search to escape justice

Gerhardt awoke in the early morning fully drenched with the sweat of another restless night.

For weeks Gerhardt had a recurring dream about his family racing through the streets of Kassel and seeking safety from the bombing. He heard the screams of his children as they entered the bomb shelter pleading for him to save them. Nightly he woke drenched to the bone and often could not resume his sleep. He was more and more physically and psychologically drained by the horror of their deaths. The past two nights Gerhardt's sleep was not haunted by memories of his family. The slumber had been fitful but appeared to be his first subconscious exploration of his new plan. Was it possible for him to leave the SS, Germany and even Europe to find a new identity? There were so many untested challenges in his musings and he realized that timing and details could not be blithely ignored. As he rose, the image of Adolph Hitler immediately struck him. On his bureau was his most prized possession, an autographed photo of himself and Hitler taken at the Berghof in late 1942. He, Reinhard Heydrich and Adolf Eichmann as architects of the Final Solution had been invited for a medal ceremony. The recognition was never openly stated or put in writing. The award was for the expansion of Auschwitz and the extermination program that had been conceived at a Lake Wannsee mansion. That moment was the peak of his military career, and even now it evoked a sense of pride. He could not deny the exhilaration that he felt when the Fuhrer shook his hand, and he glowed at the applause rendered by Goebbels, Himmler, Goring and the cast of the inner circle. He never shared with his wife the origin of the notoriety and was satisfied with her beaming pride that he had actually met the Fuhrer. He had cloaked his conscience with the belief that the end goal would be a Germany that would rule the world with compassion and be so powerful that peace would be more than the idle dream of poets. It would be the second wave of Pax Romana. Somewhere in the process he ignored the reality that temporary inconvenience for the Jews of Europe would not warp into complete annihilation. This moral blindness was supported by a hatred of the Treaty of Versailles, because as most Germans, he believed it unfairly blamed Germany for the Great War. He resented making Germany pay for the entire war was the primary cause of Germany's economic woes. In addition, he concurred with the fallacious belief in the world-wide Jewish conspiracies honed and perfected by Dr. Goebbels.

As he prepared to go to SS headquarters, he tried to purify his mind and move away from the consequential fears that had plagued him for weeks. The pithy plan for his removal from active duty and a way to save himself was rudimentary and not yet based in fact. Money was not an impediment because during the last few years he had amassed a fortune from his nefarious deeds. Three large accounts in Swiss banks plus the portfolio of stolen Degas drawings would ensure a comfortable living for the rest of his life. He was multi-lingual and had a particular expertise in English so leaving Germany from a language standpoint was not a problem.

Caffeine always helped his thought process and after his third cup he started to meld the unconnected challenges into practical steps. He could not embark on this venture alone. He would need documents, passports, letters of transit and a host of official papers to wind his way through the Nazi net. He scoured his memory for anyone who he could trust. There was one name that was plausible, Heinrich Mueller. They had been boyhood friends, as well as rivals in Regensburg and members of the Bavarian youth orchestra. Heinrich had become one of the premier pianists in Germany and Gerhardt believed that he was currently stationed in Rome. He learned from his wife before her death that Heinrich was severely wounded in the battle of Stalingrad but was now back on active duty. Initially he thought that Heinrich would be a person he could trust, but further reflection raised the issue that in Germany today it was almost impossible to trust anyone. Despite this without an ally the maze that faced him had no route to his new-found goals.

He needed help, but also some sort of insurance policy if he was caught.

Chapter 23

April 1944, Rome
Gerhardt engages a willing accomplice

    Heinrich Mueller wished he could shed his soldier's uniform as he crossed the street in front of the Victor Emmanuel monument. The circle at the Piazza Venezia was already frenetic and crossing against Italian drivers seemed more perilous than any combat assignment. He loved Rome but had noticed a marked change in his life since the Italian government had collapsed. The murder of more than 350 Romans had completely turned the population against the Germans. The massacre was ordered by Hitler in retaliation for the March attack by Italian partisans on the Via Rasella that killed 32 German soldiers and wounded 38. Hitler was livid when he heard of this attack. His response was to kill 10 Italian civilians for every German death. In addition to this massacre, the Gestapo in the city had taken over the Jewish persecution and the concept of Italy as an ally to Germany was damaged beyond repair. When he entered a crowded cafe for a morning espresso, conversation ceased and he was totally aware that he was an occupier. He loved Rome but despised the lack of courage and commitment to the cause on the part of the Italians. He often mused to himself that God should never have given such a beautiful city and country to the lazy, cowardly Italians. He was a bureaucrat in the Nazi killing machine responsible for the meticulous documentation of seven concentration camps. He, like his closest friends, was enthusiastic about Hitler even though he lost a brother at Stalingrad. As a member of the communication unit in Stalingrad, Heinrich was severely wounded by a Russian tank attack. He was fortunate in that he was airlifted before it was impossible to leave Russia. His left leg was permanently affected and he needed a cane to walk. Fortunately, he had full use of his right leg and continued daily to play the piano. Today he was excited because his closest friend, Gerhardt Stark, would be in town for a few days. He began to shape the tour and restaurants where he would share with Gerhardt the city that he had come to love.

Train to Rome

The overnight train ride from Munich to Rome would take approximately 12 hours and would provide Gerhardt an opportunity to format his conversation with Heinrich. How could he be sure that the reaction to leave the army and go AWOL would not provoke the need to have him arrested? He knew Heinrich before the war but that was meaningless. He, for example, was a completely different person far removed from the boyhood chum in Regensburg. In those days he was a carefree upbeat student who had wondrous dreams of being a world class architect. He resisted thoughts of his childhood and the temptation for self-examination during the night and tried to assemble a rationale for the next steps. What would he ask Heinrich for if he did not resist the initial idea? Should he involve him directly realizing that any assistance would make him an accomplice?

Pulling into the Stazione Ferrovia in Rome at precisely 8 a.m., Gerhardt decided he would go directly to the hotel, shower, freshen up and meet Heinrich at his office around noon. The Hotel Navona was perfectly located near the Corso and literally a three-minute walk to the Campo di Fiori, the outdoor vegetable and food market in Rome. Even in these days of rationing the market was alive and active. The sounds of the merchants and customers bargaining was a new experience for him.

Chapter 24

The Emerging Plan
Heinrich helps Gerhardt avoid justice

Gerhardt would have preferred to shed his uniform but realized access to Heinrich's office would be a simple matter attired as an SS officer. After the formal process of entry Gerhardt was escorted to a foyer and informed that Captain Mueller would soon be with him. Within moments he spotted Heinrich, assisted by his cane, walking toward him. He had aged and apparently been severely wounded but the boyhood grin was still there. Gerhardt rose to greet him and before he could decide on whether to merely shake his hand Heinrich embraced him in a bear hug that seemed to last for minutes. "I have so missed you. Come let's go to my office." The room was like every other Nazi office that Gerhardt had seen for the last three years. There was an opulent stretch of carpet, ornate ceiling moldings and a huge oak desk in the center of the office. Photos of Hitler and prints of past victories adorned the walls next to the ever-present Swastika flags. The French doors at the end of the office and the Palladian window showed off an exquisite view of the Borghese gardens.

Heinrich motioned for him to sit in one of the antique black leather chairs positioned next to each other. "Before we go to lunch let's catch up. The last time I saw you was in the God-forsaken battlefield outside of Stalingrad. Where are you stationed?"

"In Munich but I hope that there is some way for me to be transferred to somewhere in Italy, hopefully Rome."

Heinrich smiled broadly. "That would be wonderful. I would love to have a chum who I could see on a regular basis. How is your family?"

Gerhardt was silent for a few seconds and Heinrich apprehensively suspected what was to come. "They were killed in the firebombing of Kassel."

Shocked, Heinrich asked, "All of them?"

Gerhardt then described the horrid details. "I am so sorry Gerhardt. I cannot believe they are gone."

Gerhardt wiped a tear from his eye, blew his nose. Once composed, he asked Heinrich, "How is your family? Are they safe?"

"I feel guilty after what you have just shared telling you that they are with my parents in Passau. There have been literally no bombings in the area. I moved them from Regensburg last summer."

Gerhardt said, "That was a smart move. I am glad they are safe."

Wishing to change the subject, Gerhardt asked, "What are your duties here?"

"I am in charge of the printing and issuing of any major official documents and this office coordinates all of the registration and documents from the concentration camps. I have become a bureaucrat Gerhardt. What about you?"

"I am still actively working in the field and primarily involved in the Jewish Question."

Heinrich said, "So am I, not directly but my office supports the registration and planning for each of the major camps in Poland. The paperwork is overwhelming. It's almost impossible to document thoroughly the history of each inmate. There is a feeling here in Rome that we should slow down the process and use the trains and military personnel for battle situations. I could care less about the Jews but the camps are draining our resources."

Perhaps it was because of their past friendships before the war but Heinrich had a sense that Gerhardt wished to speak about a personal matter. "Gerhardt, we have known each other almost from birth, and you are my oldest and closest friend. Is there anything you wish to discuss with me?"

Gerhardt paused and glanced over one shoulder and then the other. "This may be an insane question but are there any hidden microphones in your office?"

Heinrich shook his head and said, "I understand your question because in these times everyone is becoming paranoid. I can assure you that there are no listening devices in my office. Why do you ask?"

"Because I am about to take a leap of faith. I do not want anyone but you to hear what I am about to tell you."

Heinrich offered Gerhardt a cigarette, then lit his own, took a deep drag and said, "I can assure you that we are truly alone."

Gerhardt paused for what seemed like minutes. He lit his cigarette before speaking. "Heinrich, what I am about to reveal may put you in a compromising position. I realize that the end is near and I need to flee Germany as soon as possible. I must not only cease direct involvement in my SS work, I also need to create an insurance policy."

"I am not sure I follow you."

"I plan to leave Germany and I need to create a bargaining chip if I am caught by the allies. That is why I need your help. Shall I stop? Are you sure you want to hear this?"

Now standing, Heinrich placed his hand over Gerhardt's mouth. "If I am to put myself in harm's way, I choose not to hear about it here. I have a place that will weather favorably anything you are about to reveal." Heinrich picked up his phone and called his favorite restaurant near the Piazza Navona.

The Joint Venture

Despite the cool, damp weather Heinrich insisted they walk from his office in the Borghese down the Spanish Steps. Winding their way through tiny streets they passed Trevi Fountain. Heinrich was giving a running account of each monument and paused when they arrived at the Pantheon. Heinrich went on for five minutes recounting the history of this magnificent edifice. Prior to the war Gerhardt would have been mesmerized by the history and architecture. This morning he barely noticed the wonderful historical monuments. Heinrich said with relish, "Before you tell me something that may alter my life, I need three experiences. The first will appear in about four minutes."

True to his word they crossed a busy street and entered Heinrich's favorite Piazza in Rome. "My friend, this is the Piazza Navona, my second home in Rome. Gaze at that beautiful fountain which represents the four continents that were known at the time of the sculpture. The fountain portrays the four great Rivers the Danube, Nile, Ganges and Rio Plata. The sculptor was Bernini and it is called Fontana di Quattro Fiumi, the fountain of the four rivers. Also, it makes you realize that we Germans are not the only historical plunderers. The Obelisk was stolen by the Romans from Egypt. My first experience is done and now we must proceed to number two"

Heinrich turned and despite his gimpy leg walked briskly toward a beautiful church in the middle of the Piazza. "This is San Agnese; my parish church and I wish to say a prayer here before we eat." As he ascended the steps he turned and asked, "Do you still believe in God Gerhardt?" There was silence and Heinrich said, "It does not matter I am still on good terms with Him and my prayer will benefit both of us."

Making the sign of the cross, Heinrich blessed himself with Holy water and genuflected. He went to the last pew and for a few moments was engrossed in silent prayer. He saw no contradiction in his devotion to a religion that had its roots in Judaism and the current persecution of the Jews. Gerhardt stood motionless in the rear and was increasingly uncomfortable being in a church.

Henrich rose and said, "Ok my friend two down and one to go."

Gerhard was somewhat surprised by the religious devotion that his friend had maintained. Down the stairs at great pace Heinrich walked through an alley and made a right turn in front of the Hotel Raphael. "If you are in Rome when it is warmer than today, I will take you up to the hotel's roof garden for a marvelous view of the city."

The brisk pace continued. After a few minutes they arrived at Ristorante D'Amore.

"This is my third wish because for me this is the finest restaurant in Rome. We Germans are good at many things, but we cannot compete with the Italians when it comes to food. For them it is a three-act play. The first act is anticipation. The second is the actual meal and the third is the ongoing conversation and evaluation."

The foyer of Ristorante D'Amore was quite elegant and filled with large leather chairs and two Victorian sofas. On the walls were paintings of ancient historic Roman scenes and the main dining area had a silver glow from the Venetian crystal chandeliers. The dining room was crowded and noisy but the waiter escorted them to a side room where they would be afforded significant privacy. It was apparent that Heinrich was a regular and despite the German uniforms they were received as valued guests.

"If you don't mind Gerhardt, I will order for both of us. He turned to the waiter and said, "We will begin with the fish appetizers, the sautéed mussels and clams, sea-bass carpaccio, and the oysters. Also, the house specialty, cold anti-pasta and eventually we would like small dishes of pasta carbonara. And for the entree we'll have Saltimbocca Romana."

The waiter made no attempt to write down the order and apparently had it memorized. "And to drink?" the waiter requested.

"Aqua minerale Frizzante and Bottiglia di Gattinara."

Gerhardt found it decidedly impressive to listen to Heinrich's exchanges with the waiter. "Well done, obviously you are fluent in Italian."

"Yes, I am. It began at the conservatory years ago. Many of the terms and musical movements had Italian names and I was attracted to the beauty of the language. If I recollect correctly, you are also multi lingual and have a great facility for language. Now that we are outside the confines of required repulsion of anti-German humor, I can tell you what Charles the Seventh of Spain said. 'When I write poetry, I write in French. When I speak to God, I speak Spanish. When I am making love, I use Italian and when I speak to my horse, I speak German.' Of course, he was at war with Germany when he uttered those profound words."

Heinrich gustily ate course after course while Gerhardt simply nibbled at the sumptuous repast. He sat with a grim distracted silence. Finally satiated, Heinrich ordered two glasses of Sambuca but as the waiter left with the bottle, he said, "Waiter, please leave the bottle of Sambuca. I am afraid I will need it in the next hour."

Gerhardt took a sip of Sambuca and said, "If I am caught, I would like some witnesses to verify that I was not involved in the death of

Jews. It seems to me if I could have a few influential Jews give testimony that I had saved them it would prevent me from being tried for war crimes."

Heinrich paused. "You realize that if you aid any Jew and are caught it would mean instant death without even a trial. You will immediately be charged with treason and tortured before being hung"

"I understand that but I don't want to spend the rest of my life looking over my shoulder."

Heinrich lit a cigarette and blew the smoke from his nose. "Why do you need me? If I remember correctly, you had a Jew friend, Abraham, from the University who became a doctor. Maybe he would vouch for you."

Gerhard shook his head. "There are two problems with that. He would know my real identity and also, he is probably dead. He came to me last year and pleaded for me to save his family. I agreed and urged him to bring other hidden Jews to a point outside of Munich. I met them with a full force of the Gestapo and all were sent to Treblinka. I am sure they were all eventually transported to Auschwitz."

Heinrich paused and offered, "I could probably find one or two names of prominent Jews in my files." He was not even slightly disturbed by Gerhardt's betrayal of a friend. "Auschwitz would be the best place to start to select a few prominent Jews."

Chapter 25

Rome, 1944
Heinrich's Reflections and Doubts

Heinrich stayed up until the wee hours of the morning examining the events of the day. What initially seemed to be a welcome visit from an old friend turned into a significant challenge. He had no hesitation in helping his friend but realized there were many steps to be taken. The easiest part would be the forged documents for Gerhardt and possibly finding the two Jews he needed. However, there was the hurdle of Gerhardt vanishing so the Nazis would not pursue him. Also, there was the danger if Gerhardt were caught and tortured, he would reveal the fact that he had been aided by Heinrich.

After hours of going through the proposed plan he finally decided to go to bed. Exhausted both physically and emotionally he immediately fell into a deep sleep. He woke early with the mixed emotions of dread and opportunity. Slowly he sat up in his bed and began to design the necessary tasks that would fill his day. He reached for the cigarettes on the night table, lit one and walked to the French doors at the end of his bedroom. The cool air caressed his face as he threw open the doors to the bourgeoning sunlight of a new dawn. Putting out his cigarette he made his way to the bathroom, showered, shaved and put on his shirt and trousers. Suddenly he was grasped with a host of worries about the coming involvement with Gerhardt. Every dimension that seemed possible in the restaurant yesterday seemed daunting today. The two old friends had been chatting as though they were writing a war novel. It was somewhat invigorating talk. However, risking their lives in a plan bourgeoning with known and unknown pitfalls seemed extraordinarily foolish this morning.

Besides the realization that he risked his life in this escapade there was the stark reminder of his family. Yes, they were temporarily safe, but how would they survive after the war without him? Though still fully a believer of the Nazi world view, he, too, knew the end was coming. Pretensions for a world conquest by Germany were not even remotely possible. There would be pain, hunger and all sorts of retribution once the war ended. He was aware that even the relatively easy life he lived in Rome was, in a short period of time, going to come to an abrupt halt. The Allies were marching toward Rome and he was certain they would occupy the city by late spring. He tried to dismiss the ugly thoughts spinning through his head while he finished dressing.

Before going to a local café for his morning expresso, Heinrich opened his briefcase and reviewed the series of questions to be answered. He had carefully coded the parts of the plan and laid out the components on the dining room table. Each item in daylight had essential complexities that did not immediately challenge him earlier.

The café near his apartment was crowded with Italians quickly draining small cups of espresso that would fuel their morning activities. The tables as well as the counter bar were filled with patrons discussing a myriad of issues. This cacophony immediately ceased when Heinrich entered the area and made his way to the counter. This experience was nothing new for him but still made him uneasy. Quickly he ordered his espresso and drank it basically in one large gulp. He then quickly made his way to his office and began to scour the concentration camp records for possible candidates. In the midst of his search, he came across the name of a world-famous pianist who had once been his idol. He had the opportunity to attend a concert given by maestro Svi Contini who was the gold standard of classical piano music that Heinrich wished to emulate. He adored his talent, but in fact today he was just another Jew who could easily be discarded. The other name he discovered in his search was Dr. Lorenzo Kaplan, a noted Italian psychiatrist.

Thursday, before making his way to the office, Heinrich rose early and went for an extended walk before calling a cab. He stopped to say a prayer at Trinita Monti church before making his way down the Spanish steps and weaving a path to Trevi Fountain. He had on a few occasions thrown coins into the fountain hoping the gesture would allow him to return after the war. Flipping coins into the water over his left shoulder was more imperative this morning and directly linked to the hope that he would actually survive the war.

The Trip to Auschwitz

Fortunately, Heinrich was the sole occupant of a compartment on the train. He was able to spread out the puzzle pieces that had been finished; as well as the parts that would be addressed today.

He had to find answers to the following hurdles:

Documentation for Gerhardt and a new identity.

A plan for Gerhardt's death and the closing of his file.

Selection and transit papers for the two Auschwitz Jews.

A safe place for Gerhardt to take the Jews.

A re-assignment for Gerhardt under a new name and an eventual exit route from Germany.

Arriving at the Krakow station he was met by a beefy middle-aged driver and transported to the camp, which was two hours away. Last year he was driven in style in a Mercedes sedan but an indicator of the downward spiral of the German war effort was reflected in the shabby two-seater auto with a cracked windshield and a broken heater that was to be his transportation. Heinrich barely noticed the condition and was more aware of the beautiful Polish rural countryside and what a contrast it was to the shabby buildings of the Auschwitz concentration camp. Upon arrival he was quickly passed through the main gate and delivered to the administration office. A low-level guard welcomed him and guided him to the main records area.

"Thank you for escorting me to the document office. Do you know captain Klaus Lubok?"

"Yes, I do sir."

"Is he stationed here or in Birkenau?"

"He is stationed here sir."

"If he is available, will you please tell him Captain Heinrich Muller is here and would like to have a cup of coffee with him?"

"Yes sir, I am sure he is in his office."

Heinrich took off his coat and hung his cap on the top of the coat rack. He began to examine the files to learn the status of the names that he had compiled. For the first time, the files were out of order and he had the distinct impression that the systemic processes of the past were no longer in place.

Twenty minutes after his arrival at the document office there was a knock on the door and he saw his colleague, with two cups of coffee, waiting for him to release the internal latch. Heinrich rose to greet him and once the coffees were safely placed, he warmly greeted his former colleague. Klaus sat down and began to sip his coffee. Heinrich said, "I have not seen you since our graduation from the war college."

Klaus, who had gained significant weight, appeared to have lost his boyish enthusiastic presence. He sported a prison haircut and his mouth appeared rigid and tense. At the college he was bright and a total prankster and bon vivant in all social environments. Today he appeared sad and his attire was just short of slovenly.

"Those were different days, Heinrich, and certainly much happier."

Heinrich asked, "In what way?'

Klaus' response appeared to be hesitant and measured. "Everything we did after graduation turned out well. The events in the early battles and occupations proved to us and the world that we were the premier military force. I believed all of the military expertise we were taught would work infallibly in any campaign."

Heinrich listened intently but decided to proceed slowly and with great caution. "Where were you stationed right after graduation?"

Klaus responded in a low voice, "It was the beginning of the war and I was assigned initially to a field unit in North Africa. I spent 14 months there and was transferred to an infantry division first in France and then in Russia. Why do you ask?"

"No special reason, just trying to catch up with an old friend."

Heinrich then asked, even though he knew the answer, "Who was your commander in North Africa?"

Klaus looked puzzled. "Colonel Johann Stauffer. I was on his general staff."

Heinrich let out a slight gasp. "My goodness, were you caught up in the aftermath of accusations of his being a British spy?" That question appeared to make Klaus nervous and he seemed reluctant to answer the question.

"Klaus, I feel that my inquiries have made you uncomfortable and I wish to clearly state that this is not an interrogation. If it makes you more comfortable, we can chat about other subjects."

"Klaus seemed assured by this remark. "I was interrogated on three different occasions by the Gestapo but fully cleared of any knowledge that he was working for the British government. I had no involvement with his spy activities and after that was assigned here. It was a frightening experience and at one point I thought I would be cast in with anyone who knew Stauffer."

Klaus softly uttered, "It was almost impossible to believe he was a traitor; but he was. The firing squad was too simple a way for him to die. He and all the other ones that have betrayed the Fuhrer should be hung by piano wire at public executions."

Heinrich reached out and gently touched Klaus' shoulder. "I am sorry to cull up such a trying time in your life. So, you have been here for quite a while."

Klaus muttered, "It seems like forever."

Heinrich saw an opening. "I gather it is no picnic to be in a concentration camp." Klaus agreed. "At times it feels like we members of the staff are also prisoners."

Henrich probed this remark. "Not sure I follow."

"The climate is awful and the place is filled with human dregs that have every possible disease. Typhus is a frequent visitor and a constant fear for all the guards and their families. Auschwitz is a dismal assignment."

Heinrich asked, "Then why don't you ask for a transfer?"

"I have on two occasions and the last time I was singled out by the commandant and warned that there would be serious consequences if I asked again." Heinrich took out his cigarette case and offered a cigarette to Klaus. He lit both cigarettes.

"Klaus, I love Rome, despite the fact that the German uniform is an object of scorn. However, I am keenly aware that my life soon will change. The Allies each week gain significant ground in southern Italy and I estimate that they will capture Rome no later than spring."

Klaus concurred with Heinrich and offered, "I am not surprised because we are also vulnerable here. The Russians at some point will be at the gates. We are between commandants here but the next one will have a difficult assignment. The world has no idea what the Jews did to the German people in the Great War and the bleeding hearts will seek revenge."

Heinrich agreed. "Klaus, I believe that the war is lost and we are both in peril. I am sure you are keenly aware that we must individually make plans for what is coming. One of my dear friends needs a favor and I require your assistance. Can you find out if two Jews are still alive in the camp?"

"I'm not sure why you want this information, but If you have their names, I am sure that I could determine their status."

An hour later he returned to the office and informed Heinrich that both Jews were in Stalag 23 and were still alive.

Chapter 26

April 1944, Munich
Leaving Munich Forever

The night before he left for Rome, Gerhardt was frightened by a new nightmare. He dreamt that he was in a dark, damp cellar and kept trying to find a staircase or exit. He stumbled twice and realized the cellar was not empty but rather filled with the corpses of women and children. Panicked by the smell of corroding bodies he eventually saw a tiny light that he hoped would be an exit. He reached the light, which had come from under a large oak door. He opened the door but three men in judges' robes prevented his leaving the cellar. He began to shout and that is when he woke. Soaking wet from fearful perspiration Gerhardt instinctually reached over to the night table and took his silver case. Lighting a cigarette, he sat at the edge of the bed and gazed around the room. It was filled with overflowing ash trays. Wine bottles were scattered on the floor.

He barely had eaten for days and found wine was the key ingredient that allowed him to sleep. This silent apartment had once housed his children's laughter. Gerhardt wandered aimlessly through each room with the only sound being his shoes on the wooden floors. He envisioned past Christmases when the living room was filled with the joyous sounds of the season. The memory of his playing the piano while his wife sang "Stille Nacht" to the children was temporarily vivid. This, before the war, had been the center of his world and now it was a haunting reminder of what he had lost. Munich resembled his emotional life because it was in shambles due to frequent Allied bombings. His once idyllic life was in tatters and he was about to leave the city and place where he had known love and happiness. He was uncertain about his future.

He slowly filled his duffle bag, carefully placing in it the photos of Hitler and his family. He took a deep breath and made his way to the bedrooms in the apartment. In the main bedroom he opened the large wooden wardrobe and took out one of Frieda's dresses. He held the dress to his face and inhaled the aroma of her perfume. He fell onto the bed and began to weep. A man so bereft of feelings for those lives he had destroyed lived in a bubble of personal loss. After a few moments he went into the children's bedroom and picked up a teddy bear whose face was covered with lingenberry stains. His youngest, Wolfgang, had insisted that the bear was hungry and needed to eat. He held the bear to his cheek and pressed against it trying to recapture that blissful moment with his son. After a few minutes he zipped up the duffle bag and walked through each room in the apartment trying to somehow cast himself back into the past. Tears began to flow and he tried to compose himself before leaving for the train station. As he opened the door, he closed it with the realization that he would never see Munich again

The melodious sounds of water cascading in the Four Rivers Fountain made their way into the open windows of the Tre Scalini bar. It was a warm Roman April night filled with thousands of stars. Large groups of Italians visited the bar after work and the overcrowded social oasis was filled with loud songs and laughter. The bartenders seemed oblivious to the raucous noise and in robot-like fashion filled the drink orders of the patrons. Heinrich sat in the rear of the bar and had ordered two glasses of red wine. He glanced at his watch and anticipated that Gerhardt would arrive in the next 15 minutes. He laughed to himself with the thought that he could predict the exact time because Italian trains even in peacetime were always late. Gerhardt eventually appeared at the bar's door and Heinrich rose and waved to indicate his position at the rear of the bar.

There was no warm hug greeting between the uniformed figures but rather a formal handshake. It would not be appropriate for German officers to show any public sign of caring or friendship. In the next few minutes there was conversation but it seemed awkward and almost unnatural. They barely touched their glasses of wine. Gerhardt said, "When we were in your office the first time I came to Rome you sensed that I had something on my mind. I am having a similar feeling about you at this moment. Have you decided against helping me?"

"No. I have concerns but there is so much to cover that I want to make sure all of the pieces are in place. The first piece of good news is that I have secured the names of two famous Jews in Auschwitz. One is a musician with a world reputation and the other a psychiatrist and author. Both apparently are frail but will survive. I have counseled my friend to place them in a secure facility until you arrive. Gerhardt was pleased at this news and inquired, "When can I arrange to have them released?"

Heinrich raised an eyebrow and cautioned him. "Do not leap frog the many other steps that must be taken. The next challenge is for you to cease to exist and this must not be an AWOL situation. Deserters are being tracked and immediately executed."

"All right but how will we achieve this?"

"By having someone take your place.

Do you have any jewelry that has your name on it?"

"Yes, but what does that have to do with your plan?"

"Again, patience. What is it?"

"My watch, given to me by my wife when I received my military commission." "Take it off and give it to me."

Heinrich finished his wine and urged Gerhardt to do the same.

"Drink up. We have work to do."

Gerhardt seemed surprised by that statement. "It is almost 10 o'clock. What is there for us to do tonight?"

"You will see. The first thing is that we must return to my apartment and get my car. After then we will go to my office and requisition another auto."

Gerhardt was puzzled. "Why do we need two cars at this hour of the night?"

"Patience my friend, you must have patience."

Arriving at Heinrich's apartment Heinrich suggested that Gerhardt wear one of his friend's non-SS uniform. In addition, Heinrich counseled Gerhardt to take a pair of Heinrich's boots as well as the SS uniform.

At precisely 11:30 both cars were secured and Heinrich finally let Gerhardt in on his next step. "We are going to the Gestapo prison on Via Sasso and we will secure two Italian partisans."

"Ok, then what?"

"We will have them immobilized and handcuffed and then drive them to a place off the Appian way. Once there we will kill them and we will burn my car with one of the partisans in it. Near the car we will place your watch, part of your documents and the other partisan will be near the burnt-out vehicle. It will appear there was a shootout and both perished. I will leak this to the local police and then I will close the file on Gerhardt Stark. You will no longer exist."

"My Heavens Heinrich, you have thought of everything."

"Not quite. Remember this is the easiest part of your escape."

Via Sasso was the infamous Gestapo prison that had once been an apartment house. Each room was transformed into a cell without a bed or toilet. The head of the gestapo was a sadist by the name of Herbert Klapper who personally enjoyed torturing prisoners over a period of seven days. One of his pleasures was to have Jewish prisoners chant "We love Hitler." He would also have Jewish prisoners beat each other to within an inch of death. In addition to his daily sadistic practices, he was the person behind the retaliation for the Via Rasella attack and the deportation to Auschwitz of more than 2,000 Roman Jews.

Arriving at the prison, Heinrich took the lead and requested that he speak with the officer in charge.

"We are here to obtain two members of the Italian partisan group for a secret mission. Preferably, we would like the two most recent ones who are still able bodied and have not been tortured. Also, we will need confiscated weapons and red scarves that are worn by partisans. Do you have a way to drug them as well as handcuffing and shackling them?"

The officer did not seem suspicious and after reviewing their papers took them upstairs to the second floor. "These are the new arrivals and you can pick any two. I will need you to sign for their release and will have the physician on duty give them strong sedatives so they will not cause trouble once you leave here."

Ironically, the first man was about the same height and build as Gerhardt. The second was younger and appeared to be somewhere in his 20s. After a short time, both were placed in the Mercedes sedan driven by Heinrich. He turned to Gerhardt and said, "In the trunk of your car there is a can of petrol we will need when we arrive at our destination. Follow me closely and when I put on my emergency lights it will be a signal to pull off the road. It will be dark in Rome but if you get lost follow the signs for Via Francigena toward Viterbo. When we are about six kilometers outside the city, the area will be rural and I will find a place to stop."

Gerhardt closely followed Heinrichs's car and about 15 minutes outside the city he observed the Mercedes' lights go on and off. This was the signal to stop and pull onto a deserted country road.

The road was narrow and one seldom used by automobiles. It was more like a well-used tractor path filled with large ruts on the exposed earth. The moment was very still except for the wind whistling sounds through the Roman pines. Both sides of the road were covered with thick bushes and the air was filled with the pungent smell of cow manure. As Heinrich and Gerhardt exited the cars, they were engulfed in the blackness of a cool spring night. The only light was the small flashlight Heinrich held in his left hand. He removed his Luger from his holster and urged Gerhardt to have the prisoners leave the back seat of the Mercedes. Once out of the car, they appeared confused and unstable. The strong sedatives were still working. They had trouble walking. Heinrich told Gerhardt to remove their shackles and handcuffs. Once this was done, he ordered the man that resembled Gerhardt to disrobe. Once accomplished, they ordered the man to put on Gerhardt's SS uniform. The man was hesitant. In Italian he said, "Perche devo mettere su quest divisa?"

Heinrich forcefully responded, "Perche ho detto cosi."

Once dressed, Heinrich told Gerhardt to lead him to the auto and place him in the driver's seat. While this was happening, he stood the second partisan up and placed a red kerchief around his neck. "Move away from the car, Gerhardt."

Heinrich reached into the trunk of his Mercedes and took out a partisan weapon. He placed a clip in the machine gun, turned and let fly two blasts from the machine gun, which shattered the other vehicle.

He witnessed the prisoner's body heave and jolt due to the force of the bullets.

He said to Gerhardt, "See if he is dead."

Meanwhile the other partisan was whimpering and had fallen prostrate on the ground. Gerhardt checked the interior of the car and felt the pulse of the bleeding partisan. "He is dead."

"Good."

With that Heinrich forced the second prisoner to lean against a large pine tree.

"Gerhardt, move to the side of the car and shoot this one twice and use the rest of the bullets to hit the tree."

Gerhardt stepped away, cocked his weapon and fired twice hitting the weeping prisoner in the head and chest. He died instantly. He then fired the remaining rounds into the tree.

"All right now get the boots, cap and petrol out of my trunk. I will tear your watch band and leave it with your cap and wallet 10 yards from the car. Sprinkle the petrol inside the car."

Once achieved, Heinrich lit a presoaked rag and threw it toward the vehicle. The flames were small at first, but then there was an explosion and the car was totally engulfed in flames, sending a black cloud of poisonous air into the sky. They waited until the flames subsided before returning to the Mercedes. Heinrich was walking behind his friend. He called out "Gerhardt!" With that Gerhardt turned to face him. Heinrich sharply rebuked him. "You must never do that again. Gerhardt Stark is dead."

Chapter 27

April, 1944
Gerhardt assumes a new identity

It was the first time in weeks that Gerhardt was not visited by disturbing nightmares. The past week he was running on fumes trying to sort out his escape plans. The events of last evening exhausted him and his body actually ached. He slept peacefully through the entire night. In the early morning sunlight streamed through the open blinds as he felt a hand on his shoulder. "Wake up my friend because our work has just begun."

Barely opening his eyes, Gerhardt stretched and sarcastically uttered, "Heinrich you are a cruel task master."

Heinrich sharply replied, "Need I remind you that we have plunged into the world of insanity and we are far from out of the woods?"

"Can I at least have a cigarette and coffee before addressing your concerns?"

Heinrich shook his head in disgust and said, "Look nameless one this is no laughing matter. We only have a few days to figure out the next steps of your new life."

Siting up and reaching for a cigarette from the side table, Gerhardt said, "Sorry, I appreciate your concerns and am most grateful for what you have already done. What do you want me to do?"

"Well, this morning when I go to the office, I will start the paperwork to draw up the necessary documents that you will require. So, the first order of business is for you to pick a new name."

Gerhardt thought and said, "I have always liked the name Georg. It has a classical ring to it."

"Ok, now how about your last name?"

"How does Baum fit with the name Georg?"

"I think it is perfect. Ok then it is Georg Baum. You are never to respond to your prior name under any circumstances."

Continuing with his serious thoughts, Heinrich said, "I have some concerns about your plan to free the two prisoners from Auschwitz. My fear is that someone there will remember you from prior visits. I assume that persons there know you under your real name."

"I don't think that will be a problem except for the commandant Hoss. I have been with him on numerous occasions and he would know that my name is not Georg Baum."

"Well, that is not a problem because if we act this week there is no current commandant at Auschwitz. My contact informed me that they are between leaders so we must put our plan into operation immediately. Is there any business you have before that?"

"Well, I will need to go to Zurich for one day."

"For what?"

"To transfer money from accounts with my prior name and to visit an art gallery that is holding some of my art work."

"How will you do that?'

"With your help and a new passport, I will go through the security with my new name but will use my passport with the old name to transfer all funds to Georg Baum."

Heinrich was writing as though he was possessed. He had delineated a series of questions and was most concerned that they had to be answered.

"We are fortunate that my schedule is quite light this week and my subordinates can handle the day-to-day details of my office. I think I should create a fictitious bio for you, one that cannot be traced because there are no surviving records. I know that any mention of the city of Kassel is painful for you but I believe we should make your past history there. I will create a birth date, schooling and say that you completed your architectural studies there. The city, as you well know, was fire bombed and the municipal buildings were completely destroyed. There will be nothing you need to fear about past records. Also, I will insert a military history. My preference today is to assign you to an office in Zurich, Switzerland where you can work in isolation. I will have to give this more consideration.

You mentioned that you have some assets in Switzerland. Your transition and escape will have serious financial implications. Also, you will need money once you leave Germany. I worry that you will not have adequate funds to support your new life."

"That will not be a problem Heinrich. I believe I have adequate funds for the rest of my life."

Heinrich was shocked by this statement.

"How nice, I think I should have been in your line of work."

"Heinrich, after I deposit the Jews should I seek a Red Cross letter of transit and immediately leave the country? As of now my initial thought is somewhere in South America."

"I understand your desire to move quickly to your new life but it is still precarious to venture out of Germany by ship. The danger has lessened in the past year because so many U boats have been sunk but it is still a risky proposition. I would counsel you to wait until the war ends. Also, you are a sponge for language and this will give you the opportunity to learn Spanish."

Heinrich shuffled the papers in front of him. "Next on the agendum is what you do with the Jews once you leave Auschwitz. I will tactfully investigate some of the files in our office and hopefully find a landing place for the two Jews in Rome. Under no circumstances are you to bring them here. I know there is a Catholic monsignor at the Vatican who is known to house Jews and enemy combatants. I am not sure, but I think his name is Monsignor O'Flaherty. If he is the person we identify then I will get specific instructions for the exchange. Once you arrive at the Oswiecim train station phone me and I will give you instructions where you are to take them in Rome."

"All right. I have to go. There is food in the refrigerator and coffee and a carton of cigarettes in the cupboard. Do not leave the apartment for any reason. I will return tonight with your necessary documentation."

Later that evening Heinrich returned from the office with a large manila envelope that he placed on the dining room table.

"How are you Georg?" Heinrich asked, testing him with his new name.

"I am anxious but all right."

"I think I can lower your anxiety. I worked tirelessly today with total success. In the envelope on the table are the passport and the letters of transit. They are valid for seven days so I suggest you take care of your business in Switzerland tomorrow and either the next day or certainly before the weekend go to Auschwitz. It is quite a long trip so I would advise you to get there early in the morning and take the noon train back. There is no direct train to Rome and the trip will take approximately 20 hours with the transfers.

"I had to be very careful with regard to the Catholic priest who we discussed. I used an outside intermediary to find out whether we could use him. His movements are closely guarded by the Gestapo so my source contacted him and after being assured that this was not a trap, he gave two possibilities for the exchange. The first is the Vatican and

I will write down explicit entrances where you will be met. If this for any reason is not possible you are to take them to the Casa Santa Maria, which is at 30 Via del Umilta. It is very close to the fountain of Trevi. The password is the same for each locale. It is 'The Shamrocks of Erin.'

"Monsignor O'Flaherty is a thorn in the side of the local Gestapo in Rome. It has been well documented that he is involved in hiding Allied soldiers as well as Jews. Herbert Klapper, head of the Gestapo in Rome, has made catching him in the act his highest priority, but so far, they have been unsuccessful. From his dossier he appears to be an interesting character."

Gerhardt picked up the folder and began to read about O'Flaherty.

Monsignor O'Flaherty, is fluent in Italian, English and German. He is brilliant with three academic doctorates. He was an amateur golf champion. He provides Vatican sanctuary for escaped prisoners of war, partisans and Jews. Despite constant surveillance he has eluded many attempts to catch him in the act. He resides in the German College, nestled right beside Saint Peter's Basilica.

He is a master of disguise and was even rumored once to have dressed as a nun to avoid a raid on the college.

After reading the short biography Gerhardt asked, "I am not so familiar with Rome. Will I have specific directions that will enable me to find the meeting places?"

"Yes, I am sure those details will be defined if he is the choice."

Again, checking the list in front of him, Heinrich continued, "One of the key issues in your complete change of identity is that no one will recognize you. Is there anyone other than former soldiers or office personnel who might recognize you?"

"I have had literally no contact with my birth family and the only two persons who could be of concern are my brother-in-law, Rolf, and a cousin, Micah."

"Where is your brother-in-law?"

"Last I heard he was stationed in Cologne at the central SS office."

"How about your cousin?"

"No idea. But he is a Jew. He lived at 16 Boltzmangasse in Munich."

"Good, I will check the files and see if he has been transported. I know you are thinking about where you will go once you leave Germany. We mentioned it earlier but have you given specific thought to where you will go?"

"I know there is a haven in Argentina for Germans but my initial choice is to stay away from a German center. I think it will be easier to get to Spain and the government is still very pro fascist."

"Do you plan on working as an architect?"

"That would be the ideal but I have no idea what will be available."

"With all of the preparations we are making to completely change your identity there is one consideration that we cannot overlook."

"What is that?"

"Your tattoo. It immediately indicates that you were a member of the SS. I strongly suggest that before you get to Spain you have it removed."

The next morning Gerhardt, or now Georg Baum, left for Zurich to arrange his financial matters. He had no anxiety about first dealing with the Swiss Bank where he had large accounts and four safety deposit boxes. He would empty the safety deposit boxes and transfer all of his accounts to the name of Georg Baum. In addition, he intended to visit Strasberg Gallery and have them sell at the appropriate time the original Degas ballerina series, French Impressionist masterpieces as well as the Rodin sculpture that he had stored in their museum section.

Gerhardt had no trouble with the Italian and Swiss customs. He used his new name to get through the process but carried his old passport in his briefcase. Once inside the city he was pleased that this could possibly be a place where he might work. Initially, he was impressed by the beauty of the lake and the view of the snowy Swiss Alps.

This charming compact city was situated on the picturesque northern shore of Lake Zurich with the Limmat River, which flows out of the lake and runs through the town center. It had more than 1,200 drinking water sources that spread within the city, which made Zurich one of the fountain richest cities in the world. In addition, there were public parks like the Platzspitz which extended the city area.

Leaving the station, Gerhardt glanced at his city map and found the route to his destination, 45 Niederdorfstrasse. This lovely thoroughfare was the main lane through the Old Town. It was for walkers only. Part of the charm of the street was the many sidewalk restaurants and cafes, shops and bars.

As an architect, he admired the elegant towers of Fraumunster Church, with its colorful glass windows.

After approaching the intersection point of the Old City, Bahnhofstrasse and Zurich Lake, he had the full image of Zurich, an unforgettable mix of old and new.

He checked the time. He had an hour before his bank appointment so he stopped at an outdoor cafe and ordered coffee and a chocolate croissant. Paying the check, he asked the waiter where Niederdorfstrasse intersected with Blumenstrasse. The waiter said that they crossed each other barely five minutes away. The waiter asked for his destination. He was pleased that the bank was barely two blocks to the left.

Gerhardt had dealt with the bank manager, Jonas Richter, on many occasions but never in person. He had been recommended because, although he was a Swiss citizen, he had a plethora of German relatives. Unlike many of his Swiss peers, he was pro-Nazi and completely understood the sources of the wealth that his office was receiving from the SS members.

Gerhardt was cordially escorted into the private office of Richter. The office was rather spartan with no gentle touch of beauty or art. It fit the impression that Gerhardt had of Jonas Richter. Although he was tall and well-dressed, there was a coldness about his interactions.

After explaining the purpose of his visit, Richter assured Gerhardt there would be no issue in the transfer of his funds to any destination in the world. All that was required was the signing of some official documents and notification as to the date the funds would be transferred. This completed, Richter led Gerhardt to the safety deposit box area where Gerhardt emptied the four boxes of jewelry and currency into his leather bag. Because of his uniform, he knew he would not have to open the bag at either customs place.

Bank business completed; Richter invited him to have lunch at a restaurant near the train station. In the middle of the meal, testing the confidentiality of Richter, Gerhardt explained that he needed the name of a physician who could be trusted, Richter took out one of his business cards and wrote the name Dr. Ernst Vogel and a phone number. "He is an excellent surgeon and a personal friend. Use my name and I am sure that he will accommodate your requests."

Another completely successful piece was now in place. Next stop was the Strausberg Gallery where he had substantial art pieces that he wished to sell. The owner and international art expert, Dr. Myron Sven, assured him that he would selectively market all of the pieces. However, the Degas ballerina collection was the most valuable but would take a considerable amount of time to sell. Gerhardt also set up the transfer of money to Georg Baum, for when pieces were sold.

He returned to Rome, feeling confident that his future was growing brighter by the day.

It all went smoothly. The Swiss pretense to be neutral served them well. Villains like Gerhardt could secretly hide their plunder with an absolute guarantee of secrecy.

He decided he would go to Auschwitz on Friday.

Heinrich stopped at Tre Scalini to pick up dinner for the two of them. He called out to Gerhardt from the bottom of the stairway, "Open a bottle of wine. I have dinner we can eat as soon as I heat up the main course."

Gerhardt found a corkscrew. As Heinrich entered the kitchen, he poured him a glass of Gattinara red wine. "How was your day?"

"I have found your cousin. He is in Theresienstadt, serving as a physician in the infirmary. What would you have me do with him?"

"Is it possible to have him transferred to Auschwitz?"

Heinrich applied with certainty, "I am sure that can be arranged."

Gerhardt was reassured by Heinrich's statement. "If so, then his termination would be another link that does not exist."

Chapter 28

1944, Auschwitz
Micah is saved from certain death

In reviewing the paperwork on his desk, Captain Armand Verner was surprised by one of the documents that came the previous night by courier. The document did not state the name of the prisoner who arrived the previous afternoon but the instructions were quite clear. Captain Verner was personally to see that the prisoner was terminated on arrival or soon thereafter. Verner thought this must be a political prisoner because individuals of less importance do not arrive at the camp with singular paperwork. He picked up his phone and because he was curious ordered his assistant Corporal Klaus Schoendienst to come into his office. "Good morning captain. How may I help you.?"

"I have received orders to deal directly with the prisoner who was transferred yesterday afternoon from Theresienstadt. Go to the administration office to find out who the prisoner is and once that is determined bring him here."

An hour later Corporal Schoendienst returned with the prisoner. Shackled, Micah Goldstein waited in the outer office before meeting Captain Verner. After a few minutes he was led to the office. When he entered, Captain Verner was looking out the window. The corporal knocked and announced the prisoner. Verner turned from the window. His jaw dropped when he saw Micah. He ordered the shackled prisoner to be seated. At this point Micah did not recognize Verner and had no idea why he had been moved from Theresienstadt.

"The paperwork on you does not list your name but I know who you are."

Micah was confused by this statement but knew enough not to speak without permission.

"You are Dr. Micah Goldstein."

Still silent Micah could not fathom how this Nazi could know his identity. "Although I know who you are, your facial expression tells me you don't know who I am. Do you have any idea where our paths crossed?"

"Am I allowed to speak?'

"Certainly. Now answer the question."

"I do not know who you are and I have absolutely no idea why I have been transferred to Auschwitz."

"It would be very simple to inform you where our paths crossed. However, I think instead of telling you I will give you some hints. I know without any official paper work that you are from Munich. Isn't that true?"

Micah was totally confused by this game being played by the German captain. "Yes."

"Is it not true also that by training you are a physician?"

Again, the answer was yes.

"And further investigation tells me that you are, or shall I say were, a pediatrician?"

"Obviously, you know a great deal about me."

"I do, and instead of dropping a ton of hints I will give you one specific hint that may jar your memory. Does the name Anna Verner ring a bell?"

Micah paused before answering. "I am sorry but that name is not one that I recognize."

Captain Verner lit a cigarette. He offered one to Micah who politely declined, being a non-smoker. "In Munich before Jews were forbidden to treat Aryan patients, Anna Verner had a seriously high fever and was literally close to losing her life. She was taken to the children's hospital in Munich and after hours of dedicated service the team saved her life. At one point her heart stopped but the team refused to allow her to die and she was resuscitated. Four days later this beautiful 4-year-old child was released from the hospital and is now a healthy 10-year-old living with her mother and grandparents in Bavaria. That child is my daughter and you were the head physician of the team that saved her life."

Micah now remembered the child but said nothing.

The captain continued, "That reality poses a problem for me this morning. I don't know why someone thinks you are so special but the fact that you have been escorted here individually is a sign of that. Also, doctor, you come with orders that you are to be terminated upon arrival or soon thereafter. Can you tell me why someone has singled you out?"

"I have no idea," Micah choked out.

"Well because of your presence in my past and the fact that you saved my daughter's life I am immediately in the midst of a serious challenge. Let me share a few facts that may help you understand my predicament. Two years ago, in Russia I refused to issue an order that immediately had me lose my field command. I was ordered to have a group of Russian women and children in a village shot. I refused to issue that order and my commanding general, in reviewing the case, decided that the adequate punishment would be to assign me to Auschwitz. His reasoning was based on the belief that I was a weakling who could not kill Jews so he would send me to a place where thousands of Jews would be killed daily. Please understand that I am no fan of the Jewish race but directly shooting women and children was not an order that I could issue."

Now Micah could not remain silent. "So, you traded that decision for one that allows you to murder women and children here?"

"I can understand how that would be something you could believe but it is not true. I do believe that Jews have done great harm to the German people but killing them instead of forcing them to leave Germany is not part of my belief system. I make the choice to live and also to have my family live and so that is why I stay here. A second refusal would put me and my family in danger. Again, do not take from this that I am some hero who wishes to protect Jews. However, I have a special affinity for my children and Anna is alive and well today because of you. The question for me is what do I do with you? If I follow the order to have you killed immediately there is no personal risk but what are the consequences for me emotionally? Every time I see Anna's beautiful face will today put a blemish on that experience? I order you not to share any of this conversation. I will search to learn if there are any alternatives in carrying out the orders that I have received about you."

With that Captain Verner picked up his phone and summoned the guard.

"Take this prisoner to the infirmary and place him in a solitary room. He is not to be mistreated and I will give further orders as soon as possible."

Captain Verner sent a communique to Theresienstadt stating that Micah Goldstein had been terminated. Once this was accomplished, he visited Micah in the infirmary. He informed Micah that his name was no longer Micah Goldstein and that he would now assume the name of Israel Ross. "The reason that I am making you assume this name is that I have informed my superiors that I had you terminated. For now, I will assign you to assist the German physicians treating the children of those who are stationed here. This will allow you to have better living conditions while you are imprisoned here."

Micah had mixed feelings about being treated in such a privileged way, but his desire to live and someday take his revenge against Gerhardt Stark allowed him to accept the decisions made by Captain Verner.

Chapter 29

April 1944, Rome - Auschwitz
Gerhardt frees the two key Jews from Auschwitz

The Station was relatively empty as Gerhardt boarded the train. He had an increasing level of confidence that within the next year he would successfully leave Germany to start a new life. Weeks ago, he was mired in the belief that he would be incarcerated or even hung for his participation in "so called war crimes." Heinrich had been a gift. The next few days would be critical to this life-saving adventure.

Gerhardt was pleased that he had an entire compartment to himself in the first-class smoking carriage. It was ironic that the place where he had organized massive atrocities was key to a new life. He had visited Auschwitz-Birkenau on many occasions while planning the construction of the new site but never once did he feel any pang of conscience about what he was doing. The legacy of his murders to this day has never penetrated the soul of one who owed so much to his Jewish relatives. On the train he was focused only on self-preservation. He gazed out the window and pressed his face to the glass. In the beginning of the trip the view was filled with the ram shackled remains of Munich. The city had been literally obliterated by American and British nightly bombing raids. However, an hour outside the city the countryside changed to rolling green hills with the dark mountains rising in the distance. The train route passed through picturesque towns, dense forests and rolling landscapes. As he gazed out the window he was caught up in his hopes and dreams for the new life that was slowly evolving and becoming more and more possible.

He took out of his briefcase and mentally addressed the steps to the new life that Heinrich proposed.
1. It appeared that the release of the two prominent Jews was a given. He was aware that appearances mattered so he would be harsh in his initial dealings with them. He was somewhat concerned that they did not have passports but the transit papers and his uniform should be sufficient in getting them through the borders.
2. The trip to Switzerland was a complete success. He had transferred all of his accounts to his new name and his substantial art collection would now be selectively sold through the Strasberg Gallery. His collection of the Degas ballerina series was incredibly valuable as well as the 17 French Impressionist paintings. He had made a wise decision to ship them to Switzerland when his family moved to Kassel.
3. He was pleased that Heinrich would be able to give him a false history and transfer him to a desk job in Zurich but he had not yet determined where he would go when the war was coming to a close. He knew there was a huge German community in Argentina but was leaning toward starting life over in Spain. Either way he had months to learn Spanish but that would not be a problem because he easily learned other languages.
4. The tattoo presented an issue but he was certain that Dr. Vogel in Zurich could find a solution to the challenge of removing it. Dr. Vogel, a German physician, was recommended by Jonas Richter and the only decision was to have it done now or later. He mused that the operation must not be merely the tattoo area. He thought he would have more damage to the upper arm and neck. He could claim he had been harmed in either combat or an allied air raid.

5. Part of his thoughts this morning were memories of significant assignments he had in the past. He, in particular, missed the collegial times with Speer in the Nuremberg era and longed for the opportunity to once again ply his skills as an architect.
6. Blocking out every scintilla of his prior existence was essential and he was concerned about Micah and his brother-in-law, Rolf. He had no idea whether they were alive but it would make him more comfortable if they were both dead.

Halfway into the train ride he placed all of his plans and concerns into his briefcase and decided to sleep. Because his compartment was empty, he stretched out and fell into a deep sleep. When he awoke, he thought that they were but an hour and a half from Oswiecim.

Arriving at the main gate to the camp, Gerhardt was summarily passed through customs. He informed the guards that he had an appointment with Captain Lubok. They escorted him to the administration building where he was to meet Captain Lubok.

"Good morning Captain Baum. I know you are on a tight schedule so I will take you to the infirmary to collect your two prisoners."

Once inside the infirmary they called out the names of Lorenzo Kaplan and Svi Contini. As they came forward, they were ordered to "put your coats on and come with us."

On the Monday morning roll call two days prior to this, the prisoners from Stalag 23 stood for hours. One hour into the process two names were read and ordered to step forward. Lorenzo Kaplan and Svi Contini shuddered at hearing their names because they thought this was their turn to be terminated. They had learned from experience not to question any direct orders so they merely came to the front of the line and waited for instructions. The guard taking the roll call ordered another guard to take them to the infirmary. Before they arrived at the infirmary, they were led to a warehouse filled with clothing and shoes. The guard took a piece of paper out of his pocket and after reading it said, "Pick out a suit, undergarments and shoes. Also, select a coat from the large rack in the corner." Again, they followed orders and did not ask any questions.

Once they arrived at the infirmary, they were placed in a separate room away from the patients and ordered to stay there until further notice. That afternoon, and for the next few days their isolation continued but they received three meals a day and were allowed to use the infirmary shower.

On Thursday morning they were escorted to the administration building at 10:30. There they were ordered to wait in the vestibule. A few minutes later two officers appeared and both Svi and Lorenzo were handcuffed by one of the officers.

"Excuse me sir but where are you taking us?" Svi gently asked. Furious Svi had spoken, Gerhardt slapped Svi across the face with his leather gloves.

"Be silent Jew pig. One more word out of you and you will wish you had never been born."

Guarded by two soldiers and Gerhardt, the prisoners walked quickly to the main gate where an auto was waiting to take them to the train station.

Gerhardt spoke to the driver.

"I will sit in the back with the two prisoners."

When they arrived at the gate Gerhardt exited the cab with his two prisoners and gave instructions to the driver.

"I will no longer need your presence. If either one of these Jews tries anything, I will shoot both of them."

As soon as the auto pulled away Gerhardt addressed the two in a completely different manner. "I am sorry I had to be so harsh in speaking to you and slapping you. That was for appearances. Put out your hands and I will uncuff you."

Both prisoners were totally confused by this radical change in tone and behavior.

"My name is Georg Baum and I am going to take you to a place in Rome where you will be safe."

Svi said, "I don't understand. You are a Nazi soldier. Why would you do that?"

"All of us are not monsters. I cannot make a big difference in the camp but I can save a few of you."

Lorenzo was incredulous. "But why are you doing this?"

"Because I do not hate Jews. I believe persecuting you is wrong and immoral. I have not had the courage to stand up publicly and say this but it is time to stop the killing. My plan is for us to take a train to Rome and there I will escort you to the Vatican where a Catholic priest will offer you sanctuary until the war ends. Between here and there you must act as though you are my prisoners. Say nothing on the train when we pass through the borders where we will be asked for passports. Neither of you has a passport but I have transit papers and my uniform should be the deciding factor that will allow us to pass without incident."

Svi inquired, "Why did you pick the two of us.?"

"I have a friend who examined the files and chose you because of your backgrounds and past occupations."

Svi said, "My wife and children died in the camp."

Lorenzo choked back tears and added, "My beloved wife, Ella, also died there."

"I am so sorry. I cannot believe the number of innocent persons my government has killed."

As the conversation progressed Lorenzo offered, "This is the first time since I was arrested that someone has treated me like a human being."

Svi agreed. "I cannot even find the words that allow you to understand what has happened to us."

Gerhardt put on a fake compassionate face. "I cannot change the losses you have experienced. But I hope that soon your nightmare will be over. The Russians will be at the gate in Birkenau but I had to act now to do some small part to resist the ongoing murders."

The train ride was long. The two prisoners had a plethora of questions for this person who treated them with dignity.

Lorenzo asked, "What was your profession before the war?"

"I was an architect. I'm hoping that when the war is just a bad memory, I will be able to go back to it."

"Do you plan to do that in Germany?"

"I am not sure because there is so much destruction in my homeland that it may be a decade before anything positive can happen. I may leave Europe and go to South America."

Svi stared at his hands. "It has been so long since I have played a piano. That is one of the things I hope to do again."

With a compassionate face, Gerhardt said, "I can only imagine how much rigor and practice go into your profession. But perhaps when you are safe you can dedicate yourself to restoring your skill."

Lorenzo asked. "You mentioned that you were taking us to Rome. Can you help us understand where in Rome?"

"Apparently, there is a Catholic priest who provides sanctuary within the Vatican. He has been contacted and is willing to take both of you inside the Vatican. My government, at least up to now, has accepted the neutrality of the Vatican so you will be safe there. I am to call a contact number and when we get to Rome I will walk you to a location that leads to his residence. My understanding is that he will meet us there."

"Can I ask another question? Is this dangerous for you?" Svi nodded in agreement. Gerhardt smiled and said, "I would be immediately executed for helping you. Do not think of me as any kind of a hero. I am more than a little concerned about what will happen to me if we get caught. You will no doubt be returned to a camp but I would be killed. All right, we have hours to talk but I am sure that right now it would be beneficial for you both to have a decent meal. The train has a dining car and it would be my pleasure to share a meal with you."

The first border crossing went without incident and the passport personnel only casually glanced at the transit papers after examining the German officer's passport and identification. After hours of sleep, Gerhardt knew that within a half hour they would arrive at the main station in Florence. At that moment there was a knock on the door. A tall man in a long black leather coat identified himself as a member of the Gestapo entered the compartment. "Good morning. I need to see your papers." Gerhardt took out his passport and indicated that the two men with him were prisoners. "I have been commissioned by higher authorities to transport these two Jews. They were at the camp in Auschwitz and I am taking them to a site in Rome."

Gerhardt kept his calm, but was apprehensive that somehow his story would not hold up.

The Gestapo agent inquired, "Where in Rome are you taking these two prisoners?" "The site has not been established in the orders that I received. Once in Rome I am to call the main headquarters and ask for Captain Heinrich Mueller and he will then tell me where I was to deposit the prisoners."

That information did not satisfy the protagonist and Gerhardt realized the situation had become precarious. The Gestapo agent said, "We will soon be in Florence and if everything that you have said is true, there will be a momentary pause in your trip. I will escort you to my headquarters in Florence where we can verify your story."

Gerhardt attempted to use reason. "If you understood the seriousness of this mission, I'm sure you would not consider asking us to leave the train in Florence." "That may be true, but I have a responsibility to make sure that what you are telling me is factual. There is the possibility that you may not even be a German officer and that you yourself may be Jewish."

"Would it help you to see my SS tattoo to prove that I am who I say I am?"

"Tattoos can easily be faked. If you are a member of the SS why are you not wearing an SS uniform? There is something quite out of order here and I intend to make sure that you are not lying."

Gerhardt knew if they got off the train in Florence the entire plan would blow up in his face, so he decided that he could not allow himself or the prisoners to wind up in Gestapo headquarters. There was no way out unless he was willing to do something startling. He asked, "Is it possible for the two prisoners to go into the bathroom so I could speak with you in confidence?"

The agent stared at him for a moment. "I will allow that but first you must frisk these Jews to make sure that have no weapons. Also, you must remove your revolver and hand it to me."

With that, both Svi and Lorenzo were patted down and then ushered into the bathroom. Gerhardt passed over his Luger, but what the Gestapo person did not know was that Gerhardt had a dagger up his sleeve. He had been taught in his SS training that the sleeve is an area that is rarely searched for a weapon. Slowly he slid the knife from his sleeve into his hand. It was still totally concealed. His heart was pulsating. He could feel the adrenaline racing through his veins. He took a deep breath and with all his strength plunged the knife into the Nazi's chest. He withdrew the blade and placed his hand over his opponent's mouth. He struck again and again. Blood sprayed high into the air, staining Gerhardt's jacket. As the blade entered there was a series of squishing sounds in the Nazi's stomach. He heard the gurgle in the throat. He let the body slump to the floor.

He then opened the bathroom door. In staccato commands he barked, "Hurry. Help me get him into the bathroom. Pick up the towels. We have to get these blood puddles off the floor."

Lorenzo and Svi were aghast at what they were seeing. Having no choice, they immediately responded to Gerhardt's commands. Once that had been accomplished Gerhardt washed his hands but realized that the blood had splattered on his uniform. Fortunately, he had a coat to wear passing through security. The next 40 minutes before the train arrived at Florence were tense. As soon as the train was within a few minutes of the station Gerhardt and his captives left the compartment and headed toward one of the exits.

He reminded them, "You must remember to be docile and act as though you are frightened of me when we get to security."

Fortunately, there were only two Italian policemen and one German soldier at security in the Florence station. Gerhardt quickly explained that he was taking these two prisoners to Gestapo headquarters. His authoritarian manner and his paperwork, unlike on the train, allowed them immediately to pass through security. Finally, though he pretended to be calm, Gerhardt could breathe more easily and he assumed a peaceful demeanor. On the way out of the station he asked a train official if there was another train station in Florence. The official answered yes there were two, the closest is Firenze Statuto.

"Is it possible to get a train to Rome there?"

"Yes, but they run infrequently. You would be better off getting one here."

"I understand that but we have some business in Florence before we go."

The attendant took out a schedule. "Let me check. The next train to Rome from there is at 1:30. It arrives in Rome at 3:12."

"Thank you. You have been most helpful."

Once outside the terminal Gerhardt hailed a cab. "Please take us to Stazione Statuto."

Svi and Lorenzo were unnerved by the train debacle and feared that the plan was unraveling. Lorenzo nervously asked, "What will we do for the time before the train?"

Gerhardt had regained his composure. "We will act like tourists and find a café until it is train time. I need to check to see if our tickets are still good."

The security here seemed simple, with only one Italian official scrutinizing the paperwork. He seemed bored and barely looked at the transit papers before passing them through.

On the train Gerhardt warned his prisoners that the tightest security they would face would be in Rome. "Once through the security I must make a phone call before we go to your place of sanctuary."

The line for security in Rome was long and Gerhardt decided he would walk past the line and speak directly with the German officer in charge.

"I am Captain Georg Baum. I am on a mission to deliver these two prisoners to Captain Heinrich Mueller. We are a bit behind schedule thanks to the ridiculous lack of timeliness in Italian rail service. Why did God give this beautiful country to a race of idiots?"

The officer laughed at his comment, then asked for passports and transit papers. "Where are their passports?"

"They are Jews who have been in Auschwitz. They do not have passports."

The officer seemed to understand. He ordered the guards to let them pass. Relieved and seeing the goal in sight Gerhardt found a public phone. He dialed the number Heinrich had given him.

A voice answered in Italian. Gerhardt said, "I have two packages of Shamrocks from Erin. Where should I leave them?"

"At the Porto Branzo in the Vatican. Once you are in St. Peter's Square the gate is to the left. There will be two Swiss Guards in front of the gate. I will be there to receive the packages."

Gerhardt hung up the phone and examined his map of Rome. He said, "Now this is the last step but if we are stopped for any reason you must act as though I am in charge and you are fearful that any act of disobedience will be harshly treated."

Lorenzo said, "No matter what happens we are so grateful for what you are doing." Svi nodded in agreement. "You have been incredible to risk everything for two strangers. I hope that when the war ends, we will be able to meet you again."

Gerhardt feigned being moved by their gratitude, when in fact he could not care less about them. They were merely part of a puzzle he needed to complete. A cab took them to the head of the Via della Conciliazione. They exited the cab and there in front of them was St Peter's Basilica. Gerhardt tried to ascertain the best way to approach the square and to identify the area that was suggested on the phone. There were hordes of pilgrims even in the middle of the war so he decided to try and meld with them walking toward the Basilica. He could see the obelisk in the center of the square above the heads of the crowd. Once in front of the basilica he saw to his left in the distance two Swiss guards and a gate. A cleric in priestly garb stood in back of them.

Gerhardt said, "We are going to cross the road and bear to the left where those guards are."

Once they were close, the cleric walked to the front of the guards. "I am Monsignor O' Flaherty and I am expecting two packages."

Gerhard responded, "Yes Monsignor. The packages of Shamrocks from Erin have arrived."

Before entering the Vatican, Svi and Lorenzo warmly shook Gerhardt's hand.

"We will never forget you."

Gerhardt turned and walked briskly toward the Castel San Angelo on his way back to Heinrich's apartment. He had already forgotten both of his grateful prisoners.

Chapter 30

Late April 1944, Zurich
The Swiss connection

Three days after the rescue from Auschwitz, Gerhardt prepared for the next step in his plan. Aided by Heinrich he had been posted to an isolated German government office in Zurich. He would report to Heinrich on an official basis. Before officially assuming his post he would see if he could have his tattoo removed by Dr. Vogel. So far, the transformation from impending doom had miraculously occurred in a brief period of time. None of this would have happened without the interventions of his dear friend Heinrich. Before leaving for Zurich Gerhardt made a reservation for lunch on the outdoor patio of the Hotel Rafael. He wanted to show his gratitude. On one side, the Roof Garden directly overlooked he beautiful Church of San Agnese and the Piazza Navona.

Gerhardt raised his glass of wine to toast his friend.

"Heinrich you literally saved my life and I am eternally grateful to you for all you have done. I am sure there is no way I can repay you for giving me the gift of a new life. There was a time just months ago when I seriously considered suicide. You have given me a gift of a future without worry."

Heinrich accepted the compliments. However, privately he was worried and somewhat jealous. The Allies would soon occupy Rome. Heinrich did not have the depth of financial resources to keep himself safe. It was true he was not literally a war criminal but his bureaucratic role as a record keeper of the concentration camps would certainly warrant incarceration. Gerhardt was wealthy and would be set in his new environment but Heinrich had little in comparison. How would he care for his family if he left for some place like South America? He resented the fact that he would not have the financial or political influence to have his family leave Germany.

The following day Heinrich began to make plans to vacate his post in Rome. The first step was to contact Bishop Hudal and arrange for an international Red Cross refugee visa. It was common knowledge in the German government offices that the bishop was involved in arranging exit strategies for high-level members of the Nazi party.

As Heinrich approached the bishop's residence, he was again impressed by the building that in the 17th century had been a residence of Cardinal Biaggini. It was located in the Aventino area. It had a breathtaking view of St. Peter's Basilica and the Eternal City. The exterior walls sparkled as the morning sun shone on the terra cotta exterior. Heinrich ascended the marble steps and knocked on the huge wooden door. A seminarian greeted him and led him through the marble hallway to the bishop's library.

After he finished celebrating Mass, Bishop Hudal removed his chasuble and knelt to say a series of morning prayers. It was his custom before reading his breviary to identify the groups that he wished to single out for special consideration. In the last few weeks, the focus of his blessings was German officials who were seeking aid in leaving Europe due to concern that Germany would soon be defeated. This morning after breakfast he had an appointment with a local member of the SS who he presumed would ask for his assistance.

Austrian Catholic Bishop Alois Hudal was a Nazi sympathizer, and the rector of the Pontificio Istituto Teutonico Santa Maria dell'Anima in Rome, a seminary for Austrian and German priests. He had been an early church supporter of Hitler. He believed the stories of Jewish persecutions were grossly exaggerated. He used his position and relationship with The International Red Cross to aid the escape of those he felt would be unjustly persecuted by the Allies. He justified creating false identities for German soldiers and officials on the basis that war requires persons to follow legitimate orders. As the war was drawing to a close, he provided passports and assistance that enabled so-called refugees to apply for Red Cross verification. His involvement was not sanctioned officially within the hierarchy but it was commonly known that he believed he was performing acts of Christian charity in abetting these escapes.

This morning after celebrating Mass in the chapel his secretary reminded him that he had an appointment with a German officer after breakfast. Lately, these types of appointments were often related to personal requests by German officers wishing to flee Europe.

Bishop Hudal was in his middle years and was not in particularly good shape. Taller than the average Roman, his once muscular frame had been altered by his sedentary existence. He had cold intense blue eyes and strong Germanic features. He entered the lobby outside his office and found an officer seated in one of the leather chairs there. The officer had difficulty rising and was aided by a cane. He introduced himself and the bishop invited him into his office. After preliminary introductions Heinrich informed the bishop that he was there to seek assistance in moving to a new locale.

Bishop Hudal asked Heinrich, "Are you getting ready to leave Rome now or will you stay until the Allies come? I am sure you are aware that the Allies will seek revenge for what they perceive are war crimes. I resist this interpretation. I view men like you as victims. The church must resist the growth of communism and liberalism by protecting those who had the courage to fight these evils. These are the great dangers to our church as well as western civilization. I will help any and all who come to me for assistance. Like you, many of these men are Catholics in good standing and have been treated grossly unfairly. The Allies will take at face value the stories of the Jews and that will lead to severe punishment for many who were merely doing their duty."

Heinrich nodded in agreement. "I am one of those innocents your grace. I have merely been a record keeper but fear that my role will be miscast by the Allies once they invade Rome. I will probably leave in the next two weeks but I have not yet ascertained where I will go".

The Bishop offered, "If you need a place to stay until you firm up your exit plans, I can arrange for you to stay in a monastery on the outskirts of Genoa. If Argentina is a possible destination, it will be feasible for you to book passage on a freighter there. I am sure you are aware that there is a sizeable German community in Bariloche, Argentina. There has been a vibrant German community in Bariloche for at least 100 years. You would be welcomed there."

"I know that your grace, but I have reservations about boat travel in the Atlantic at this stage of the war. Also, I have a wife and children and intend to have them join me eventually."

Heinrich picked up his cap from the side table and rose to leave. "You have been most kind your grace. As soon as I have firm plans, I will return. Now will you please give me your blessing?"

Heinrich tried to kneel but the bishop, realizing kneeling would be difficult, helped him up and made the sign of the cross over his head.

Heinrich knew that the assistance of Bishop Hudal was merely a temporary solution and he began to alter his feelings toward Gerhardt. He had taken great risks in assisting his friend and yet what was the return from Gerhardt? The response was a few words spoken in gratitude and a parting lunch. He literally risked his life for Gerhardt. He now realized that as the Allies got closer to Rome all he had was a fragile exit plan. Morning, noon and night he began to be possessed with the belief that Gerhardt owed him more than a fancy lunch and a thank-you. He wanted substantial resources that would enable him to do better than merely survive. Also, the possibility he might have to leave Europe without his family completely depressed him. Finally, he decided that he would confront his friend and negotiate a just settlement for his past assistance.

Gerhardt had surgery recently and according to plan the debrasion technique to remove his SS tattoo was accompanied with further scarring on his upper arm and neck. The scars gave the impression that he had been a victim of fire and a war time bombing. Dr. Vogel insisted after the surgical procedures that he remain in the hospital because of potential infections. After four days he was released and returned to his apartment. He notified Heinrich that he would report for work in a few days.

Initially he was happy to receive a call from Heinrich but shortly into the conversation Heinrich's tone changed dramatically. For 10 minutes he complained about what he had risked for Gerhardt and at one point bluntly stated that he should be compensated for his troubles. Gerhardt was troubled. He thought he was being blackmailed. He asked if he could call back in an hour. He hung up the phone. He was livid that his friend was threatening to blackmail him. He never envisioned this would be an issue. The idea of living forever with this threat made him sweat. Collecting his thoughts, he decided the best way to deal would be face to face.

He called Heinrich and said, "I have just had surgery but will be able to travel next week. Are you in immediate danger or can our meeting wait until then?"

The positive response from Gerhardt calmed Heinrich who agreed that next week would work. Gerhardt said, "Fine. I will come to your place to totally share what my resources are, and I am sure there will be adequate money to protect both of us. I think next Tuesday will work for me. Is it possible for you to spend the entire day with me?"

Feeling completely relieved, Heinrich was apologetic for the way he approached their initial conversation. Gerhardt assured his friend that he completely understood and had no hard feelings.

"Why don't we have lunch out and then return to your apartment and openly discuss how I can help you."

Heinrich was now relaxed. He welcomed the visit. "Fine. What time do you believe you will be here?"

"I will take an early train. Why don't I take a cab and meet you in the Piazza Navona at about 10? We can have a light lunch and then figure out the best way to help you."

Gerhardt moved from concern to rage during the next few days. Just as he had acted in the past with anyone who did not continue to help him, he began to justify whatever would be required to stop the threat Heinrich had become. Initially he thought he would give him a firm sum of money with the understanding that there would be no further payments. But what guarantee would that provide him? Heinrich would always be able to identify Gerhardt and if he was interrogated by the Allies, he probably would bargain by giving up a war criminal. He began to entertain more sinister possibilities.

The Architect of Auschwitz

Gerhardt arrived at the Piazza Navona 10 minutes early. He saw Heinrich standing in front of the Fountain of the Four Great Rivers. Gerhardt immediately embraced Heinrich and said, "It is wonderful to see you again."

Heinrich observed the bandage on Gerhardt's neck. "Are you in any pain?"

"Very little. It is merely slightly uncomfortable. Let's go eat."

They selected the Tre Scalini restaurant. Both ordered Pizza. Heinrich selected the Margarita pizza while Gerhardt chose one with fungi and salciccia.

Heinrich began. "I have good news for you. Micah has been transferred to Auschwitz. I left instructions for him to be terminated on arrival. In addition, there is a bonus for you. Your brother-in-law, Rolf, was killed in a Cologne air raid. Now you need never look over your shoulder."

Gerhardt thanked him for the update but thought to himself -- there is now only one person who can cause trouble for me.

After they finished the meal Gerhardt suggested they purchase dessert and have it with coffee at the apartment. He suggested they take a cab.

Once they arrived at the apartment Heinrich prepared coffee and placed cups, spoons and forks as well as the almond tort on the table. Gerhardt asked, "What did you have in mind regarding financial aid.?"

"I think one third of all your current wealth as well as one third of the future art sales."

"Well, I have to tell you that number takes my breath away but you have certainly earned it. I will do that and put it in writing but I need a guarantee."

"What kind of guarantee?"

"I will need you to stipulate in writing that you will in the future not request any additional funds from me."

"Isn't my word good enough?"

"I think it is, but I would have no doubts if you are willing to sign a paper saying so."

The coffee was percolating. Heinrich went to shut the gas. He then brought back a typewriter and sheets of paper. He sat down, typed the message of what they had discussed and then dated and signed it. He took the paper from the typewriter and handed it to Gerhardt.

"Now let's have dessert."

He poured two cups of coffee and then returned the typewriter to the other room. Removing a packet from his pocket, Gerhardt placed two capsules in Heinrich's coffee. Heinrich returned, cut two slices of tort and took a bite. Gerhardt raised his cup and said, "Let's toast our future."

Heinrich raised the cup to his lips and swallowed the coffee in one gulp. In a matter of seconds, he felt faint, collapsed against the table and then onto the floor. The cyanide killed him instantly.

Gerhardt went into the other room and brought back the typewriter. He typed a suicide note stating that he could not live with the thought that he would be punished for his role as a Nazi administrator. He said he was sorry for his family but he could not live with what he knew was coming. Gerhardt took the original sheet and forged his friend's signature. He sat down, finished his coffee and ate a slice of the almond tort. He then returned the rest of the tort to the box. He washed the cups and placed the silverware back in the drawer. When finished he went to the bathroom, washed his hands and prepared to leave. His gaze swept the street out the front window to make sure the area was empty. He hurried out of the apartment. He walked down the stairs and hailed a cab in front of Trinita Monti Church.

Now there was no one who could identify him.

Chapter 31

March 1945, Rome
Svi and Lorenzo deal with survivor guilt

Monsignor O' Flaherty periodically touched base with Svi and Lorenzo. The priest was keenly aware that Svi in particular was experiencing a deep sadness at the loss of his family. He had contacted Lorenzo and asked that he meet him for breakfast. After a few cups of coffee and a marvelous breakfast served by Sister Anita, a Swiss nun, Monsignor O'Flaherty asked Lorenzo how he was adjusting.

"Most days I read. Also, I am trying to reconstruct the manuscript I wrote before I was imprisoned."

"How is that going?"

"I have finished about half so far. The last two years have engaged me in further developing some of my initial premises."

O'Flaherty was intrigued by this statement. "Like what?" he asked.

"Well, as you already know my field is psychiatry. Since living under the Nazis, I have been focused on what one can do when his physical freedom is stolen from him."

"Have you made any conclusions?"

"Yes, but I would like to see if they are applicable in other situations where it appears that the choices are limited."

"I am not sure I follow you."

"Well, Monsignor…"

O'Flaherty placed his hand on Lorenzo's forearm. "Before you answer may I interrupt you? I would be more comfortable if we did away with titles. I will not call you doctor and you need not call me monsignor."

Lorenzo smiled. "That is one of the things I love about you Not only did you save my skin but you also are so human and accessible."

Sean urged him on. "Please continue with your thought."

"There was literally no physical freedom I had once I was transported to the death camp. I was totally restricted. They controlled where I went, when I ate. Every minute of my day was in their hands. However, they could not control my mental freedom. Each day I vowed that if I lived, I would live as a free man. Now the challenge for me is that soon I will be physically free to decide what I will do with that freedom."

"Have you made any decisions?"

"I know that I wish to practice medicine again and I probably will go back to Milan but I am uncertain as to whether there will be any opportunities there."

"Do you have family there?"

There was a long pause. Sean waited patiently for Lorenzo's response.

"I am not sure you know this Sean but my wife was murdered in the camp and I am unsure about my brother, sisters and other family members."

"I knew that from our initial conversations on the day you arrived here. I am so sorry for your tremendous losses. How is your friend Svi doing?"

"It has not been easy on me but I think he is in worse shape than I am. I see him every day and it appears that he is significantly depressed. He lost his wife and twin sons in the camp and is feeling grief and tremendous guilt."

"Why the guilt?"

"It is not rational, Sean, but we both have it. The question every waking day is why them and not me."

"That must be an unbearable burden to carry."

"It is. In my head I know it is irrational, but still, it torments my heart and soul."

"Is there anything I can do to help him, help both of you?"

"I am not sure but obviously he owes you his life. He may be willing to share his feelings with you."

"Would it help if I spent time with both of you so it does not look like I am interrogating him?"

"I think that might be helpful. What did you have in mind?"

"I know that our faiths are different but the three of us are well educated and I would presume that we share an interest in things like art and music. I am familiar with Svi's musical background. I think maybe a tour of the Vatican art treasures might be a neutral place where we could chat. For instance, I would love to take you both to the Sistine Chapel to discuss the magnificent art of Michelangelo."

"Honestly, Sean, there is nothing to lose by trying. When will you do this?"

"I will ask permission from the curator and hopefully schedule a visit after breakfast tomorrow morning. Should I ask Svi directly or will you suggest it to him?"

"I think it might be better if I brought it up."

"All right. I will get back to you this afternoon."

The next morning Monsignor O'Flaherty shared breakfast with Svi and Lorenzo. The conversation largely focused on the news that the Germans were seriously considering surrendering to the Allies. Lorenzo was enthusiastic about this potentially rewarding news but Svi was relatively silent. Monsignor O'Flaherty said he had permission to lead them on a tour of the Sistine Chapel after breakfast.

"I hope you will enjoy the beauty of the chapel. I have been privileged to be there on many occasions but I am always stunned by the glorious art."

When they opened the door to the chapel Monsignor O'Flaherty pointed to an area where he suggested that Svi and Lorenzo seat themselves. Smiling, he said, "I am always looking for ways to play professor. I will talk about what I know about the chapel and its history. Let us begin by looking upward at the ceiling.

"In order to frame the central Old Testament scenes, Michelangelo painted a fictive architectural molding and supporting statues down the length of the chapel. These were painted in grisaille (greyish/monochromatic coloring), which gave them the appearance of concrete fixtures.

Some say that when Michelangelo painted, he was essentially painting sculpture on his surfaces. This is clearly the case in the Sistine Chapel ceiling, where he painted monumental figures that embody both strength and beauty."

Lorenzo was deliberately silent and did not offer his impressions of the chapel. The silence continued for minutes when Svi finally said, "I feel like those hurling into damnation represents what has happened to us. The violent eruption of bodies being hurled into space feels like the inferno of my tormented thoughts. I feel anger and guilt at the same time looking at this scene."

O'Flaherty gently probed, "I am not sure I understand."

"I am angry at those who took my most precious family and I am angry at myself for not leaving Europe before it happened."

Lorenzo interjected, "But Svi how were we to know that it would be so horrible?" "We should have known. And it was up to us to protect our loved ones."

"I am not sure that there was any way I could have protected Rosella," Lorenzo said.

Svi asked, "Don't you feel guilty?"

"Certainly, I do but my life has to go on even without her."

Svi shook his head. "I am not sure that I can find any way to do that."

"This may not be appropriate, Svi, but what would Rosella have dome if it was you who perished?"

He paused and said, "I cannot be sure but she was stronger than me and she would have gone forward."

"What would she expect from you now?"

"I have no idea."

Lorenzo said, "Svi there are no simple answers but we must find some way to have a purpose or meaning."

"That sounds good but how?"

"I guess it means that my work has to make a difference and I have to use the pain and suffering that we have endured to help others," said Lorenzo.

O'Flaherty had listened intently. He then asked, "Svi are there any moments when the pain is less intense?"

"I am not sure that there are but when I play the piano it momentarily takes me away from my sadness."

"If the opportunities are there, will you pursue your musical career?"

"I am not sure and frankly I may have lost the ability to perform at such a high level."

The hours in the chapel were followed by days of conversations among the three men who would be bound together for all the days to come.

Three weeks after the visit to the Sistine Chapel, Monsignor O'Flaherty informed Lorenzo and Svi that soon the war would be over. He suggested they should start to make plans to leave the Vatican.

Recently Svi had thrown himself into rigorous practice sessions as though he would one day resume his world concert tour.

Chapter 32

Early April 1945, Zurich
Gerhardt's plans to live in Spain

There were fewer and fewer footprints in the snow that could lead to the door of Gerhardt Stark. Thanks to Heinrich, he had eliminated his former self. Plus, there was documentation in the Roman police files as well as the German headquarters in Rome that he had been killed by partisans. He had documents that created a new identity and enough stolen treasure to afford a new life. Witnesses, like his brother-in-law Rolf and cousin Micah, had been eliminated and he had personally killed Heinrich. So that was it. There was no one who could identify him.

There was no change in philosophy within Gerhardt. He bore tremendous resentment toward all who had sabotaged the glorious thousand-year Reich. He felt no regret or remorse that he had actually been one of the architects of the genocide. There were no moments of breast beating or soul shattering guilt. Not for one second did he think of himself as an evil person. In addition, he bore hatred for those who took the core of his soul: Frieda and the children. This was a man who had built an emotional moat around his Nazi past and filled it with mental bridges that made access to an alternative reality possible. His lust for power and privilege created a myth of certitude that ignored the truth.

For Gerhardt there would be no time spent in justification or moral gymnastics to prevent the moral confrontations of conscience. His conscience was clear. Everything he did was in the context of creating a world that was purer and more righteous. Now all of his energy had to be focused on the new life: transition and destination for the future. The desire to live in South America remained the ultimate goal but his initial rejection of Argentina grew stronger every day. The thought of exile with a group of Nazis left him vulnerable and too connected to his past life. There was a slight possibility someone would recognize him there. Spain, on the other hand, had positive predispositions toward Germans and he could be less vulnerable in a place like Madrid. The war was winding down. Still, there were challenges before he could actually leave for Spain. The first problem was the Spanish language. He was multi lingual but the transition would be simpler if he were fluent in Spanish. In order to achieve this goal, he chose informal strategies rather than traditional academic Spanish lessons.

The Spanish restaurant El Cocodrillo was a central habitat for Spanish ex-patriots in Zurich.. Gerhardt slowly created a presence there by eating lunch twice a week. He then increased his presence to dinners nightly. The restaurant had an extensive dining area with oak paneled walls and a twenty-foot ceiling adorned with painted beams. Chrystal chandeliers hung from long black chains and created gentle strains of light through the area. One evening while having a cocktail he exchanged glances with a beautiful woman seated at the end of the bar. After a period of flirtations back and forth he moved his seat and asked if he might sit next to her. She smiled and said yes, pulled a cigarette from her engraved sterling silver holder and asked him for a light. She stared into his eyes and held his forearm as he lit her cigarette. He used his few Spanish expressions to initiate the dialogue but she assured him that she was fluent in German. Her name was Aniceta Velasquez. Instantly he was struck by the darkest brown eyes he had ever seen and they were complimented by her perfect olive skin, supple and glowing. She was relatively tall with a tiny waist and curvaceous breasts. As they chatted, she tossed back her long black hair, which cascaded down her back like a peaceful waterfall. She had lived in Zurich for the past seven years because her father had been transferred from Madrid to the Spanish embassy in Switzerland. He found that fact interesting and thought at some point her father might provide some assistance in the future. In the flow of conversation, he learned that she was the oldest of four siblings, a brother and two younger sisters. She was single, and worked as an assistant planner in the embassy. Her younger sisters and brother were still living in Madrid. He tried not to be too forward but he thought to himself this woman could be critical in the next chapter of my new life. After an hour of background chats, he invited her to dine with him and by the end of the evening he had positioned himself well to further grow the relationship.

Eventually the relationship became intimate. One night in his apartment a long period of touching and French kissing led to further sexual sharing. It appeared that both were waiting for the other to make the final move toward the bedroom. She pressed against him and could feel the stiffness of his penis against her legs. She reached down and gently caressed him and that signal allowed him to swoop her up and carry her to his bed. They kissed again passionately and he placed his hand inside her bra and caressed her breasts. He then moved his mouth to her nipples and slowly eased her onto the bed. She kissed his neck and folded her arms around him. His kisses were deep. She was excited enough to have trouble breathing. From that evening forward they daily enjoyed sexual hours in his apartment. However, they could not live together because that would create a scandal for her family. Despite this factor they often spent many nights and days together. Spanish was the preferred language between them and in four months he was close to fluent. She had fallen deeply in love with him. Of course, he was enjoying their relationship but for Gerhardt, she was merely a pawn to be used and eventually discarded. The bonus for him was her knowledge of Madrid's culture. He knew he would hit the ground running once he left for Spain.

On a few occasions Gerhardt attended social events at the Spanish embassy where he was reassured that Madrid would be the perfect site for his new life. The ambassador indicated that Spain had turned a blind eye to the atrocities committed against the Jews. Gerhardt shared the possibility that he would seriously consider becoming a permanent resident of Spain. The Spanish ambassador was Aniceta's father and was pleased by this, hoping that Gerhardt and his daughter would wed. He shared the name of Charles Lesca, an anti-Semitic journalist and Nazi collaborator living in France, as one who could connect Gerhardt with influential resources in Madrid.

The following week Gerhardt contacted Charles Lesca by mail and used the name of Ambassador Velasquez as his entrée. Lesca quickly responded. During a four-week period they exchanged letters and three long phone conversations. Gerhardt conveyed his intention to live in Madrid and assured Lesca that there were no legal impediments. Lesca was most supportive and suggested that when it was time to leave Zurich, he come to Marseilles on his way to Madrid. In the interim he gave Gerhardt the name of Clarita Stauffer. She was a Spanish woman with deep Germanic roots living in Madrid. He said she had been instrumental in assisting many Germans who recently decided to leave Germany.

Of course, true to his nature, Gerhardt spent two days investigating Clarita Stauffer and discerning how she could help him.

Clarita was the daughter of Konrad Stauffer, a German master brewer, and Clara Sofía Loewe, who came from a wealthy family of German origin.

In his search he found that Clarita Stauffer was an excellent athlete and had been a vigorous supporter, along with her father, of Hitler and the growth of National Socialism.

Gerhardt contacted Clarita Stauffer. He used the name of Charles Lesca to gain access and trust. She immediately responded and in a 10-day period they had spoken twice on the phone. In these conversations she asked him many questions in German, which were somewhat coded. When he visited Madrid would he require a residence and would it be helpful to provide leads for employment? She also noted that at the border to France there would be serious consideration to certain physical attributes like tattoos. This was an obvious code for "if you have an SS tattoo there is the possibility that you will be identified by the French resistance." With all of the pertinent questions answered by Clarita, Gerhardt had now positioned himself to take the next step. Maintaining his government position was no longer an issue because the government in Berlin was literally nonexistent and since Heinrich's death, he had been a solo flyer. He contacted Clarita and she told him that arrangements were complete and she would secure a hotel once she had a specific arrival date. She informed him that a courier would deliver a package to his home in the next week.

Over the past month Gerhardt struggled with the best way to sever his relationship with Aniceta. He had become more and more aloof but wanted to end it in such a way that it would not present future difficulties in Madrid. He decided he would relate a story about the death of his wife and children and that he loved her but was unable to commit because the haunting tragedies of their deaths have revisited him. He stated that he was depressed. He said he would contact her in the future, but the reality was whenever the utility of a relationship ceased the relationship ended. It was simply another shipwreck on the reef of Gerhardt's narcissism.

He received good news that one of the original Degas ballerina paintings sold for a price three times the original estimate and all of his Swiss investments were doing handsomely. It was time to move and this financial news gave him breathing room to establish himself under the radar in Spain. He decided that the best way to make the trip was to enter Spain by taking a train to Marseilles, France. Clarita had provided him a Spanish Passport under his new name and a fictitious address in Madrid. As he was packing, he received a tearful phone call from Aniceta and he pledged that he would contact her as soon as he was able to sort out his sadness.

Upon entering the train station at Marseilles, he was surprised to see a horde of men with automatic weapons stationed in the security area. None were in police uniforms but nevertheless it was obvious that they were in charge. He was fluent in French and thought this would be a formality. However, one of the men identified himself as a member of the French resistance and seemed suspicious regarding Gerhardt. He examined Gerhardt's passport and began to ask a series of pointed questions. "Are you a German or a Spaniard?"

Gerhardt politely answered, "My parents were German but I grew up in Spain."

"Where are you coming from?"

"I had business in Zurich and am now returning home?"

"Have you ever served in the German army?"

"No, I have not."

The man continued to press Gerhardt and at one point he said, "Stay here." He went to speak with another armed man. The two came back and said, "Please come with us."

Gerhardt knew enough not to escalate the situation but politely asked, "Why?"

"Never mind. Do as you are told."

"But I am to take the train to Madrid."

"There is plenty of time. This will take but a few minutes."

They led Gerhardt to a room off the main section of the station and ordered him to remove his shirt. Gerhardt responded, "Why in heavens name do you want me to remove my shirt?"

The one man pointed a gun at him and said, "Do what you are told."

Gerhardt removed his jacket, tie and then his shirt. "Lift up your arms."

The scars on his arm and neck were obvious. He knew they were looking for the SS tattoo. "How did you get those scars?"

"As you probably know Spain was involved in a Civil war. One evening the section of Madrid where I lived was heavily shelled. Our residence took a direct hit and I was burned while fleeing the building. That is when I suffered these severe burns." His calmness and cooperation worked and after receiving their apology he was escorted to the train bound for Madrid. The new life was about to begin.

Arriving at the main train station he passed through security with no difficulty. Once outside the station he hailed a cab, which took him to the Hotel Achoa. After a shower and breakfast, he called Clarita and she suggested that they meet for lunch. She asked him to come to her residence at 14 Buena Vista Drive and from there they could walk to the restaurant.

Clarita was waiting for him in the garden in front of her building. His first reaction was that she had the body of an athlete but was gaining weight. She was tall, semi muscular, big boned with golden blond curly hair pulled back into a perfect bun. Her face was full of pockmarks and she wore thick makeup and dark red lipstick. Her handshake was powerful. Still, she exuded a warm welcoming presence.

She first spoke Spanish in the hope that he had a fundamental knowledge of the language. "Welcome to Madrid." She was stunned by his facility and the responses in Spanish thrilled her. "I am so pleased that you speak Spanish, it will make your transition to this community fairly simple. Tell me a little about yourself."

She sat in one of the chairs placed at the side of the garden and gestured for him to be seated. Gerhardt gave her a sanitized version of his past but before she inquired about some issues that were of concern, she wished to explore his architectural background. "Madrid has many problems but one of the most pressing is housing. The Civil war has brought many Spaniards to the outskirts of the city and there are huge areas of shanty housing. It is a major issue and the reason I want to explore your work intentions is that I have contacts within the government."

Gerhardt graciously thanked her for this but said, "I really do want to get involved but would like a short period of adjustment before I commit to work."

"All right, then it would be worthwhile to discuss your current situation. It would be helpful to me to know your status with regard to what you have done during the war in Europe."

"I am not sure what you are asking."

"Well, Gerhardt, I am aware that some members of the Nazi party are going to be hunted by the Allies for so-called war crimes."

Gerhardt placed a cigarette in his mouth and offered one to Clarita. She shook her head. "That is the only vice I do not have. Food, on the other hand, is what I struggle with."

Gerhardt said, "I can assure you that I was not involved in anything that could merit someone searching for me. I held a bureaucratic position that was never connected to the issues you raise."

"I am glad because this government is very receptive to Germany but one never knows what will happen in the future. Now there are the questions of housing and finances. I do not wish to be indelicate but how can I help you with those?" "Actually, due to family inheritance, I am well positioned to live here without financial assistance. However, I would love your guidance on where I should look for an apartment and eventually, I would appreciate access to those dealing with the issue of housing."

Clarita was pleased that Gerhardt's was a simple case that would require no financial aid and would not be the target for vengeance. After a series of lesser questions, she took him to a local restaurant and introduced him to Enrique Paco Marias and several prominent members of the Spanish government.

Chapter 33

January 1945, Auschwitz
Russians at the gate of Auschwitz

It was becoming more and more obvious that the Russians would soon be at the gates of Auschwitz. Captain Verner learned that Himmler ordered many of the prisoners left in Auschwitz be taken on a death march. The German high command was insistent that the horror they had created in this death camp be erased as much as possible. Verner knew that Micah Goldstein would be one of the prisoners selected for the death march. He did not want that to happen. He struggled with a solution regarding Micah and finally concluded that the only way to save him was again to create a totally new identity. He summoned Micah to his office one evening and said, "I'm taking you to the administration building this evening where I will have access to a camera. I will take your picture."

Micah, who by now was comfortable addressing Captain Verner in a normal manner, said, "Why?"

"I will share something with you that you are not to tell another living soul. The Russians will soon be here and this camp will be liberated, but in the interim many of the prisoners will be forced on a death march. In all probability you will be included in that march and the only way I can save you is to create a new identity for you. The reason I'm going to take your picture is I'm going to have a new passport issued for you, but it will require that you be in the German uniform. My plan is for me personally to leave here and create transit papers and head toward Berlin. Once I have a passport and transit papers you will be able to come with me as my assistant."

Micah was stunned. "I really don't have any words. You have prevented my death in the past so whatever is required, I will gladly do."

During the next two days, Captain Verner took Micah's photo in a German uniform and created a passport and transit papers as well as a series of orders for both of them. The orders were critical because Berlin was in such a state of chaos that the German military had ordered immediate death for anyone viewed as a deserter. On the morning of January 4th, two hours before dawn, Captain Verner and Micah, dressed as a German soldier, requisitioned an automobile and started their journey toward Berlin. They took mostly back roads to avoid the invading Russian army. Verner, who had grown up in the idyllic city of Breslau, had no idea that the city was under siege. Breslau now resembled the ruins of Stalingrad. It was almost totally destroyed. Once in the city they were confronted by marauding groups of German soldiers who were not only fighting the Russians but were also in search of deserters. Once a deserter was caught, he was immediately hanged. They had on three separate occasions met these groups but their paperwork allowed them to survive these inquisitions. The real issue confronting them now was where to stay. The city was under constant bombardment. The Russians had completely broken through the German lines. There was literally no German garrison or fortification where they might stay. Captain Verner suggested they make their way out of Breslau, which turned out to be fatal for Captain Verner and perilous for Micah. When they were on the outskirts of Breslau, they were confronted by Russian soldiers who began to fire their weapons at them. They attempted to run into a deserted building when a burst of gunfire hit Captain Verner. He was killed instantly. Micah instinctively raised his hands in a form of surrender. Two Russian soldiers grabbed him and knocked him to the ground. Micah, who could not speak Russian, kept repeating in German and then in English, "I am not a German soldier. I am a Jewish prisoner." These words had no effect. One of the soldiers hit Micah on the head with a rifle, knocking him unconscious. When Micah regained consciousness, he was in an area enclosed by barbed wire with thousands of German prisoners who had been captured by the Russians. Once the battle of Breslau was completed, Micah, who had escaped Auschwitz, would now spend the next 11 years in a Russia.

Chapter 34

April 1945, Poland
Esther confronts her past

Esther found days of working with Dr. Hobbs in the clinic kept her occupied and gave her purpose. However, the nights were a totally different story. Often, she fought sleep knowing the price her spirit would pay for rest. Most nights were filled with the dreaded visions and sounds of the eventful day and night when she lost her family. She often had a recurring dream. She would twist and turn before sleep came. Almost every night the voice of the evil one would startle her. She could see the face of the German officer, Stark, speaking in such civil tones. His orders to assemble in groups were concerning but none of the innocents could foretell the murders that were to follow. She could often feel her clothes being stripped away and the searing pain as the soldiers thrust into her virginal body. The sounds of sobs and the flashing of machine gun fire as she rolled down the hill into the cascading crowd of lifeless bodies often woke her. She had been counseled that time would ease her memories and at one point life, though different, would have meaning. The words, well intentioned, never penetrated her belief and she feared that all the days to come would be tainted by what she had lost. In particular, she often wept at the loss of her father. It was not that she did not mourn the intense pain of losing her mother and brothers but no one had understood her like her father. It was as though he had a complete understanding that could answer all of her hopes and dreams. He had encouraged her learning when the culture cast doubt and obstacles in her way. Now in the clinic she often found his emotional presence while giving treatment or consoling a fearful patient. Medicine was the area where he still lived and she more than ever wanted this to be part of her life. It was this constant that made her want to spend all her days caring for others.

Six months after the village massacre, she finally decided to go back into the woods where the murders had transpired. She did not tell the Hobbs her intent to stand on the precipice where she had been shot. They might have tried to stop her. But she believed if she were ever to be whole again, she had to experience this on her own. The memories of that day were as sharp as broken glass. She recaptured the words of Gerhardt Stark in her mind and wondered how anyone could so calmly give orders to massacre innocent civilians. As she entered the woods there was the normal tendency to turn back but she deeply inhaled the cool air and pledged to move forward. In the bosom of the beauty and splendor of nature it was hard to imagine the desecration that happened under the tree bows gently swaying through the breeze. The stains of the innocent blood had been washed away by the rain. Still, the sounds and images remained as she stood on the precipice and gazed at the gentle flow of the river below. She wept but these were not only tears of sadness they were the birth of resolution that somehow, she would find the resolve and strength to live again. She returned home with an internal pledge to do everything possible to survive the war.

She had willingly assumed the German identity of Luise and was most grateful for the safety that the Hobbs had provided in this perilous time. She realized that they had taken enormous risks and despite the fact that they were German citizens they could be put to death for harboring a Jew. The Hobbs had in many ways become her foster parents and she loved them. But she hoped to connect to her blood relatives if she survived. Her father's sister lived in America and she remembered as a young child how loving she was whenever she visited them in Poland. Her father had a special relationship with his sister and often he would regale her with stories of when they were children. She often wondered whether it would be possible for her to join her aunt in America.

As the war was apparently coming to a close it meant joy but also potential loss for the Hobbs. Being childless they had grown to see Esther, or Luise as she was called, as their child. They had totally committed themselves to her welfare and were willing to risk their own lives to save her. In the beginning, taking her in had been a commitment to the memory of his colleague, her father, but over time Dr. Hobbs and Selma had grown to love her as their own child. They knew that when the war ended there was the possibility that she would leave them and perhaps join her relatives in America.

Rome May 9, 1945
The War Ends

Finally, it came. VE day! Church bells rang all over the world. The moment held different meaning for persons who had been engulfed in six years of war. For Svi Contini and Lorenzo Kaplan physical freedom presented the monumental tasks of rebuilding their lives. For Esther it was a venture into the unknown to visit the last remnants of her family. For Gerhard Stark, known as Georg Baum, it was a bitter moment because it signaled the complete and utter destruction of the Aryan nation, an idea that had literally transformed his life. The path ahead presented challenges for all.

Wonderful sounds of St. Peter's bells as well as the bells of all churches in the city of Rome rang simultaneously to announce the end of World War II. The celebration in the city was not as jubilant as those in New York, Paris, London or Moscow but it was still a day of great relief and joy. Lorenzo Kaplan and Svi Contini were at breakfast when

Monsignor O'Flaherty made them aware that Germany surrendered the prior evening. Both men responded by reaching out to hug each other. From the day they were rescued from Auschwitz they had become brothers. The bond of their friendship born on the day of their rescue had grown. Lorenzo had consistently reached out to lessen the pain of Svi and had been instrumental in his again trying to find hope for the future. The news of the war's end enabled both men to create a temporary plan regarding where they would go and what plans they would pursue.

Lorenzo decided he would go back to Milan and immediately seek information on the rest of his relatives. Svi was uncertain whether he should stay in Rome or go back to Bologna. After many discussions Lorenzo convinced Svi that he should join him in Milan. The plan was to share an apartment while they were figuring out the next steps of employment. Svi began to practice the piano for hours at a time. The rust of not having a daily practice schedule did not immediately disappear but the last two weeks before they left for Milan the magic of his ability began to reappear.

After the war Lorenzo and Svi shared an apartment in Milan but both men were burdened by a continued sense of guilt. The feelings were not rational but they were emotional drains on their everyday existence. The haunting reverberations of their loved ones dying in a gas chamber gnawed at their very souls. In addition to their personal struggles there was the reality that Italy like many of the European countries was facing enormous challenges and many of the institutions were in complete disarray. In the midst of this chaos their search for relatives and friends was not successful. They spent weeks combing the records at refugee centers but only Lorenzo could find a few distant cousins. When the search period ended, both men believed that work and activity would be the best therapy and they had extended conversations about their next steps. Despite the mammoth challenges they both decided that they would return full time to the work before the war. Lorenzo initially worked as the medical director of a refugee center in Milan. However, after seven months he left Milan and accepted the position of medical director of The Carino Psychiatric Clinic in Rome. Svi had been contacted by Arturo Benigni, the music director of La Scala, and agreed to perform a series of concerts in Milan. His talent as one of Europe's premier musical artists spread quickly and within two years, he returned to perform on concert stages worldwide. Both men realized that living the rest of their days as mourning widowers would do nothing for them nor the memories of their loved ones.

Chapter 35

May 9, 1945, Poland
Esther seeks her family in America

A mixture of joy and sadness lived in the heart of Dr. Kristopher Hobbs as he ascended the stairs to the second floor of his home. The war in Europe was finally over and Germany had unconditionally surrendered. This was the source of happiness. But the end also meant that Esther, having lived as his niece Luise, would probably leave Poland and move to America. Not only was she a remarkable young woman but she was also a vital support to the medical practice. Kristofer hoped that her talents would be utilized in a place that presented more opportunities for women.

Esther had grown fond of Kristofer and Selma Hobbs, and in many ways, they had been her foster parents. However, she knew that her father had a sister who was living in New York and she yearned for some connection to her blood family. The Hobbs completely understood this, though they were shattered by the thought that this wonderful young woman, who had become an intimate part of their family, would leave them to join her relatives in New York. After long discussions with Esther, Kristopher decided he would take her to Vienna to the refugee headquarters to see if they could track down her aunt in New York. Dr. Hobbs enlisted one of the local army veterans, Johann Wochna, who had been part of the underground to drive Kristofer and Esther to Vienna. He was aware that the roads were filled with desperate persons in search of food and shelter and he wanted some assurance that the trip would be without peril. They found lodging in a village just outside of Vienna and daily they visited the refugee centers with the hope of securing the necessary information that would make it possible for Esther to emigrate to America. Hours spent in the refugee centers were painful for Esther because the horror stories of loss on the part of others were overwhelming. She heard first hand of the camps and the ordeals that persons had experienced. Her losses were mammoth but the safety and the security of hiding were vastly different than the day-to-day nightmares of the concentration camps.

After weeks of failed attempts, they were successful in finding her aunt, who immediately responded and was overjoyed at the possibility of Esther coming to live with her and her husband in New York. Once Esther received a new passport and permission to gather a visa, she was to be on the first ship of refugees bound for New York. She was required to go to Germany where the ship would leave for New York the following week. The ship contained many orphaned Jewish children. Because of Esther's maturity and medical experience, she was chosen to be one of the guardians to accompany the children to New York.

As she prepared the children for their places in the steerage area, she experienced a wave of mixed feelings. Despite the fear and pain, she had experienced in the last six years, she was about to embark on a path that was completely unknown. Poland and Europe had been her world and now she was going to a new land and living with a family that she barely knew. In a very real sense, she was saying farewell to her family, culture and the only life that she had known. She had a physical sensation to bolt from the ship to go back to the familiar but she knew that was a choice she could not make. Despite her decision to stay with her plan, her insides were tightened by fear of the unknown. She steeled herself to the present responsibilities of caring for the children on the ship and put on hold the anxieties of her new life.

On the ship she again had anxious thoughts because she had only 10 years prior met her aunt. That was a short visit to Poland and all she could remember was that her aunt had a contagious laugh. She knew that her father had a special relationship with her but she was uncertain how that would translate to her. Fortunately, the care of the children was so immediate and necessary that she was distracted from constantly reflecting on her own personal concerns and worries.

Once the voyage was underway, some children, most of whom had presumably never before been at sea, were overwhelmed by the discomforts of an ocean expedition. Initially the children were all sick and many cried day and night. Caring for them was physically exhausting. Fortunately, Esther was not at this time seasick. However, after the ship docked for 10 hours at Liverpool it ran into heavy winds and large waves on the next leg of the journey. For the rest of the trip the ship was engulfed in high seas and violent storms. The waves became hills cascading over the bow of the ship causing it to roll and stagger. It was as though the ship was slowly trying to ascend high mountains of turbulent water. The hammocks in the steerage deck swayed from side to side and the area was filled with the penetrating sounds of creaking doors and strained wooden floors. After each lurch of the ship water would seep through the portholes and the floor was filled with inches of sloshing sea water. The water was mixed with the remnants of vomit that had spotted the decks during the inclement weather. There was a two-day period in which Esther was so sick that she was confined to her hammock.

On the final day of the voyage the sea was calm and unruffled. Esther, somewhat recovered, went to the top deck and realized by the number of flying sea gulls that land was rapidly approaching. They elegantly swooped across the sky high above the ship. Although seasonably cool, the day was sunny as the ship slowly entered the Hudson River. She marveled at the luminosity of the water's surface caressed by the gentle rays of the morning sun. It was one of the few tranquil moments she experienced in months. In the distance she had her first glimpse of the Statue of Liberty. She had been a solitary figure on the deck but now she was joined by a multitude of adults and children. The ship was now surrounded by a series of tug boats. The passage from the sea to the Hudson River resembled a parade. As they approached Pier 44 where the ship would dock it was apparent that there was a crowd waiting to greet the ship. Once the mooring lines were secured, passengers pushed to the rails of the deck trying to find loved ones. At first, Esther could not find her relatives because there was such a huge crowd and because she was not sure of her family's appearances. Finally, she saw a sign in Polish and English that said, "Welcome Esther." Frantically she waved and felt the tears fill her eyes. It was at least an hour before she disembarked. Almost immediately, she saw her aunt and uncle in the crowd. She raced to them. The three embraced, unwilling to let go.

Hoping to make her more comfortable Esther's relatives started a conversation about her voyage. Her aunt asked "How was the voyage?" Ester said 'the first part was fine but we hit high seas for the last part of the trip and everyone was seasick." Her uncle smiled and said" I still have nightmares about our voyage from Germany. I vowed then that I would never go on a ship again." Esther listened to the myriad questions but she was mesmerized by the huge buildings as they drove from the wharf to their apartment on New York's east side.

The traffic was heavy as thousands of cars wound their way around the busy streets. The constant sounds of honking horns and drivers shouting obscenities at each other was overwhelming for Esther. She had no realization that the city would be this large and active. The sounds and activity were somewhat startling but also thrilling.

New York was in the midst of a building boom and it appeared that every street was being altered to adapt to the thousands flocking to the city. Arriving at their home she was struck by the shabby condition of the apartments and the pungent smell of urine on the street as she exited the auto. She lugged her suitcase up five flights of stairs. The interior of the building seemed shabby and the walls were in need of a paint job. Esther's first reaction was that the apartment was tiny and narrow. The railroad room apartment was four rooms cobbled together. It had paper-thin walls and rusty plumbing. The kitchen was tiny with a small dining area that could only accommodate three or four persons. The bathroom, with an old-fashioned tub with clawed feet, was down the hallway. The apartment had just the one bathroom. Her aunt helped her remove her coat. "I am sorry that we do not have a more lovely place for you to stay Esther but we are thrilled that you are here."

Esther said being with them was more important than any living conditions. However, she had thought that in America everything would be exceptional and glorious. She maintained her enthusiasm when she was informed that there was no separate bedroom for her and that she would have to sleep on the sofa bed in the living room. Certainly, this was a far cry from the lovely accommodations that she had experienced at the Hobbs' home. Her aunt and uncle were kind to her. And they also peppered her with dozens of questions. Esther was very open about the last six years but did not go into detail about the worst day of her young life. Aunt Miriam, not wishing to overwhelm her on the first day, suggested that if she was up to it, they could take a walk around their neighborhood. She had provided warm clothing, an overcoat and fur hat for Esther to wear. After the walk Esther rested and collected her thoughts before joining them for dinner. The rest of the evening was spent looking at family photo albums. This provided a bonding experience with her new family but also a wrenching of her soul at the visions of her parents and brothers.

Exhausted but filled with gratitude, Esther changed her clothes. She put on her nightgown and unfolded the sofa bed. Initially she was aware of the sounds of the city especially the elevated IRT which made the window next to her sofa bed rattle as the trains whisked past the apartment. However, she easily slept that night free of the images that had haunted her in Poland.

In the following weeks Esther became aware that life had not been easy financially for her aunt and uncle. When they left Germany, they had no investment funds but believed that because Isaac had so many business connections in New York he would be able to secure investments that would allow him easily to establish a high-end clothing manufacturing enterprise. For a variety of reasons this dream did not materialize and currently Isaac was the owner of a small café in the center of the Jewish east side. In order for Esther not be a total financial burden, she would work as a waitress in the café after becoming acclimated to the New York way of life.

The café was really a Jewish deli and was filled daily with all sorts of Jewish refugees who came to New York before and after the war. It was a tiny, narrow storefront that by fire laws could accommodate no more than 40. Usually, another 50 patrons waited inside for the next empty seat. The cops and firemen who were regulars looked the other way regarding the fire laws. The great pastrami sandwiches, coleslaw, potato salad, matzo ball soup, borscht and potato pancakes helped officials ignore local ordinances. The jukebox played all day and night long while the waitresses and short order cooks spoke a language that no outsider could possibly understand. Uncle Isaac, with his rimless glasses perched on his nose, was like the neighborhood rabbi in that he knew every customer. He would wander through the deli engaging regulars in playful banter. Aunt Miriam also played the role of welcoming hostess. In her sixth decade, wearing brightly colored dresses, she still had the energy of a younger woman. She was the cashier and was intimately involved in the lives of the families who made their weekly visit to the deli.

Esther was keenly aware that some of the regulars had been in concentration camps and almost all of the patrons had lost loved ones in the Shoah. The deli was a landing place for the Jewish patrons to openly mingle with their Jewish brethren. Despite this, no one spoke about the Nazi years and she never shared her own experience. At this point, her life was largely governed by tragedy. Beneath the surface of composure and steadiness were pain and doubt. Despite the hectic world of the café, she spent time trying to fathom the future and where this new life would take her.

Her aunt and uncle were appreciative of her service in the café but were aware that she was exceptionally intelligent and hoped that she would be able to work and go to college part time.

There was a great deal of trial and error in Esther's first six months in New York. She loved the complete freedom that she experienced but initially was intimidated by the immense city. She reveled in the reality that she could freely walk through every part of the city without fear. No police or government officials stopped her or asked to see her papers or passport. She was not afraid to identify herself as a Jew. She felt like this marvelous metropolis seemed to embrace her.

New York, which had been spared the ravages of the war, was in the midst of a building boom and it now was even more prominent on the world scene. Although she had minimal resources, the city was magical for her and the darkness of the past slowly started to disappear.

Before her shifts at the café, coffee cup in hand, she would sit for hours reading college catalogues. She hoped that at some point her relatives would address the question of her educational needs.

Aunt Miriam and Uncle Isaac were attentive to Esther and consciously tried not to overwhelm her during this whole new part of her life. Aunt Miriam saw so much of her departed brother in this marvelous young woman and enjoyed every moment of their time together. Almost every evening they would go through old family albums and shed tears seeing the images of her parents and brothers. Despite the pain Esther felt seeing images of her family, she loved the stories and memories. It was in those moments that she felt they lived again through her.

After weeks of settling into her new life, her uncle and aunt began to explore academic opportunities for Esther. Her Uncle Isaac was a regular member of the Temple and made an appointment to talk to the rabbi about his niece's situation. Rabbi Emmanuel was on an advisory board at Columbia University and had a strong personal relationship with the provost, Dr. Brian Bradford. He asked Dr. Bradford to examine Ester's abilities and propose an academic plan in light of her extenuating circumstances. Bradford understood the request but wishing to remain objective he agreed to have three scientific faculty members conduct the interview. He informed Rabbi Emmanuel that he would not be involved in the final decision.

The three scientists interviewed Esther and were impressed by the depth of her scientific and medical knowledge. In addition, she was trilingual and incredibly poised and articulate. They recommended she be placed in an accelerated program with the goal of receiving a BS in science in a two-and-a-half-year program. Esther welcomed this opportunity but declined because of her work at the café. She felt loyal to her family. She did not share the recommendations of the scientists with her family. Instead, she applied for a part-time undergraduate program after discussing the situation with her aunt and uncle. Her plan was to add summer courses to the part-time yearly classes. She figured she could graduate in four years. This was exceptionally strenuous and physically taxing because between classes, work and study she lived on four hours of sleep a night. In addition, she at times felt exceptionally lonely and had little opportunity to share the wondrous opportunities of New York arts and culture.

May 1947 New York
Esther seeks advice regarding medical school

Esther excelled in all of her classes. She managed a 4.0 average in all of her courses. She wished to apply to medical school but had no idea how to begin. One of the regular customers at her uncle's café was a physician. Perhaps he could give her some counsel. One morning while the doctor was having breakfast she asked if she could speak with him about her desire to enter medical school. He had encountered Esther many times in the café and was impressed with her efficiency and upbeat personality. He said his office was merely three blocks away and she should make an appointment so they could speak without interruptions. His response was so warm and gracious that

Esther called him that afternoon and made an appointment for late the next day. As she entered the building and waited to take the elevator to the doctor's office, she experienced both anxiety and hope. She had not received much encouragement from any of the undergraduate faculty regarding the possibility of a woman being accepted to medical school. The little advice she received was to go for an advanced degree in chemistry. In the office, she informed the secretary that she had a 5:30 appointment with Dr. Meiner. She was told that the doctor was with a patient but would be with her shortly. After a brief time, Dr. Meiner appeared and waved her into his office. He pointed for her to be seated and before discussing her issues Esther explained that she had brought her transcript from the University. While scanning the documents Dr. Meiner asked why she wished to become a physician. She was aware this question would probably come up and she skillfully gave him the background of her father and the years she had spent as Dr. Hobbs assistant. He was silent during her explanation but was obviously engaged in trying to understand her motivation. When she finished, he talked about the issues she would confront in seeking admission to any local medical school. He said he believed she had all the essentials to be an excellent physician. Ahead of his time, he did not believe gender should preclude anyone from practicing medicine. However, Dr. Meiner was a realist. He knew it would be a major achievement for a woman to get into med school. He honestly told Esther, "You will be asked questions that have absolutely nothing to do with medicine. However, if you answer them honestly your chances of entry will be slim."

Esther asked about the questions.

"You will be asked if you're married. Or are you in a serious relationship? Do you have or intend to have children? If you want a shot at a position you will have to answer these in such a way that you indicate that medicine is your sole goal and that no relationships could ever stand in the way. It is a shame that you have to play the game because it is what it is. I can tell you that every medical school has similar numbers of women they accept. Approximately six percent of the incoming class will be female. In addition, though this is not public, there is also a Jewish quota. In many ways, Esther, you have two strikes against you."

Dr. Meiner was absolutely correct in his counsel.

During her medical school interviews, Esther was asked questions such as "Do you plan on getting married?" And, "Are you going to have children?" Of course, they were all questions not remotely related to one's qualifications to become a doctor. While these questions may have seemed harmless, their answers could have drastic impact on whether a woman would be accepted or denied into med school. Much to her surprise one of the interviewers asked about her experience during the war in Europe. She did not offer specific graphic details but she candidly shared the horror of losing her entire family. It was not her intention that this would weigh in her favor but it apparently did. She skillfully answered all the offensive questions and although the school would have preferred to have no female candidates, she was one of those who would be admitted. It was one of the first times anyone asked Esther about her experiences in Europe during the war. For some unknown reason she shared with the interviewers that her father was a physician and that she was the sole survivor of her family.

The forecast that only six percent of the new class would be female was correct. From day one it was apparent that the women students would be treated differently than the men in the class. Often the professors ignored them in the classrooms and there were more than a few comments about how they were occupying the seat of a male who would totally dedicate his life to medicine. Esther, having experienced years of fear and terror, was not in the least swayed or intimidated by the realities of the chauvinistic environment. She even made a joke out of the fact that she was called "Momma Esther" by some of her classmates. She never took her eye off the prize and as the years progressed, she began to change the minds of some of her colleagues and professors. She was the number-one student in the class and despite the resistance to her it was impossible to ignore her skills. When it came time for her to choose her medical specialty, she selected Obstetrics and Gynecology. Her losses in life were somewhat tempered by the thought that she would bring new Jewish life into the world.

Despite the fact that she first in her class she was not invited to be part of any medical group in her area of specialty. Throughout her career in organized medicine, Esther would undergo many setbacks due to her gender. Although her experiences may not have been as severe as others who came before her, it was evident that women still faced many struggles.

Chapter 36

Madrid, December 1943
Gerhardt is fully acclimated in Madrid

After a difficult period of boredom, Georg Baum was assimilated into the culture of daily living in Spain. His Swiss investments had tripled in the last year and a half. He had a beautiful villa in Torre Blanca on the Costa del Sol and an apartment in Madrid with a luscious terrace overlooking an elegant boulevard. Georg was now extremely comfortable with his new life in Spain and slowly but surely, he had begun to lay the ground work for becoming active as an architect. In many ways, Madrid was in worse shape than Germany and it was conceivable that he could be on the ground floor in rebuilding this great city.

The years following the end of Spain's Civil War in 1939 were at best chaotic. In addition to the physical damage done to many of the country's cities there was a severe drought that lasted three years. Hunger was pervasive and as Georg explored the outskirts of the city, he was stunned by the living conditions. His environment in the center of the city was plush, refined and removed from the squalor of the shanty towns that were pervasive in the outskirts of Madrid. Food was scarce for those living in shacks partly because the fields had been neglected during the war. Even after the fighting stopped, Franco was intent on rounding up as many "enemies" as possible. Amongst the general population, illness and malnutrition caused innumerable deaths.

The realities of poverty and poor diet were rife.

Ever the opportunist Gerhardt saw opportunities in the post war climate and sought to have Clarita introduce him to the minister of welfare and housing, Juan Maria Cortez. He thought the best way to achieve this was for Clarita to have a party and invite key government officials who could be helpful in providing architectural opportunities. At a gala event held by Clarita she introduced the two men and Gerhardt skillfully questioned the minister about the great challenges that currently faced him. The minister had the aura of a patrician and was dressed impeccably in a stylish military uniform. He was a distant relative of Franco, a fact he made known almost immediately after meeting Georg. The conversation quickly focused on Georg's background. Juan was duly impressed with the conversations and suggested they meet the following week to explore the possibility of Georg consulting with the government. In their follow-up conversations Georg made it clear that the cost of his consulting services would not be an impediment because Georg's investments in Switzerland had grown exponentially the past year. He had recently had serious interest in the Degas ballerina series which enabled him to provide consulting services to the Spanish government at a discounted rate.

Over the next six months the two men had extensive conversations but Georg began to realize that the Spanish bureaucracy and approach to solutions were vastly different from his Germanic strategic sense of immediacy. Eventually he turned his energy to writing articles for the International Journal of City Planning with the intention of consulting in other cities.

Chapter 37

November 1955, New York
Gerhardt seizes the New York opportunity

Mark Mahoney was a tall, solidly hewn, handsome man from the depth of his sparkling blue eyes to the warm sounds of his deep compassionate voice. As he entered his middle years, he became even better looking with silver hair tinged with black strands and a ruddy Irish complexion. He had the gift of gab, and never lost the fun-loving lad who grew up in New York's Hell's Kitchen.

For years Mark Mahoney, a principal in the architectural firm of Mahoney Properties was disturbed as he witnessed the ongoing destruction of neighborhoods in New York City. Mahoney, a strong supporter of retaining the integrity of neighborhoods, wished to preserve historic buildings and at the same time create environmental habitats that were more than filing cabinets for the disenfranchised. His views had not been taken seriously by the city administration, and many of the other real estate firms in the city, including the most powerful man in New York City. Robert Moses was hell-bent on destroying much of what Mahoney felt made the city so vital. Many of the neighborhoods as well as some of the historic buildings had been demolished due to Moses' desire to create a series of highways that literally destroyed some of the oldest neighborhoods in the city. Moses' latest intention was to build a massive highway that would destroy Greenwich Village. The plan, which would have displaced lifelong residents, had very little opposition. This changed radically when a single person took on Robert Moses. And she won.

Moses was not by title the all-powerful planner and developer of a host of New York's biggest civic undertakings. But by influence he was all powerful. Governors and mayors feared him and rarely stood in the way of his strategic plans for the city. Unlike Mark Mahoney, Moses had little concern for the poor and disadvantaged.

He viewed the poor as nuisances that should be confined to large housing filing cabinet buildings on the outskirts of cities. He believed that their neighborhoods in the city were cancers that should be torn down to make room for parks, arts centers, and expressways.

Moses met his match in Jane Jacobs, a resident of Greenwich Village. She was, in Moses' opinion, a nobody. Initially he ignored her opposition. Jacobs took exception to virtually every aspect of Moses' vision, declaring, "There is no logic that can be superimposed on a city. People make it, and it is to them, not buildings, that we must fit our plans." She saw city life as the genial co-existence of many different neighborhoods, where the residents supported and looked out for one another while enjoying access to all the cultural advantages of the greater metropolis. She believed that Moses' housing projects were sterile fortresses of concentrated poverty and unsafe streets, which sucked the soul out of people, robbed them of normal communication, and fostered stigmatization and crime. "Moses does not give a damn about people," she said. "He is like an emperor who is intent on destroying the culture of the city." By the force of her will and dynamic personality, Jacobs mobilized a coalition that killed Moses' plan to destroy Greenwich Village.

Mahoney was buoyed by the success Jacobs had in preventing the new Moses project. Complimenting this encouraging news was a paper he recently read that was published by the International City Planning Association. The topic focused on creating new environments in cities that faced the challenges of contemporary living. The author of this revolutionary approach to preservation and growth, Georg Baum, proposed creating affordable low-level housing on the outskirts of major cities. This approach, while enhancing and preserving the historic buildings within the major cities of the world, would also provide livable housing for the poor, especially those affected by war. Mahoney was intrigued by one of the concepts in the article based on the work of Greek architect Constantine Doxiadis. The basic premise was that in order to preserve traditional cities around the world, it would be necessary to create a parabolic series of smaller cities on the outskirts which would enhance the internal city and lessen growth challenges. In particular, the residents of these connecting cities would have employment closer to their homes. This would lessen traffic and allow the larger central city to address major issues, such as air quality, congestion, traffic flow. The plan included the creation of areas that would be open only to pedestrians. Mahoney and his partners believed that much of Baum's theories had implications for the future growth and development in New York City. They decided to invite him to present his theories at the international conference to be held in New York in the spring.

Mahoney was pleasantly surprised at the immediate response he received from Baum, one of the authors of the Madrid article.

Over the course of 10 months Georg Baum had been intrigued by the opportunities for an architect in New York City. Madrid had been a welcoming chapter after leaving Germany but the opportunities paled there compared to New York. His wealth had grown exponentially after the war and he began to explore the possibility that his relationship with Mahoney Properties could become more formal.

The chameleon once again adopted the community societal positions that would enable him to further his personal growth. Mahoney and his partners were impressed with Baum's proposal as the way to have cities grow while retaining the character and heritage of the past. The polluted air in slum sections of every city could be alleviated by innovative policies. Baum proposed significant government investments in smaller connecting parabolic centers outside the major cities. The planning would have sound economic strategies. In addition to creating local housing that differed from the past pattern of filing cabinets, Baum's vision would create small townhouses and apartments that were no taller than five stories. He proposed mixed living communities with small businesses, restaurants and cafes to ensure low crime and nocturnal safety. Mahoney and his partners were taken instantly not only with Baum's wealth and planning abilities, but also his compassion and concerns for the welfare of the disadvantaged. They were duped by one who had created the greatest killing environment in history and now were part of his developing web of success. Baum had been intrigued by the work of Mahoney Properties and was becoming increasingly restless with the lack of future opportunities in Madrid. What he had achieved as a consultant in South America was formidable, but Spain, Argentina and Chile paled compared to the wealth of scenarios that a New York presence would provide. He began to lay subtle hints in his ongoing conversations with Mahoney and at one point the offer to become part of the New York firm came from Mahoney. He has discussed the possibility of proposing a part ownership with the firm to his partners, Perry Adams, Linda McGonigle and Charles Cutler. They, like he, were champions of the retention of the neighborhoods and were impressed with the achievements of Baum in South America and parts of Asia. Mahoney pointed out that Baum shared a philosophical view of dedication to preservation, plus he was innovative and the influx in cash would allow them to purchase land and building sites in multiple neighborhoods.

Once again, the façade of decency and concern continued to hide the legacy of horror that was Baum's past.

The next years saw tremendous growth in Mahoney properties and after the retirement of Cutler and McGonigle, Baum became the driving force of the company and launched into more substantial building of condominiums and modern office buildings. Also, he had become one of the most significant philanthropists in the city. Legacy drove him and his vanity focused on the premise that involvement with Jewish philanthropy would make him respected and revered.

Chapter 38

New York 1956
Esther confronts her past in a new relationship

Esther drew on her father's religious convictions in her practice. He once told her that he became a better physician because of his belief in God. She found the idea of believing in a higher power comforting. Her belief in God also connected her again in a new way to her family. She began to attend Friday services with her aunt and uncle on the evenings when she was not on call. In addition, she volunteered to be of assistance to anyone in the congregation who had questions or concerns in the area of her medical specialty. She was impeccably ethical and did not use profanity. The only exception to this was when she held a newborn Jewish baby in her hands after delivery. She under her breath always uttered, "Fuck you Stark and fuck you Hitler."

By 1956 Esther had developed a very successful practice and had formed a corporation along with two other female physicians, Dr. Susan Sherman and Dr. Ellen Sipe. This allowed her to have a modicum of free time and finally she could get involved in the adult education classes at the temple. One of the courses that sounded appealing was a four-part series on "The Life of the Jewish community in America." The course was being taught by one of the associate rabbis, Daniel Rosen. The class met on Tuesday evenings for two hours and was followed by coffee and dessert. Rabbi Rosen was a dynamic speaker and Esther immediately found him to be brilliant. And she marveled at his keen sense of humor and ability to engage each of the seven members in the class. She was also aware that he was tall, athletically built and had a warm smile. She knew little about him but did not allow herself to muse about the possibility of him as a person of emotional interest because she was certain that such a catch would already be taken.

One Tuesday evening the forecast was dismal due to a snow storm that had immobilized the city. Esther called the temple and learned that Rabbi Rosen's class had not been cancelled. She decided to trudge through the snow to class. It was almost a complete white-out by the time she reached the temple. She wondered if she had made the right decision. Only three of the participants weathered the storm and Rabbi Rosen commended them on their courage and openness to learning. The other two participants left after the class ended but Esther decided to stay and chat with the Rabbi. After pouring herself a cup of coffee and selecting a Danish, Esther sat down and offered the Rabbi her view of the class. "I as an outsider found these four classes fascinating. You are a gifted teacher."

"Well thank you. I love teaching and I guess that is one of the reasons I chose to be a Rabbi."

He added with a huge grin, "Although my mother would have preferred that I become a doctor. My son the Rabbi does not have the same weight that my son the doctor has."

Esther laughed. But she did not offer that she was a physician.

Daniel inquired, "When you say that you are an outsider what does that mean?"

"I was raised in Poland and came to America in late 1945," Esther said.

Daniel was interested in this knowing how difficult it was for the Jews in Europe at that time. He asked. "How have you found it living here as opposed to your life in Poland?"

"I think that New York is an unbelievably exciting place to live and I never run out of interesting places to go and there are so many wonderful cultural opportunities," she said.

"I am a native New Yorker and honestly could not imagine living any place else."

Daniel was starting to realize that his interest in this person was not merely the usual banter between student and teacher. At the same time Esther found it interesting that despite the awful weather she was not in any hurry to go home. Daniel poured another cup of coffee and offered one to Esther, hoping this would provide more opportunity to chat. Ordinarily she would have refused because the caffeine would make sleep difficult but she accepted. Daniel decided to move the conversation to a slightly more personal level.

"Will you have difficulty making your way back home in the snow?"

"It is pretty difficult because of the wind but I only live about six blocks from here."

"Where is that?"

"I live on Park Avenue."

Daniel quipped, "I did not realize I was sharing coffee with someone from the high-rent district."

Esther said she was renting a tiny studio. She said she was not one of the New York elite.

His response changed the course of the conversation. "Doesn't your husband worry about you being out in his kind of weather?"

Esther laughed, "I don't have a husband. I live alone. I don't even have a pet! I guess I could ask you the same question: Doesn't your wife worry about you in this storm?"

Daniel said, "I do not have a wife and that gets back to what I said earlier. When I tell them, I am a rabbi the air goes out of the balloon. By the way what is it that you do?"

Esther hesitated and smiled, "I am a doctor."

"A PhD or a medical doctor?"

"I am an obstetrician in practice at Beth Israel."

Daniel laughed. "In case you meet my mother at the temple please tell her that you are a journalist because a single female doctor will trigger her matchmaking antenna."

Esther enjoyed talking with this man. She did not relish that this would be the last class that she would attend with him.

Daniel said, "Well I guess it is time for us to venture into the snow. I live relatively close to you and would enjoy the company on the way."

They dressed with all of the warmth required and left the temple. When they arrived at Esther's home Daniel took off his glove and shook her hand. "I have really enjoyed this evening and hope to see you again."

Esther agreed and said she might meet his mother at temple some Friday evening.

By early morning the snow had finally stopped as Daniel made his way to his office at the temple. He altered his usual route and walked by Esther's apartment on Park Avenue. The prior evening went so well that he thoroughly enjoyed revisiting the conversation this morning. He had the desire to contact her again but was unsure how and if he should proceed. Perhaps he could engage her in developing one of the new courses that he was about to research. He had no awareness of what her experience was during the Second World War, but he certainly would like to hear her perception of what life was like for Jews during the war. He had toyed with the idea of creating a series of lectures on how the Holocaust began in Europe and the time period before the actual persecutions. It was difficult to ascertain what age Esther would have been at that time, but based on his observation he thought that perhaps she was an adolescent. As someone that age she might have an interesting perspective on what it was like to live as a

Jew in Poland during that time. Part of this was academic but also, he had a real interest in her as a person. Not necessarily as a potential date but theirs was more than a casual exchange after a course. He was intrigued by her and quite honestly it did not hurt that she was quite beautiful and most articulate. It was rare to get the feeling after a brief exposure that you had some sort of a connection. He admonished himself because this fascination could certainly be one sided and though she was not married he had no idea whether she was romantically involved with anyone. The other reality was that he was immersed in his work at the temple and was not sure that this was the right moment to even pursue anything more than a friendship. After a lot of mental gymnastics, he decided that he would look up her file in the temple office and pursue the possibility of her being a resource in the new course he was about to design. Her phone was answered by her Aunt Miriam. He had met her on a few occasions so after preliminary exchange of pleasantries he inquired as to whether Esther was home. Miriam replied, "She is actually at the hospital, rabbi, is there a message that you would like to leave?"

"Yes. Would you please have her call me at this number? I am putting together a new course and think that some of her background may be helpful in formulating my preliminary outline."

Miriam said that she would certainly give her the message this evening. When Esther came home from the hospital, she was surprised by the message Daniel left. Expecting to have a secretary answer, she called the temple but Daniel answered the phone. "May I please speak with Rabbi Rosen?"

"This is Rabbi Rosen, how may I help you?"

"This is Esther Slawinski. My aunt said you left a message and was interested in discussing my assistance in a course that you were developing."

"Yes, I am considering creating a series that focuses on the period in Europe between 1933 to 1945 and thought that some personal reflections would supplement some of the factual historical data. It has been my experience that the course becomes much more vibrant when it is seen through the prisms of those who actually were life witnesses to the period."

"Actually, Daniel, I was quite young at the time and not sure that I could lend any valuable insights."

Unwilling to let go of this opportunity to spend time with Esther, Daniel responded, "I think a preliminary chat around some of the questions I have developed would be helpful if you have time. Would it be possible for some time in the next week or so to have coffee? I would think that perhaps an hour would be beneficial for me to establish how my questions would fit into the overall plan." Esther checked her schedule and said, "Well I would say Wednesday is my best day because it is my day off from the hospital as well as my private practice and perhaps, we could have lunch together."

Daniel was thrilled at the opportunity to spend more than an hour pursuing her insights. "Where would you like to have lunch?"

"Well, since you are the native New Yorker, you should be the one who selects the place."

"Ok, let's begin with what kind of food you like."

"One of the joys of New York is that I have been exposed to cuisines that I didn't even know existed. However, I am partial to either French or Italian."

"Ok then I will tilt the vote and take you to one of my favorite Italian restaurants in Manhattan. The good news is that the food is outstanding and the price falls in the range of a Rabbi's salary."

Esther said, "There is no need for you to pick up the tab; we can split the bill."

"No, because I am seeking personal information for my course, the pleasure is all mine."

Daniel said he would call back after he made the reservation. Both Daniel and Esther viewed this as a casual lunch that had grown out of an interesting academic exchange and potentially nothing more. Even though their lunch date was two days off, Daniel began to realize that his interest was not purely historical. He really wanted to spend more time with Esther. In a similar manner, Esther found herself recapturing in her mind the time they had already spent together. Both of them did not want to get ahead of themselves. Esther in a particular had no plans on becoming involved with anyone in a romantic way. She was totally dedicated to her career and also part of her was still locked up in the horror of that tragic day when she was gang raped by German soldiers. She had not experienced even infatuation since the day. She was unsure if there would ever be an opportunity to share herself with anyone.

Daniel, who had been outside the dating game for quite a while, started to reflect
on what he was missing and how much he enjoyed just that one personal time they spent together. This luncheon was not really a date but he felt a real connection and her image frequently leapt into his mind. He had spent only a couple of hours with her that snowy night but he loved her laugh and the gentle tone of her voice. He had not asked if she was dating anyone. But now he began to admit that engaging her in his historical venture was really a ploy. He didn't want to get ahead of himself but he was hoping that this was someone with whom he could at least be friends. If it turned out to be more than that, it would be fabulous. For a fleeting moment his sense of humor kicked

in and he thought, well if this becomes serious dating, my mother will be able to tell her friends, "Daniel is dating a doctor."

Wednesday morning finally arrived. After breakfast, Esther checked her watch. She had about 45 minutes before she left for La Traviata, the restaurant Daniel selected. She spent an inordinate amount of time trying to select what she would wear. Actually, the word date made her realize this was not just a time of sharing information, but possibly something more. Partially because of her schedule she had only had a few casual dates over the last few years. It was not that she was disinterested, but it just seemed that there were no opportunities for her to meet people to cultivate mutual interests. Miriam and Isaac had invited a few of their bachelor friends for dinners, but she did not have any chemistry with them. She cautioned herself that this may be a very one-sided thing. This may be truly nothing more than an academic pursuit where he generally is interested in what I have experienced in Poland, there was also the consideration about how candid she was going to be with him, conjuring up experiences she had tried to forget since coming to America. She thought that perhaps she should be very guarded and just deal in generalizations with regard to the time that she had spent with the Hobbs in Poland. Finally selecting a dress, she realized she had approximately 25 minutes before she would leave. When Esther arrived at the restaurant Daniel was waiting for her at the entrance. The day was sunny and they both commented that it was vastly different from the last time they met in a snowstorm. As they entered the restaurant the proprietor Angelo greeted them. "Buon Giorno Rabbi Daniel, it is so good to see you again. I see that you have brought a beautiful woman to our restaurant. Welcome signorina."

Esther was somewhat embarrassed but impressed that the owner made such a fuss over Daniel. After hanging up their coats Angelo led them to a table that had a view of the snow-covered garden. "Red or white wine?" he asked Daniel, who turned to Esther. She asked for white. Daniel chose red. Esther unfolded her napkin and said, "I gather you are a regular here."

"By luck I found this restaurant a few year ago. I hate to cook and the Hebrew University is right around the corner. One of my classmates who was raised in Rome recommended it. Angelo is a phenomenal cook and many times I just drop in for a plate of pasta. I recommend that we order the specialty of the day unless it is something that you do not eat."

Esther replied, "I am up to try whatever he recommends."

After Angelo brought the wine and bread, he suggested the pasta Amatriciana with a side dish of broccoli rabe.

Daniel proposed a toast, "Here is to us and I hope this is the last snowfall of the season. I am so ready for spring."

Esther clinked his glass and nodded in agreement.

"Before the food comes, I would like to ask you a few questions about your experiences in Europe during the war. I am toying with the idea of creating a four-part series of what the Jews experienced before and during the war. I would like to use a similar format of the course you attended on Jewish life in America."

Esther was unsure of where this conversation would go. She did not feel totally comfortable sharing the intimate details of what she had personally experienced. "Where were you in 1939 before the war broke out?"

"I was living with my family in a small village near Warsaw."

"What was it like? I ask because I have no experience living in a small village or town. I have loved my whole life in Manhattan."

"Actually, it was quite charming. The countryside was beautiful and my family was part of a large Jewish community."

"Did you have access to the city?"

"Yes, but it was infrequent. On a few occasions I had the opportunity to go to Warsaw but it was only on special occasions."

"Was the village solely a Jewish community?"

"No, even though we had a large number of Jewish residents the larger community was Christian."

"What was that like before the war?"

"It was not something I was aware of because I had literally no contact with the other community."

"Was it just distant or was it by design?"

"I am not sure what you mean by design."

Just then Angelo brought their entrees. Daniel asked, "Would you prefer to wait until we finish the meal to continue?"

"No, I think we can eat and chat. I am used to it at the hospital."

"I mean were there deliberate attempts to keep the communities apart?"

"I have no knowledge of that because all of my activities were in the Jewish community. I was never told to avoid anyone but there literally was no opportunity to spend time with anyone who was not Jewish."

"Was your family active in the temple?"

"Actually, my father was deeply religious and a member of the temple elders."

Joking, Daniel asked, "Was he a rabbi?"

"No, but he was really attached spiritually to the temple."

Now, Esther began to feel uncomfortable and did not wish to share any of her personal tragedy with Daniel. She attempted to change the course of his questions. "As you approach this course Daniel, how do you envision you will break it up as you did with your recent course?"

Daniel took a sip of wine. "I think that for the first part I would like to set the stage by introducing the life of the Jews in Europe in the early 1930s . Most courses deal solely with the war years and I always like to examine history through the prior prism to get at the underlying cultural facts that influence the decisions that affected the Jews."

"Are you going to focus on any one country like Germany?"

"Because the time is limited, I will certainly build it around Germany but one of the reasons for my asking your experience is that it widens the scope. Do you mind if we focus on when you became aware of the war?"

"No but I am not sure I can add the kind of detail you are seeking."

"I know it is impolite to ask a woman her age. However, I know that you were not very old in 1939 so I can ask without fear of offending you."

"I was 14 when the war broke out."

"Did you have any warning beforehand that war with Germany was possible?"

"Not really. My parents and two older brothers may have known but I was totally unaware."

Now Esther was very uncomfortable. She realized that she did not want to talk about her personal experience. She attempted to move the conversation away from her to a more general discussion.

"Daniel, I don't know that there's a whole lot that I could add to this conversation because really I was so young and to some degree, unaware of what was happening politically."

Daniel understood that Esther was uncomfortable so he decided to ask what she was experiencing living in New York.

"Esther I am interested in what it was like coming here after the war."

Esther paused. "Well, as you probably know, the European cities were totally destroyed. It was difficult to get a visa to come here because there were certain restrictions as regards the numbers, but as in all cases, I had no real concept of America. As most Europeans I had seen movies about New York and what it was like but there's nothing that could prepare you for the size of it. I remember standing at the rail on the ship coming into New York Harbor. It was my first glimpse of the Statue of Liberty, which is really obviously very impressive but the thing that was just overwhelming was the size of the buildings. Warsaw was a major city, but by comparison, it seemed like a tiny village compared to New York. The other thing was the activity in the streets, always the frenetic pace of life and sounds of the city. I have to tell you from my perspective it was almost an instant love affair. Fortunately, I had family here and they introduced me to so many wonderful free cultural and social activities.

"What are some of the cultural activities and places that you were introduced to?" "One of the most intriguing for me was the Metropolitan Museum. The other place that I loved immediately was Central Park. There is just something wonderful about walking through the park, especially early in the morning. I even became a Yankees fan because my uncle loves the team. In Europe baseball in my area was relatively unknown but because of his passion I actually follow the team. He has taught me that before breakfast you must check out the scores from the day or night before."

Daniel warmly replied, "Well Esther we have found common ground. I have been a Yankees fan all my life. In New York there are two teams, the Yankees, and the Mets but anyone with an ounce of sense is a Yankee fan. The Mets are perennial losers. On another note, do you enjoy the Opera?"

"Yes, I do."

"Well one of the members of my congregation is on the board of directors of the Metropolitan Opera and I happen to have two tickets to the opera this Saturday night."

"What opera is playing?"

"La Boheme."

"Ah, my favorite opera."

"Would you be my guest on Saturday?"

"I would love to but isn't there someone else you should be taking?"

"No. It would be my pleasure to go with you."

After the luncheon it was becoming obvious that this relationship might become something more than a casual one. Daniel was counting the hours until the opera on Saturday and even while making rounds at the hospital Esther was thinking about Daniel and how much she enjoyed his company.

Unknown to Daniel was the reality that La Bohème would trigger wonderful memories of Esther's family because it was one of the first operas that made a major impression on her as a teenager. She immediately felt emotionally stirred by the overture because the last time she heard it was listening to it with her father in his library. The beautifully textured opera took her on an emotional journey that was mesmerizing, but at times painfully so. It was hard for Esther to separate the beauty of the music from the tragedy of her life. At intermission she apologized for her tears but Daniel was moved by her ability to relate to the wonder of Puccini's music. The evening ended with both of them realizing that what had started out as an academic sharing was moving from that to more.

The following months it became clear that Daniel and Esther were becoming an item. Esther had shared Daniel with Aunt Miriam and Uncle Isaac at their Manhattan apartment and also spent a few days with them at the beach in Coney Island. The friendship blossomed. Daniel wanted to ask for Esther's hand in marriage. His career was blossoming. He was now the second rabbi at one of the most prestigious temples in Manhattan. He smiled knowing that if she accepted his mother would finally have a physician in the family. He knew very little about her immediate family but was comfortable that in time she would share details with him. No one had spoken about them but he was convinced that they were dead and possibly victims of the Shoah.

One issue that remained unsolved was Esther sharing with Daniel what had happened to her years ago in Poland. The relationship was wonderful but also threatening at the same time. At the subconscious level Esther started to distance herself from Daniel. She'd always found time in her hectic schedule to be with him. However, now she was finding more and more excuses to cancel potential dates with Daniel. In the beginning this did not seem to be a real problem for Daniel who understood that she, like him, had a very hectic schedule, but even in the times they were together it seemed that Esther was becoming somewhat distant. Like anyone in love, Daniel made all sorts of rational excuses as to why Esther was behaving this way. The issue had reached a crisis for Esther because of her fears that she could not have children. And what about enduring physical intimacy? She thought perhaps it would be best that this relationship no longer continue. She found herself rehearsing all kinds of scenarios that focused on "can we still be friends?"

Two months previously, Daniel thought he and Esther were on their way to becoming more than an item, a couple that would spend the rest of their lives together. Even though he could not explain what was happening, he realized they were starting to drift further and further apart. Esther had been extremely lovable but something had changed her behavior. He could not imagine that what they had experienced was about to come to an unresolved end. He thought that the counsel he normally gave other people regarding relationships was one that he should apply himself. He needed to raise this issue directly with Esther.

Daniel decided that this conversation would be best done in a place and time when both of them would feel comfortable expressing their most inner thoughts. Although Esther had cancelled two or three dates, again supposedly due to her hectic schedule, Daniel called Esther and told her that he had an urgent need to discuss their relationship. For this conversation Daniel chose the fountain area in Central Park. Daniel quickly conveyed that he had become somewhat confused as to what's going on. "I don't think it a secret, Esther, that you have become in many ways the most significant person in my life. I found what started out as a very casual academic relationship progressed early on to friendship and to be truthful more than that for me. I never intended our relationship to go anywhere in the beginning. Initially, I had no illusion that it would go anywhere more than a casual friendship. However, it has become a lot more than that for me. You have become the key person in my life and until recently, I thought you felt the same way about me. I guess what I'm trying to say is that I just need to know where you are with me emotionally because lately, I feel like there are a lot of mixed signals."

Esther had dreaded this conversation, which she knew was coming for a long time. She was unclear how to answer Daniel.

"Daniel, I have really enjoyed the time we have spent together, but recently I guess I came to the conclusion that the whole situation got ahead of us. We had a lot of delightful experiences but I guess what I'm trying to say is that I don't think that I am ready for the kind of commitment you are seeking."

Daniel asked, "Esther, I feel like I've been pretty honest with regard to my feelings toward you, but I think it's reasonable to ask how you feel about me."

"I think my remarks with regard to your question may be confusing because I found my time with you absolutely delightful. But I'm not sure whether I am ready or willing to have the relationship go any further."

"I guess that's where I'm confused. Why not allow the relationship to proceed without forcing it to some kind of conclusion that may not be good for either of us?"

Esther was unwilling to share her history and her fear that the relationship would be fruitless if she was unable to have children. "I don't want to fall into the cliché area of stating that I would still like to be friends but at this point I must admit that I am uncertain as to what is next."

Daniel was very disappointed in the outcome so far but realized that perhaps it was better to let the issues simmer. "All right. I had hoped that I would further understand where we are but I don't."

Esther responded by saying, "I understand that and wish that I could be clearer but I think maybe we should take a break for a while."

Daniel was stunned but he felt he had no choice. He figured the risk in not accepting this possibility could lead to a complete break. "All right. Why don't we consider a specific time? Does a month sound reasonable to you?"

Glad that the difficult conversation was coming to an end, Esther said, "I think that is a fair amount of time."

The next few weeks were very difficult for both Daniel and Esther and resolution did not seem any closer. What changed on the part for Esther was a realization that Daniel was truly the most important person in her life at this time. She was unsure whether the relationship could work, especially if she could not have children, but the absence had made it clear that she truly loved Daniel. In the beginning of the relationship, she just enjoyed his company but as time went on, he had become central in her thoughts and dreams. It was only when it became apparent that the relationship was headed toward marriage that her history and fears began to dominate. Now she struggled with her choice. She considered whether she should be completely frank and tell him the whole story. She was hesitant because he was such an honorable person. She worried he might look beyond the possibility of not having children because he felt it was the right thing to do. The other side of that question was if she did not share the truth with him, how fair would it be? The back-and-forth of these thoughts become almost intolerable. She decided that the only way to proceed was to be perfectly honest share her history and anxieties. She called and invited him to meet her in Central Park in the place where they had decided to take a month separation. Daniel certainly had mixed feelings about this invitation because he was even more deeply committed to the fact that he loved Esther. He was clear that he wanted to spend the rest of his life with her but realized that this could be the permanent severing of their relationship.

Daniel was so anxious that he was 25 minutes early for his appointment with Esther. He walked around the fountain 20 times and every 10 seconds he checked his watch. Finally, off in the distance he saw Esther. It was one of those very uncomfortable moments when he was totally confused. Should he shake her hand, kiss her on the cheek or just say hello? Instead of any of these he just nodded and gestured for her to sit on the bench. Esther sat, took a deep breath and said, "Daniel I am about to say things that I have rehearsed for days and would ask that you say nothing until I finish."

Daniel nodded, somewhat fearful, but he agreed.

"All you really know about me is my time in New York and when you asked me about my time in Poland, I was unwilling to share my experiences. I made it sound like I was oblivious to those times. The truth is that period was the most horrifically painful time of my life. You know that I lived in a small village near Warsaw but what you did not know was that the Nazis occupied our village in the fall of 1939. My family consisted of my father, mother and two older brothers." Esther took a deep breath, paused and forced herself to continue. "They were all murdered the day the Nazis occupied our village." Now quietly crying, Esther pulled back her hair and showed Daniel the scar from her bullet wound from that horrible day. "I was shot and through some miracle rolled down the hill but did not go into the river with the rest of the young women who were murdered. I was saved by a colleague of my father. He and his wife hid me as their German niece for the duration of the war. In addition to all of this there is another part that I have been unwilling to share with you."

Another long pause. Esther could barely look at Daniel. She forced herself to continue. "I was 14 years old and was savagely raped before being shot." Now she was openly crying. "I am unsure whether the physical damage done at that time will prevent me from having children. No doctor has been able to answer that question. I felt knowing how you are with children that I could not deprive you of being a father."

Now Daniel was crying. He was overwhelmed. He could not resist the urge to hold Esther. Taking her in his arms, they both freely wept. It was moments before Daniel could speak.

"I have no words to address what you have been through but I know I love you and the thought of anything standing in the way of that cannot change my heart. I want to love you without reserves or conditions. You must not let this fear stand in our way."

"But Daniel I know that you want children."

"I want you more than anything else and we will find a way to solve that challenge."

"But Daniel are you saying that because you feel pity because of what I have been through?"

"I am saying it because I love you."

Esther, so relieved of the burden she carried, caressed his face and kissed him. "I was so afraid and almost did not tell you."

Two months later

They set a wedding date for May. Still, Esther was worried, this time about another question.

"Daniel I am embarrassed to say this but I literally know nothing about the Jewish wedding ceremony. I have never been to a Jewish wedding."

Daniel laughed. "Marrying you is like marrying a shiksa. Daniel took Esther through the ceremony and she raised her eyebrows and shook her head at some of the customs especially the parts about acquiring the bride and unveiling her to make sure she was the right one.

"Good thing that I love you because this is getting out of hand."

"OK, now that you have had the short course in Jewish weddings are you still willing to have me?"

Esther said, "Actually you had me at the circling part. The ceremony will be a cinch."

"Esther, you must realize that your biggest challenge will be surviving the wedding reception. My mother will introduce you to every guest as, 'This is my daughter. She is a doctor.'"

Esther laughed. "I think that I can handle that part easily.'

Chapter 39

May 1956, New York
Esther experiences sadness and joy on her wedding day

As the wedding day approached, despite her love for Daniel, Esther became somewhat depressed. Everyone who should be present to celebrate this wondrous occasion was dead. Her parents, brothers, cousins and so many loved ones from her village would be absent on this meaningful day. She tried to gain a positive perspective but was so immersed in sorrow that it began to negatively affect her work. She became more and more morose. Eventually, she confided in a psychiatrist at the hospital and agreed that she would seriously consider grief counseling after her wedding.

The sunlight burst through the curtains in Esther's bedroom, producing slanting rays across her bed. It was a beautiful day for a wedding with nary a cloud in the brilliant blue skies. She'd had difficulty sleeping and though this was to be a joyous day she was saddened by the fact that her parents and brothers would not be present part of her wedding. She rose from her bed and tried to adjust her mood. The aroma of coffee and toast wafted through the hallway as she walked to the bathroom. She realized that Aunt Miriam and Uncle Isadore were already downstairs. After a shower and two cups of coffee she was able to begin focusing on all she had to do before the afternoon ceremony. Aunt Miriam joined her in the kitchen and asked what time the Hobbs were to be picked up from the Pierre Hotel. "Because it is Saturday there will be little traffic so I would think an hour before the ceremony would be fine," Esther said.

Aunt Miriam reached out and hugged Esther. "I am so happy for you and especially because Daniel is such a wonderful man."

"He is and also a terrible tease. He took me through the wedding process and because I knew so little, he said I was more like a shicksa than a real Jewish woman."

Aunt Miriam laughed and said, "A sense of humor is very important in a marriage."

Esther knew that the humor was a thin cover of the feelings she had carried for weeks. She paused before speaking again but decided to let the reservoir freely flow.

"Aunt Miriam, despite the pain I feel now I also experience a joy beyond description. Until I met Daniel, I never believed I could be so happy or excited." Aunt Miriam placed her arms around Esther and folded her into a long hug.

The ceremony was to be outdoors, weather permitting, and fortunately the day was perfect. Esther was thrilled that the Hobbs had come from Poland especially because Dr. Hobbs had been seriously ill a year ago. His condition had vastly improved and he viewed today as one in which he could honor the memory of his beloved colleague. When Esther and the Hobbs saw one another, all three burst into tears. The bond of their love was ironclad and she treasured the gift of life that their courage had given her.

Before the wedding processional, Aunt Miriam pinned photos of her brother and his family on her husband's and Dr. Hobbs' jacket. She turned to Esther and said, "They are with you on this blessed day."

The ceremony went perfectly and like the rehearsal dinner the celebration was filled with marvelous loving toasts. Daniel's forecast about his mother was right on target. She spent the entire wedding celebration by taking Esther around to every table and introducing her: "This is my new daughter. She is a doctor."

Daniel and Esther stayed at the Pierre Hotel the evening of their wedding day and left for their honeymoon in Puerto Rico the next morning.

1960

Four years after the wedding the lives of the Rosen's' had changed dramatically. Despite her fears, Esther became pregnant in 1958. She gave birth to twins without any serious medical concerns. Daniel Jr. and Rebecca were now almost two and were the center of Daniel and Esther's lives. Esther was now the associate director of Obstetrics at Beth Israel. Her private practice was thriving. More and more women were seeking a female physician for their gynecological and obstetric needs. In addition to all of her responsibilities, Esther had become a role model for the growing number of female medical students and physicians.

Daniel's life had also significantly changed. He was now the chief rabbi at Temple Beth El. He had also accepted a position on the Holocaust museum board and was active in promoting educational programs on the Shoah.

Chapter 40

1960, Italy and New York
Svi and Lorenzo rebuild their lives

Through the years Svi and Lorenzo would both marry and act as each other's best man. The friendship that was forged on the train to freedom had never wavered since the day. They treated their new families as part of one family and regularly visited each other, often spending vacations and Jewish holidays together. During one time together, in Taormina, Sicily, they were having lunch at the San Domenico Hotel while the children and their wives were at the swimming pool.

Despite the passage of time, the Shoah and what they had lost were still part of their conscious existence. Still, they found new ways to live again. Lorenzo, in particular, was consistently exploring the meaning of their persecutions and thought that perhaps together they should share their experiences in a manuscript. Lorenzo proposed they write a book about the Nazi years. Initially, Svi was unsure. He thought the memories might create new pain and he was also concerned about how the book would be received. Lorenzo understood the hesitancy but pointed out that their reflections might be helpful to others in painful life situations. After two days of considering the possible collaboration, they spent an afternoon creating an outline and they agreed to meet via the mail and phone every two weeks. Much to Svi's amazement he spent hours on the outline and after six months the two had created a full manuscript. In the midst of these sessions, they discussed the man who had saved them. A few years back they tried unsuccessfully to find him. It was obvious to both of them that they needed an editor and the search for a publisher began. One of Lorenzo's colleagues at Harvard University, Dr. Gordon Hennessey, read the rough draft and was so taken with it that he contacted a friend who was the principal owner of a major publishing company in New York. The friend, Malcom Kilbride, saw the value in the work and personally contacted the two authors. After weeks of discussions, the publishing house assigned two editors to begin the process of bringing the work to completion. The title of the book was "Life after the Shoah." Despite their incredibly busy schedules, the publisher believed the best market to launch the book would be in New York. In preparation for the tour the publisher called a friend who was an investigative reporter for the New York Times. He told him the story and asked if he could search to learn whether Georg Baum existed in South America. He explained that they had uncovered the story about the person who had saved their lives They had no contact with Georg Baum since he left them at the Vatican and were unaware that the German officer responsible for their salvation was now a prominent architect in New York. Upon learning this, the publisher arranged two key events, one would be a speaking engagement at the 92nd St. Y in New York and the other would be a concert at Lincoln Center in memory of those who had perished in the Nazi concentration camps. The publisher explained to Lorenzo that they found Georg Baum and arranged for the Lincoln Center concert to celebrate publicly what he had done for them. The thought was that they would launch the book the day after the Lincoln Center concert. After two weeks of investigation, they had fully uncovered a great deal of information about Georg Baum. He was currently a very successful real estate partner in the firm of Mahoney, Adams and McGonigle. Fortunately, the publisher, Malcolm Kilbride, had a personal relationship with Mark Mahoney, one of the principals, and he agreed to contact him regarding a secret celebration of Georg Baum's involvement in their lives. When the circumstances of the event were made known, Mahoney was thrilled to have a part in the secret celebration. Mahoney was committed to making sure that Georg would attend. The book had only a vague description of their rescue from Auschwitz and the publisher suggested that they describe the event in detail in the forward and that one of the dedications should be to Georg Baum. He recommended that on the evening of the concert they give him a copy on stage.

Rabbi Daniel Rosen was intimately involved in the orchestration of the Holocaust Remembrance Day to be held at Lincoln Center. He and members of the synagogue's board were one of the main sponsors of the event. The rabbi was fully aware of his wife's story and was uncertain whether she would attend such a remembrance. However, she enthusiastically agreed to attend and was thrilled that one of her favorite artists, Svi Contini, would be the concert's main performer. Her husband was pleased that the event was to be held on a Tuesday evening because Esther had Wednesday off and would be able to join him in attending the concert as well as the post party. He had secured tickets for members of the board of directors in the third-row center orchestra.

Mark Mahoney checked Georg Baum's schedule for the evening of the concert and informed his secretary not to book anything for that night. In turn he visited Georg a week before the event and made a direct appeal to ensure that he would attend.

"Good morning Georg. Were you at Martha's Vineyard this weekend?"

"Yes, I left late Friday and came back last night."

"How was the sailing?"

"Absolutely delightful. The sea was relatively calm especially on Sunday. Every time I am out on the water, I wonder why I don't spend more time at my summer place. How was your weekend?"

"Fine. Elaine and I spent it in the city. We saw a play on Saturday and spent yesterday with our grandchildren. Oh, by the way, I have a favor to ask of you. I, and technically the firm as well, are being honored at a concert in Lincoln Center for the work we performed for the Schnitzer Foundation. I would appreciate it if you and Perry would join me for the concert and a dinner afterwards."

"Let me check my schedule."

"I already checked and you are free."

"Certainly. When is it?"

"Next Tuesday. I will have a driver pick us up and after the party the driver will let you off at the Winchester."

"OK. What is the attire for the evening?"

"Just a business suit."

Mark Mahoney called Malcolm Kilbride and assured him he would have Georg at the event.

As they arrived at Lincoln Center, Mark said to Georg, "We do not have to use the main entrance. We will be greeted by a staff member at one of the private side entrances."

As they entered the building Georg asked what is the charity and who is performing. Mark ducked the question with a vague response as they were led to the premier box that overlooked the main stage. Mark had made sure there would be no programs in the box so Georg would have no warning about the evening's procedures.

Rabbi Daniel Rosen, Esther and members of the temple board were escorted to the third row of the orchestra just minutes before the curtain arose. Esther nudged her husband and said, "The temple will be in hock for years paying for these seats."

He smiled. "This performance will be worth every penny."

Just then the house lights flickered and large applause greeted the conductor, Paul Winslow, as he came on stage. He approached the microphone. "Good evening ladies and gentlemen. Before we begin the concert, I would like to introduce the main artist who will be featured in this evening's performance. He will address you and honored guests before we begin. It is my honor and privilege to introduce Svi Contini."

Georg seemed stunned but said nothing.

Contini began to speak. "I would like to welcome to the stage my dear friend and spiritual brother, Dr. Lorenzo Kaplan."

As Kaplan entered the stage Georg had the impulse to bolt but of course he remained. How could these two be in New York and at a performance he was attending? He turned and looked at Mahoney who had a broad smile on his face.

Taking a deep breath, Svi Contini began to speak. "As you know this evening the concert is dedicated to those who perished in the Holocaust or as I call it the Shoah. Lorenzo and I were among the fortunate ones. We were at Auschwitz and lost loved ones there. However, our lives were spared by the heroism and selfless courage of a German officer. He rescued us from the camp and led us to safety by leaving us at the Vatican where we stayed until the end of the war. Both Lorenzo and I have never had the chance to publicly thank him but we would love to do it at this moment. The man who saved us is in the box to my left. His name is Georg Baum and I would ask him to join us on stage."

Georg was stunned. An usher came to the box and pointed him to the staircase that led to the stage. There was a momentary silence as Baum made his way to the stage. The audience, which was comprised of Holocaust survivors and their families, rose to their feet and burst into thunderous applause. When Georg arrived on stage, he was embraced by Svi and Lorenzo.

Svi gave him a copy of their book and after thanking him again invited Georg to speak.

Esther was mesmerized by this figure on stage but initially dismissed the possibility. He looked like Stark but he had aged and maybe her mind was playing tricks on her. When he began to speak, she realized it was Gerhardt Stark. She was horrified, even nauseated by the sound of his voice. She could not believe her eyes. The man on the stage, although somewhat disfigured, was the one she heard on that tragic day in Poland. Feeling nauseous and physically sickened she bolted from her seat, raced back to the ladies' room, opened the stall door, but before she could reach the toilet, she vomited. She sat on the cold marble tiles sobbing uncontrollably. The memories of that fateful day when she was only 14 years old flooded her mind. She was tormented not only by the visual memory of this massacre but also by the fact that the monster was still alive. She rose from the floor, washed her face and pulled a breath mint out of her pocket. She returned to her seat and Daniel anxiously asked if she was OK.

"I felt slightly nauseous but am fine now. It must have been something I ate at lunch." At this time, she did not tell Daniel what she believed.

She attended the party but told her husband she did not wish to reveal what happened to her and her family. At the Mahoney Penthouse Georg was signing copies of the book with Svi and Lorenzo. Esther tried to get as close as possible to him without formally speaking with him. The apartment was filled with the happy sounds of many of the survivor families who attended the concert. Under different circumstances Esther would have loved this party. The atmosphere was one of joy for Svi, Lorenzo and Georg Baum as they recounted the story of how they met. Esther sat in a corner and stared stonily at the man she believed to be Stark. After hearing his interactions with other persons, she was even more convinced that it was Stark. In that moment she relived the moments when as a 14-year-old girl she was standing in front of him while he issued his orders to the people in the village. She refused the waiter's offer of a glass of champagne because her hands were trembling. She chose not to tell her husband but was completely bewildered as to what she should do. That night she dreamed that he held her prisoner in a room without a door or windows.

Chapter 41

1960, Vienna and New York
Esther reaches out to a Nazi hunter

For weeks Esther struggled with what to do about her belief that Georg Baum was really an SS officer named Stark. It had been a painful mind-numbing time after that horrid evening at Lincoln Center. She had spent hours researching Baum's biography and, on her day off, followed him from his apartment to a local café where he had breakfast each morning. Every moment spent staring at him further convinced her that she must act. This evidence had thrown her into a complete state of anxiety and confusion. Finally, she ascertained the name of a Nazi hunter in Vienna and sent him a packet of information about Gerhardt Stark.

Dr. Micah Goldstein had served multiple years as a war prisoner in Russia primarily as a physician caring for children. He had tried for years to convince the Russian authorities that he was not a German soldier but had abandoned that argument. Recently he had been transferred to Moscow to become part of a research program for children with developmental disabilities. One day a visiting associate professor engaged him in small talk. The issue of being a Jew in the Russian government came up. The professor shared that he was Jewish and though it was known he felt that his medical expertise had been respected and rewarded. This was the first Jewish person that Micah had engaged in his captivity and he shared his own background. The professor took this information to his superiors. The following month Micah was summoned to a hearing in a Russian court. With the information validated he was informed that he would be released the following week and the government would provide transportation to

Munich. Micah was thrilled to finally be a free man. Still, he vowed vengeance. It was a dream that had dulled but now it took on new meaning. Once he was situated in Munich he worked as a physician in a children's hospital until he acquired enough funds to visit Vienna. He had heard there was an office in the city that pursued war criminals and he hoped they could help him locate Gerhardt Stark.

David Bernstein had received a special delivery package in his Vienna office sent by a New York physician. He read through the pages and decided that it was a possible lead that he should follow. As one of the premier Nazi hunters in the world, David Bernstein received leads weekly on former war criminals. Very few were worth following because of his limited resources but this one could be significant and he believed it was worth investigating. In addition, he was to speak at the United Nations in New York in three months. He hoped he might meet the doctor who sent the package. In his preliminary search through the files the name Gerhardt Stark became more than just another member of the SS. He had led an Eienstazgruppen unit in Poland and Russia. However, what made him even more prominent was the fact that he had done a great deal of the architectural planning for Birkenau.

Two weeks after the initial inquiry about Gerhardt Stark, a thin disheveled man arrived at his office in Vienna and made a startling request. The person appeared to be a middle-aged homeless man. Actually, he was a Jewish physician who had the great misfortune to be at Theresienstadt, Birkenau and Russia for more than a decade. The man said he intended to spend the rest his life hunting down the Nazi who had stolen not only his life, but was also responsible for the deaths of his parents. He shared the story with David but what made it so unusual was that the man he hunted was Gerhardt Stark. David understood this was not some crazy person who had a casual interest in this search. He told the Jewish physician that if he called back in two days, he might have some additional information. After the man left, he called New York and sought to speak with the source of the first inquiry. She was in the hospital and could not receive his call so he left a message. The next morning Esther returned David's call. He told her the story about the second inquiry. He had determined that it was a sincere request and asked whether he could share her information with the other person. She eagerly agreed, hoping that he could personally identify her nemesis.

Upon receiving permission from David, Micah contacted Esther and they chatted for a brief two minutes. Embarrassed, Micah shared that he was on a pay phone and he had run out of money. Esther, eager to pursue the conversation, took down the number of the pay phone and called him back. In the course of the conversation Micah shared his history with Esther. He said that if she was right, he could absolutely identify Stark. Esther asked if there was a mailing address where she could reach him after she had more information from David Bernstein. He gave her the address of friends in Munich with whom he was staying.

David Bernstein arrived in New York weeks after the initial contact with the New York physician. He was scheduled to deliver two presentations at the United Nations, focused on the need to share information about war criminals.

He had been in touch with Esther and they agreed to meet at a local coffee shop three blocks from the United Nations.

Esther was at the café early. At approximately 10 a.m. a middle-aged man with a rumpled tan raincoat entered the café. He looked as though he was searching for someone. His dress was common but he had the body of an aging former athlete. His rumpled hair was drooping from his forehead, engulfing his bushy eyebrows. Esther stood. "Are you David Bernstein?"

"Yes."

She motioned for him to be seated. David removed his coat, hung it over his chair and sat down across from her.

After preliminary introductions, David began to speak. "Doctor, in order to frame our conversation, it might be helpful to give you some personal background."

Esther nodded in agreement.

"I spent a considerable amount of time in Mauthausen and Birkenau. Fortunately, I was liberated but I lost most of my family to the Nazis. I have spent the post war years hunting down every credible lead, considering my limited resources. I tell you this because it is important that your concerns were taken very seriously by me and my investigators. The name you referred to me was of special importance because of his being an SS officer. I am not sure you are aware that he was one of the primary architects of Birkenau. This fact moved our investigation to top priority. If Stark is alive, he would become the number-one target for my organization and we would literally move all of our focus to confronting him publicly. Do you mind if I smoke?"

Esther smiled and said, "No but as a physician I feel obligated to say it will negatively affect your health."

Ignoring her counsel, he pulled a tattered fragment of a cheap cigar from his pocket, lit it while looking past the flame into Esther's pleading eyes. His voice, tinged with a heavy Austrian accent, was deep and impressive. He bent down to pick up his briefcase and removed a black leather book.

"We have spent the better part of a month investigating your information and I totally respect your concerns, as well as those of the Jewish physician I referred to you. However, we have concluded that

Gerhardt Stark was killed by Italian partisans outside of Rome in March of 1944. He was found dead in a burned out auto on an abandoned farm road. The official government report states that he probably had been drinking and pulled off the main road to sleep it off. Somehow, his car was attacked by Italian partisans and he was killed as well as one of the Italians in a shoot-out. The body was consumed by flames but there were personal items that indicated who he was. The Italian carabinieri as well as the central German headquarters in Rome officially confirmed his death.

"With regard to Georg Baum, we uncovered very little information. He was from Kassel, a town that was completely fire bombed. There are no records of his being involved with SS activities. It appears that he held an insignificant government desk job in Munich and Zurich. He left Germany sometime in late 1944 or early 1945 and established a successful consulting architectural business in South America and moved to New York in 1955. He appears to be very private but has been enormously generous to many local Jewish charities. However, this fact has had no effect on my decision regarding your inquiry. I would publicly denounce him if he was, in fact, Gerhardt Stark."

Esther was crestfallen. She did not immediately react. She sighed and began shaking her head from side to side. "I appreciate your assistance but that dossier is wrong. I know that he is Gerhardt Stark. I not only saw him on stage but also attended a party in which he was honored for saving Jews. I stood three feet away from him and heard that same voice that condemned my family in 1939. He has aged but I am certain that he is Gerhardt Stark."

David had a deep understanding of her pain and responded, "Because I have suffered losses like you, I can relate to your pain but there is no proof. Memory often plays tricks on us and I am sure it would help somewhat to ease your pain if Baum was Stark."

Esther reacted sharply. "There is not one iota of doubt in my mind that Baum is Stark. My memory of that awful day is intact and I stood in front of that monster when he ordered the murder of my entire village. His voice is as clear in my brain today as it was on that morning. I will find a way to continue the search because I cannot live with the realization that this monster is leading such a privileged life. What kind of proof would it take for you to believe me?"

"Something that would link him to the past. I still think that he is not who you think he is so you would need concrete evidence."

"Can you suggest where I might begin?"

"Well at some point you may have further conversations with Micah Goldstein but again remember that this is a broken person who spent years in Nazi as well as Russian prison camps."

David was quiet for a brief moment but then added, "Although I don't agree with your current conviction, in order to put your mind at rest I can put you in touch with someone who may be able to help you. Have you ever heard of the Nakam?"

"No, I have not."

"After the war a group of about 50 resistance Jewish fighters decided to avenge the deaths of the six million. Led by a man named Abba Kovner the group sought to kill six million Germans in revenge. Their moto was 'a nation for a nation' The group secretly secured large quantities of poison with the intention of poisoning the water system of Nuremberg. However, the initial plot failed when British sailors found the poison on a ship. It was being smuggled to Germany.

This grandiose plan was aborted following this failure. However, the rest of the group turned their attention to 'Plan B,' targeting German prisoners of war held by the United States. They obtained arsenic. One of the group worked at the bakery that supplied these prison camps. He poisoned 3,000 loaves of bread at *Konsum-*

Genossenschaftsbäckerei (Consumer Cooperative Bakery) in Nuremberg, which sickened more than 2,000 German prisoners of war at Langwasser Internment Camp. However, no known deaths can be attributed to the group.

One of the former members of that group is a friend who has aided me in the search for Nazis all over the world. His name is Eli Kroloff. He has an apartment here as well as a residence in Tel Aviv. I will contact him and see if he will speak with you. I am not certain that he is presently in New York but I will contact him."

Esther thanked him. And though he was skeptical he did call Eli Kroloff.

Eli Kroloff grew up near Warsaw. In 1943 he was part of the group that initiated the Warsaw uprising against the German army. He was the middle child in his family and after his parents and sisters were sent to Auschwitz, he and his brothers engaged the Germans daily in open battles. As time went on it became almost impossible to survive and after the buildings were shattered, they retreated to the sewers. The conditions were horrible and many died from disease or suffocation. Eli was one of the few survivors. After the war he established a successful import business and spent most of his time in Tel Aviv and New York. He continued to aid in the identification and punishment of Nazi war criminals.

Chapter 42

1960, New York
Esther secures an ally

Six weeks after her meeting with David Bernstein, Esther received a call from Eli Kroloff. He invited her for breakfast and asked on which day she would be available. Enthusiastically, Esther said, "I am off on Wednesday and will gladly meet you next week."

They agreed to meet at The Fresh Bagel deli located in the heart of Times square, and 43rd Street.

Eli Kroloff was a large shouldered, compact man with a bronze tan and warm, inviting smile. There was a war hero look to his body, accented by a patch over his right eye. After the initial introductions he sat erect and immediately launched into what he had heard about her situation. "David has briefed me on your problem and my first question is why are you so certain?"

Esther recounted the dark events of the massacre of her village. "I have lived with that voice in my head and the image of that monster so calmly orchestrating the murder of my entire village. He stood right in front of me when he ordered the massacre. I am the only survivor."

She paused. "It may seem strange to you but I believe that God led me to find him here in New York."

Eli responded, "I don't believe in God but if it helps you then I envy you. I have not believed in God since 1940. If there was a God he died at Auschwitz. However, that is beside the point. How can I be of help?"

"I am not sure but I cannot give this up. I must prove that Georg Baum is really Gerhardt Stark."

"All right. I will agree to try but we must have proof. It is critical that we understand that our memories in these cases must be as reliable as heart beats. The horror we have experienced often creates false details and memories.

If you out him without proof it will damage the work that David does. There are strong forces that constantly deny the Shoah. If you denounce someone without concrete evidence then it supports those who deny what happened."

"I understand that but I cannot let go of this. What would convince you and David?"

"Well, the best case would be another witness. Without that we need some physical evidence. One clear proof would be an SS tattoo but how the hell would we get that?"

"What is an SS tattoo? Just 'SS' tattooed on him somewhere?"

"Members of the SS had their blood type tattooed in case they were injured in battle. The physicians would know immediately what type blood to give them if they needed a transfusion."

Thinking out loud, Eli continued, "Ok that may not be possible but it has been my experience that many former Nazis retain some personal connection to their past. It might be a uniform, medals, some documentation or maybe a passport. I will arrange to pursue this. Where does he live?"

"In a penthouse on Fifth Avenue that overlooks Central Park. The green awning in front has the name Winchester and the number is 739 Fifth Avenue."

"Do you know his usual daily schedule? When he is out of the penthouse?"

"Yes, he goes to a local café for coffee at precisely 7:30 every week day. He stays about 20 minutes and then a driver takes him to his office, which is located on Wall Street. There is also the slim possibility that another person could verify his identity. David Bernstein has had an inquiry about Stark from a relative."

Eli gently dismissed this possibility. "Ok that sounds like a long shot so with some assistance I will find a way to enter his penthouse to see if I can find any trace that he is Stark. Please remember the evidence so far points elsewhere and I cannot indict him without some proof."

Esther replied, "I understand and so appreciate your involvement."

Eli researched the blueprints of the Winchester apartment through one of his connections in the city office of permits and licenses. He determined that the best way to enter the penthouse was to create a temporary electrical shut down in the building. In order to accomplish this, he would need the assistance of an electrician and a locksmith familiar with apartment wall safes. He called Esther and said that once the plan was fully developed, he would contact her. Four days later Eli had resolved his concerns and told Esther that at precisely 9:30 on the following Monday he would access the penthouse.

It was a clear sunny New York fall day when Eli's associate Lorenz Schoenfelder, also a Nakam member, climbed the telegraph pole in the back of the Winchester building. He waited until precisely 9:35 and then severed the main feed. He then connected the phone wires to an outlet where Eli could receive any outside call from the main desk. At precisely 9:53 Eli received a call to the electric company stating there was an issue at the Winchester. Eli told the caller that they were in luck because the company had two workmen three blocks away who would immediately come to the building. Once inside, (they were wearing Com Electric company shirts) they were greeted by the concierge. He led them to the main electrical panels but after a cursory look Eli informed the concierge that the problem was probably in one of the apartments. "I think it will be necessary to determine which apartment has caused the failure."

The concierge, somewhat flustered, said, "I do not have permission from the owners to let you into the units."
Eli said, "Maybe with luck, we will be able to repair the lines from outside the building. We will use the fire escape to get to the roof because the elevators have no power."

Once on the rooftop Moishe the locksmith picked the access door to the penthouse floor. Before entering the hallway, they saw it was empty. When they arrived at the door of the penthouse the locksmith smiled, "This part is cake."

Once inside Eli and his companion were extremely careful not to disturb anything that would give them away. For the first 10 minutes their search was in vain. They abandoned looking through his desk and filing cabinet and started looking for a safe. The locksmith unfurled a large extension cord and plugged a tool into a wall socket. "This light on the tool will indicate if there is something behind a wall."

The unit was mammoth and the initial search was fruitless. Finally, the locksmith said, "I think there is something behind this breakfront."
They took one of the Persian area rugs and placed it under the piece so the movement would not leave scratch marks on the hardwood floor. As they moved the piece, they saw a wall safe.
"Can you get into that quickly?"

"Looks fairly standard."

He placed his ear against the safe and slowly turned the dials. The first few attempts failed but suddenly they heard a clicking sound and the locksmith smiled and opened the safe. It was rather large and contained substantial amounts of cash, business statements and a few large envelopes. The first two envelopes held a series of real estate documents. The third appeared to have multiple photos. In the middle of the packet was a family photo of a woman and three children. Next there was a photo of Adolph Hitler with a German officer. The photo had an inscription: "To Gerhardt Stark." It was signed by Hitler with the date, June 1942. Eli took a camera out of his pocket and took six photos. They then replaced the breakfront and put the rug in its original place. Leaving the apartment, they went to the roof. Eli gave the electrician the sign to restore the building's power. They went down the fire escape, entered the lobby and assured the concierge that the issue had been resolved.

When Esther finished her rounds late in the morning there was a series of phone messages in her office. Most were medical issues but one was the most important. She dialed the number and a voice said, "Doctor I need to see you."

Breathlessly, she replied, "Can you tell me what happened?"

"No, not over the phone. I think it is best if you come to my apartment on the east side. I am at 443 Donald Street at 76th and Third Avenue, Apartment 11C."

She felt anxious and terrified at the same time. Was the hunt in vain, and was he going to tell her they uncovered nothing in his penthouse? What if they found something? What would she do then? He had saved the lives of two prominent Jews who had dedicated their lives to creating peace. Would it shatter them? And why had he saved the two Jews? And what of the charities that he had aided? The solution would not be simple. Would the funds dry up? What if they killed him? Would it bring back her family? Up to this point she had been enthusiastic to bring this to a conclusion but now if it truly is him what would her choices be? She was so firmly committed to bringing life into the world but could she in this instance kill him? Could she with Eli's aid force him to hang himself and if so, what happens to the charitable funds that he had pledged? If it was not him then she will be deflated. If it is him then the choices are more complex than blind vengeance.

Arriving at the apartment building she scanned the listings and pushed the intercom. A buzzer sounded and the front door opened. She made her way to the elevator. She pushed 11. She did not have to knock because Eli was standing in the doorway. He shook her hand and led her into the parlor. He motioned for her to be seated in a deep comfortable chair She feared that this gracious gesture was a prelude to bad news.

"I took this assignment because I understand the pain that lingers on and on for those of us who have suffered such losses and I had hoped that in some way I could lessen your anguish. I was most skeptical because I know that memory of murderous events is often unreliable and I honestly thought that perhaps we might find something that proved he was not Gerhardt Stark."

She felt deflated. She was sure he was going to tell her that the search had been in vain. He then opened his briefcase and took out a large manila envelope.

"I know that what I am about to show you will further complicate your life. Are you sure you want to see what I am about to reveal?"

A sympathetic smile crossed his face but she did not notice it. Esther took a deep breath. Her cheeks turned red. Physically she braced herself for this moment of truth. Without hesitation she clearly replied, "I am ready to be disappointed or vindicated."

She opened the envelope and gasped and then burst into tears. "I knew it was him. I knew it."

"You were right and I must admit I did not think there was the slightest chance that it was him. Now the hard part comes. What do you want to do with this information.?"

Esther was trembling as Eli went to a cabinet on the other side of the room and took out a bottle of whiskey and two glasses. He poured a small amount in each glass and handed her one. "Drink this."

She almost dropped the glass but swiftly recovered and drank the whiskey in one gulp. She coughed and sat motionless for a few moments. "Do you have any suggestions? What do you think I should do?"

"I don't mean to be flippant but this is your show. I have no sympathy for this monster and I am not sure you know a 10th of what he was responsible for at Auschwitz."

"Why do you mention Auschwitz?"

"Because he was the second in command of drawing up the plans for the Birkenau expansion. My family perished under his watch but I still believe that you should determine the course of action."

"It is ironic. Since finding him on that evening I have thought about nothing but this moment. But now that it is here it is not as simple as I imagined. What do you think are our choices?"

"Well, I am not sure but remember this is a powerful man and we obtained this information illegally. He could deny it and play hardball by destroying the original. It would be the word of a 14-year-old child against his word. He would probably sue you for defamation of character. The other issue is that he saved the lives of two prominent Jews. He would probably appeal to them and I am certain they would support him in the press."

Esther was taking Eli's words seriously. "There is another bump in the road. Apparently, he is a regular giver to Jewish charities and that might cease if we take the other option."

Which is?"

"I am going to ask you a question and I want you to think seriously before answering

Should we kill him?"

"As much as I hate him, I am not sure I could do that,".

"It would not have to be you. I could arrange for that to happen but it does not solve the issue of the charitable funds."

"I honestly don't know what to do."

"Have you shared this with anyone like your husband?"

"No, I have deliberately kept him out of it. He has been my anchor in dealing with the past and I do not want him involved at this level. Especially if the choice is to kill Stark. I am a bit overwhelmed at this moment. I think I need some time to clearly lay out my choices. Will you still be available to help me?"

"Yes, there is no way I will abandon you at this time."

Chapter 43

1960, New York
Esther confronts Gerhardt

Esther stewed on the choices for weeks but finally realized that inaction was not a solution. She decided she would make Stark aware that he had been discovered. She invited him to Paolo's, a high-end Italian restaurant on the east side. She requested a private booth so the conversation would not be heard by others. Pretense for this meeting was that because he was a major donor, she was interested in having his ideas on designing the new women's section of the hospital. She had four conversations with him and initially he had suggested that one of his junior partners should be the point person. She used the Lincoln Center evening and the party to connect to him on a more personal level. He agreed to meet her with the understanding that eventually he would subcontract the design work to one of his junior partners.

Esther arrived at the restaurant early. There was no fear that Stark would harm her because he was a public figure and the restaurant would be crowded. She was resolute but fidgety and kept rehearsing what she would say. She kept compulsively glancing at the time so she decided to take off her wristwatch and place it in her handbag. She entered the restaurant to make sure that her request for a private dining room had been fulfilled.

She checked her briefcase which contained the photo copies from his penthouse safe. She took a series of deep breaths. Within minutes he appeared. Of course, he believed that this was going to be a very cordial engagement. He was led to the private dining area where his client was already seated. She rose to greet him. They shook hands. Esther inquired, "What would you prefer, dinner or a cocktail?"

He thought for a second and then asked the waiter for a very dry martini. She asked for a glass of Merlot. For a few minutes they talked about the weather. When the drinks arrived, they clinked classes.

He began the conversation. "I'm not fully up to speed on the project in the hospital. My firm is a major donor to the new wing but I was not aware that the project had been scheduled for this quarter. I know a little bit about the initial discussions but thought that the architectural designs were dependent on the actual location. Is it still the intention to have the addition facing east?"

She fended off that question by saying, "Before we get to the particulars, I have a few pertinent questions that I would like answered."

He sipped his martini. "Go right ahead."

Esther gently put down her wine glass. Her cheeks reddened with anticipation.

"How long have you lived in New York?"

"I came here in 1955. And before that I spent some time in Spain."

"Where were you living in Spain?"

"I was in Madrid."

Esther said, "That is one of the places along with Barcelona that I would love to visit."

"It is a marvelous city. I enjoyed my time there."

"If I may be so bold, why did you leave?"

"For many reasons but I guess the main one was that the Spanish way of doing business was vastly different from what I desired."

"In what ways?"

"Well, it took forever to get a project started and manana was the order of the day. The other compelling reason was that New York was an intriguing opportunity. It was for me then and now the center of the universe with unlimited business opportunities."

"I understand that you grew up in Germany. Is that correct?"

"Yes, actually my formative years were in Munich before I came to the United states."

"I also grew up in Europe and came to the United States after the war. Where did you live in Europe?" he asked.

"In Poland, in a very small village on the outskirts of Warsaw."

"Perhaps you have heard of the village called Wiegrowicz?" she asked.

He showed no signs of recognition and just then the waiter came to ask if they were ready to order. She suggested they wait to order, saying they were discussing an intricate business matter.

She continued to explore her questions. "Were you in Poland during the war?"

This was the first sign of discomfort Baum showed.

"I am not sure why we are discussing Germany or Poland during the war. I thought we were here primarily to discuss the architectural possibilities of the new addition to the hospital."

She saw his back stiffen and realized if she did not get to the point he might leave. She decided to abort the subtle approach and go right to the confrontation. "Please bear with me because I believe that what we are discussing will have relevance to both of us at some point in the evening."

Somewhat annoyed at the mystery of the process, he agreed to go along with it.

"Were you in the German military during the war?"

This question made him even more uncomfortable. "I don't see the relevance in my answering that question so would you please focus on the reason we are meeting?"

She realized: it is now or never. He was about to leave. She cleared her throat and stared at him with cold contempt. "Did you know Gerhardt Stark while you were in the army?"

"Who said I was in the army and what the hell does this have to do with your hospital?"

Becoming increasingly irritated, he pushed his chair back from the table.

"Before you go, there is something I would like to show you."

She reached into her briefcase and pulled out two photos.

"Do these look familiar to you?"

Staring at the two photos, his face became ashen. He slumped down in his chair. His mouth was open. He was speechless.

Esther paused. She spoke deliberately, slowly, with care. This was the moment she had waited for since the night of the concert.

"I know you are Gerhardt Stark. Let me tell you how you have ruined my entire life."

In detail, she described the bloody scene that occurred in the village. He sat stone-faced, listening, beginning to sweat, going from ashen to red-faced.

"I never thought I would have to relive over and over what happened to me and my loved ones but I attended a concert in Lincoln Center and horror of horrors I was confronted with the man who killed my entire family. Through a bit of luck, I was wounded but I survived that massacre. You know what? Your voice and face have haunted me for years. I knew it was you but I needed concrete proof."

Now catching his breath, he accused her, "So, you broke into my penthouse and stole those photos?"

"So, you do not deny that you are Gerhardt Stark?"

"Gerhardt Stark is dead. So, what is it you want?"

"I want you to admit not only the direct blood on your hands but also your involvement in designing the Birkenau camp."

He now seemed totally under control. All emotion was gone from his face. Only his piercing eyes revealed his anger.

He glared at her with contempt. "Why should I? You seem to have all the facts. Of course, what you have left out of your story is context."

"What do you mean by context?"

"First, you have no proof that that photo was taken from my penthouse. The second challenge is that besides you there is no link to me. All of the official records of Gerhardt Stark prove that he is dead. I barely resemble that photo and have proof that I am Georg Baum. I will vigorously contest this and will sue you for defamation. Besides all of this, you have put together a story that leaves out the context of the days in which your so-called villain lived. You have established a colorful scenario of the German monster who did all these dreadful things without knowing what happened to the German people after the great war. The Jewish phenomenon was something that had to be dealt with and I will not apologize for what we did. You have scenarios of German atrocities but you have left out what happened to the German people after the great war. The Treaty of Versailles was an outrage and a criminal act that punished millions of German civilians. There was no world outcry then so if you are looking for me to apologize or beg your forgiveness do not waste your breath."

"I am not the least bit surprised at your lack of humanity. Your life here has been a complete fraud."

"All right. Apparently, all the cards are in your hand. Where do we go from here?" She paused and said, "I do not know. Part of me wishes to kill you at this moment but that would ruin the lives of my husband and children. Also, it would destroy the lives of those you rescued under false pretenses and yet I cannot let you go. There must be some sense of justice."

Esther had completely discharged her volley of facts, but realized she had lost the upper hand in the exchange. She was stunned at how quickly he recovered from seeing the photos.

With that he stood up and said, "Good luck but let me tell you I have on retainer the finest law firm in this city. And by the way, the partners are all Jewish. I will sue you for everything you have and at the end of this charade you will be penniless and have achieved nothing."

Returning to his penthouse Stark went to his safe, took out the two photos, and placed them both in his fireplace. He rolled up the New York Times, added kindling and burned them. He thought, "Now let me see what that bitch can do. She is stuck because she illegally entered my penthouse and that photo barely resembles me now." He would change the locks on his penthouse door, install a security camera and replace his wall safe. He viewed this situation as transactional and as a master chess player he welcomed the next step in the story. He had come too far to be sidetracked by some inept Jew.

Esther was confused as to what she should do next. She was amazed at Stark's response. Somehow when confronted with the photos she had expected him to panic but instead she actually felt at the end of the meeting he held the upper hand. She telephoned Eli and asked if she could meet with him.

The next morning Esther showed up at Eli's apartment and shared the discussion that took place the prior evening. "I was very confident going into the meeting that I would be calm and I expected that when I confronted him with the photos, he would collapse. But it was the opposite. There was not one ounce of contrition and he actually lectured me on what the Jews did to the Germans and why they deserved their persecution. He also pointed out that the evidence was flimsy and illegally obtained. He threatened me with a lawsuit and spitefully told me that his lawyers were all Jews and that he would destroy me."

Eli listened intently. "The bastards are incapable of sorrow and guilt. Anyone who could do what they did to us is soulless and that core does not change."

"I have to tell you that I am devastated by this turn of events and part of me wishes that I had never found him."

"So, are you willing to drop it?"

"I don't know. As much as I hate him, I don't know if I could actually kill him. Also, there is the reality that a lawsuit of that kind would destroy my family. He has unlimited funds and even if I could win, the financial costs would be astronomical. The other factor is that even though he is a monster he supports Jewish charities. I found a source that said he contributes more than $3 million a year to the central Jewish charity organization in New York."

"OK, so are you willing to let it go?"

"I am between a rock and a hard place. Do you have any ideas?"

"Not at this very moment but I have to know how far are you willing to go?"

"What does that mean?"

"You have said you can't kill him but does that exclude someone else killing him?"

"I am not sure but that still does not address the funds that end when he dies. I have no idea whether his will provides continuity for continued giving. Revenge would be sweet but not at the cost of making others' lives more painful."

"OK let me ask another question. If we could find a way to make him pay and still get rid of him, would you be able to handle that?"

"I am not sure. What you are proposing?"

Eli laughed. "I don't have a clue at this moment but my gut tells me that this bastard cannot go on living his privileged life without paying the price. Somehow there has to be a solution that addresses all of the major hurdles and still ends up with his death. By the way, who is the other person who could identify him and how do I contact him?"

"His name is Micah Goldstein and he is a cousin of Stark's. They grew up together but Stark betrayed him and his family. He is currently in Munich. I have that information at home but not sure what good that will do."

"Neither do I but I need to have every bit of information possible before I allow my sinister mind to plan Stark's demise. Let me put it this way. Now that I know who he is and what he has done I personally cannot shrug my shoulders and walk away. I will do nothing without your consent but somehow there has to be an answer. One last question, can you pay for Goldstein to fly here if in any way I can utilize him in my plan?"

"I am certain I could arrange that but if he comes where will he stay?"

"Don't worry about that. I have an extra bedroom and he can stay with me."

After Esther left, Eli began to write down a series of questions on yellow pad. "All right. Now that Stark knows someone is capable of entering his penthouse what does he do? First, he destroys the photos. His argument will be since they do not exist, they are fraudulent and because they are old it is possible to believe that it is not him. The next thing he does is to change the lock on his door and probably create a new series of numbers for the wall safe. The most important change is that he probably installs a motion camera that he activates whenever he leaves the penthouse. I could make him uncomfortable if this cousin turns out to be the real deal by sending him pieces of his past via the mail. This can be things that Esther could not possibly know. It will create psychic pain and I would like the bastard to feel the anxiety before we finalize whatever I decide."

Eli went into the kitchen to make coffee. He placed the yellow pad on the kitchen table as he walked around the apartment trying to answer the challenges of moving forward.

"The camera presents an obstacle but I bet that he has it positioned to face the wall safe. If I remember correctly there is a bookcase on the wall facing the safe. It would be the ideal place to place the camera."

He heard the coffee percolating. After pouring himself a cup of coffee he picked up the phone and checking his address book, dialed a number. Once the phone was answered he identified himself. "If someone was to install a motion camera and money was no obstacle, what would they choose?"

There was slight pause and the party on the line said, "Either a Ramson 200 or a Brandon x26. Does this have anything to do with that site we visited?"

"Yes, Moishe it is that site."

"Then I would bet it is the high-end model, which is the BrandonX26."

"Is it possible once they are activated to remove the cartridge and replace it?"

"If it is either of those two models it can be done in a matter of minutes."

"Would the person who installed the camera be able to tell that the cartridge had been changed?"

"No because the change is not visible and even if they were an expert nothing would indicate that the camera had been tampered with. The other good news is that the Brandon comes with a remote that you shut off as you enter. The only thing that would be on the tape is someone who entered while you were out. If the tape is replaced it indicates that no one has been in the site."

"Do you have access to those replacement tapes?"

"Yes, as well as the remote for the Brandon, because those are the only two that we use. I am sure that in the past whether you know it or not they were utilized in some of your past assignments."

"OK, next question. Our last meeting was relatively simple but there will be changes to the front door and I suspect a more complex series of numbers in the wall safe. Do you see that as a problem?"

"Not at all. I have yet to encounter a door that is very complex and the safe is merely trial and error."

"I will get back to you as soon as I finalize my thoughts."

He picked up the yellow pad and started to answer the questions.

1. Front door and safe do not seem to be a problem.

2. Camera is a risk but if he is wrong what is the downside? We will have masks on and Stark is not going to report this to the police.

3. The question of his charitable giving is still unsolved. There is no way we can force him to sign over his assets but what if we had his will? That safe was so loaded with documents that possibly there is a copy of his will in it.

4. He is going to stagger his schedule so that he will be less predictable. Unlike the last time when we accessed the penthouse in broad daylight this time it will have to be at night. I will have to use Esther as a lookout. I am sure that is not going to be much of an issue.

Micah was surprised by Esther's invitation and immediately agreed to come to the states. He was met at Kennedy airport by Esther and Eli and then after lunch in Manhattan Esther went back to work. Eli drove Micah to his apartment. Over the next few days Eli peppered Micah with information about Stark. The plan had begun to be operational.

Chapter 44

1960, New York
Eli makes Gerhardt aware that he has been discovered

The evening in the restaurant with the Jewish physician had been unnerving but the lack of a future response calmed Stark's concerns and he believed there was nothing left to fear. He had altered his schedule for the last few weeks but now decided that he could get back to his normal routine. As he entered his office his secretary greeted him with a cup of coffee and the overnight mail. One manila envelope had no return address and as he opened it he dropped the cup of coffee. The envelope contained a sheet filled with cut out newsprint that said, "Do you miss Frieda?"

After brushing the coffee off his pants, he asked himself, how did she know my wife's name? The frightening thought was that in all probability it was not her but who else could know that?

Over the next few weeks every three or four days there would be another manila envelope with something personal about his past life. One asked if he ever forgave his stepfather? Another asked if the weather was good on his wedding day in Passau. Eli created the level of anxiety in Stark that made his life painful. He called Esther and told her that Micah had provided invaluable information. He wished to keep her out of the next segments of his plan but there was one part only she could play. He had in mind an attempt to re-enter the penthouse and the need for her to be a lookout. It would be at night and he would tell her where to stand on the southeast corner of Fifth Avenue with a flashlight. If she saw Stark come back, she was to flash the light on and off.

In full disguise, before Stark would get there in the morning, Eli entered the office of Mahoney Properties with a large floral arrangement. Stark's secretary admired the floral arrangement. She put it in Stark's office. Eli made small talk with the secretary, advising her to gently water the arrangement. He suggested that she put the flowers in a container or vase with water. She thanked him and walked to a closet near her desk and searched for a vase. As soon as she entered the closet he went to her desk and opened the calendar. Stark had a dinner engagement at Portofino restaurant on Thursday at 7:30. He closed the book and made his way out of the building.

Stark arrived a half hour later and was informed by his secretary that a florist had delivered an arrangement. He inquired, "Who is it from?"

"I am not sure and there is no florist name on the gift. However, there is a card." Stark hung up his coat and read the card. It read, "To Gerhardt with love from your Einsatzgruppen friends." His secretary asked cheerfully, "Who is it from?" Trying to compose himself, he said, "Oh from a business friend. They are lovely."

Now closed in his office, Stark was completely unraveled. Who could this be? There was no one who knew him from those days who was alive and yet these notes and now this arrangement were from a source that knew him. What did they want?

It was a moonless night and perfectly pitch dark as Eli and Moishe climbed the fire escape dressed completely in black clothing and fully masked. Once opening the door that leads to the penthouse, they quietly approached the front door. "Just as I thought, he installed a top-of-the-line triple lock but it is really simple to jimmy without leaving any marks. As soon as I open it get ready with the flashlight because if he has installed a motion camera it will begin as soon as the door is opened. The door swung back and Eli turned on the flashlight. It took a few seconds to get used to the room and then they headed for the bookcase. "Shine the light on the bookcase." After a few seconds they found the camera.

"Bingo. It is a Brandon."

He removed the camera and opened the tape drawer. "Appears it is only rarely activated." He took the current tape out and replaced it. "When we leave it is important that we crawl out. I am not sure that it will not swivel and catch us so we have to be careful. Ok, let's get the rug and move the breakfront."

Gingerly they removed the piece and Moishe immediately addressed the new combination. "Actually, he has replaced the safe but it would not make any difference. I can still crack it."

Wearing gloves, he began to turn the dials. It was not as simple as the last time but it finally opened.

Georg had not thought of himself as Gerhardt for years and seated in this restaurant he was completely unnerved. He made an excuse about having a migraine headache and decided to return to his penthouse. Esther, nervously pacing back and forth on the corner, was horrified when a cab pulled up in front of the Winchester and Stark got out. He paid his tab and entered the building. She was so flustered that she dropped the flashlight and it shattered. She had no way to warn Eli.

Eli was going through the huge section of documents when he found the last will and testament of Georg Baum. It was a lengthy document but he was only interested in two pages. He took out his camera and flashed three pictures. They placed the breakfront back and prepared to leave. With the remote, Moishe activated the camera. At that moment Eli heard the sound of the front door lock. He and Moishe dove behind the long sofa in the foyer. Stark entered the penthouse and immediately clicked the remote to shut off the camera. He then opened the hall closet and hung up his coat and hat. Eli had been in many tight situations in his life but this one was difficult because the only choice if discovered was to kill Stark. That would leave many loose ends. Fortunately, Stark entered the main bedroom and closed the bathroom door. They crawled out and knowing the camera was off they left the penthouse. Once on the street they found a complexly shaken Esther and assured her that despite the lack of the signal all went well. Eli told her, "Do not have any contact with me. I will contact you when it is appropriate."

Chapter 45

Martha's Vineyard
The Final Solution

Eli began to focus on Stark's weekly schedule. He learned that on most weekends he went to Martha's Vineyard where he sailed. He usually came back Monday morning. Eli and Micah decided to drive to Cape Cod, to Woods Hole to take the ferry to the Vineyard.

On the morning of their trip, Micah seemed tense and relatively silent. Eli understood that this venture was probably not one with which Micah would be comfortable. He decided to tap into the feelings. He asked Micah, "I think it would be a good idea if we had a full breakfast before leaving. I am going to make some scrambled eggs and toast. Would you be interested in that?"

Micah said yes and offered to make the coffee. When they were seated and ready to eat Eli began the conversation.

"Did you ever believe that the opportunity to actually meet Stark again would happen?"

Micah was silent for a brief period before responding. "When I was in Theresienstadt and Auschwitz there was nothing else I thought about. But when I was in Siberia, I did not think there was a chance that it would happen. I had resigned myself to the fact that I would die in Russia."

Eli nodded. "I can relate to that. When I was in the sewers of Warsaw, I did not believe that I would survive and certainly did not envision that after the war I could bring some of those bastards to justice."

Micah said, "For years it was so hard for me to accept what had happened to my cousin. Gerhardt was truly a fine person before the war. He was like a brother to me and it was impossible to believe that he had become a Nazi. For a long time, I thought he would come to his senses and reject the Nazi propaganda, but he only got worse. The turning point for me was when he did nothing to release my father from Dachau. That and my mother being sent to Auschwitz."

"What are you feeling now?"

"I am all over the lot. Part of me feels like the avenger who finally has the opportunity to get revenge and yet in reality I am not by nature a killer. Human life has always been precious to me. It was one of the reasons I became a physician."

"I get that Micah. Before Warsaw I could never have imagined some of the acts I have performed. What they did to us makes us go to places that we never knew existed. I have long lost any compassion toward any Nazi who killed our people. Besides losing my parents, sisters and brothers, my younger brother died in my arms in the Warsaw sewers. The smells of that moment and his tormented last breaths often come back to me and steel my will."

Micah nodded. "I think I am there intellectually but it still goes against everything that I was taught by my parents. Coupled with that, is my training. I dedicated my life to alleviate pain and suffering."

Eli took a swig of coffee before responding. "I could support that if we had not experienced the hell of what they did to us. However, I will tell you that our loved ones cry out for justice and this bastard cannot get away with all the blood that is on his hands. I have to ask you, are you up to doing what is necessary or would you prefer that I confront him by myself?"

"I have to do this. I don't know how I will feel or act when we meet him but there is no way that I can avoid being there with you." The two men were momentarily silent lost into their memories and thoughts of loss and pain.

Eli was smiling but his smile quickly faded. He raised his coffee cup and in a loud angry voice shouted" Here's to killing that Nazi bastard."

Micah with some degree of discomfort touched his cup to Eli's and said" Here's to killing my cousin."

On the drive from New York to Cape Cod, Micah was almost totally silent. Eli's tried to lessen the tension by telling Micah what a beautiful ferry ride they would experience. Micah barely responded and gazed out the window in deep thought for the rest of the trip.

Saturday evening, they arrived on the Vineyard as dusk began to set on the island. They parked the car blocks away from Stark's residence. In the car, they put on dark clothing. There was no need for masks because they wanted him to know who they were. Arriving at the water's edge they cased his house and determined that it did not have a security system. Stark's home was a significant distance from the next property. It had a private dock and long stretch of beach. Apparently, the building was more than 100 years old. It had been completely redesigned, including a modern addition that overlooked the water. The good news for Eli and Micah was that the house was isolated and located just outside of downtown Vineyard Haven. The main part of the house was tucked away on peaceful Anchor Road. It was just a few minutes' walk from the yacht club where Stark often had dinner. They were betting that there would be no one in the area once darkness came. They made sure that there were no people in the area as they crossed the road and made their way to the wall surrounding the property. The moon was resting over the sea, providing just enough light for them to negotiate without a flashlight.

They stood in the shadow of the massive oak trees in front of the perimeter wall for moments while they assessed the best way to enter the house.

Eli scaled the wall that surrounded the property first and assisted Micah in climbing to the top. "Be careful jumping down. The last thing we want now is a sprained ankle."

They walked around the house and saw Stark seated in what appeared to be the living room. They lowered their bodies under the windows moving quickly and quietly crawled to the other side of the house. Eli took out a series of keys and prepared to enter the hallway through the double doors that led to the kitchen. Carefully he opened the door and motioned for Micah to enter. Once in the kitchen Eli said, "Stay here until I call for you."

Eli walked from the kitchen down the hallway toward the living room. Stark was having a brandy and listening to Mozart's opera *Der Fledermaus*. Stark heard footsteps. As he stood up a tall figure was facing him.

"Who are you and what do you want?"

"I am your conscience Gerhardt Stark. I have come to try you for your war crimes."

Eli pulled a pistol from his waistband and said, "Sit down. It is fine that you have music playing. That usually does not happen at a trial. Before we start is there anything you want to say?"

"Was it you sending me those messages?"

"Yes, but I was merely the postmaster. The witness and source of most of the information about you will be revealed in the next few minutes. Is there anything else that you wish to say?"

"I have friends in high places. If you kill me, you will be hunted and eventually caught."

"How nice of you to be concerned for my welfare. You don't know me but you have had a lasting effect on the life of my family. My father, Abraham, and my mother, Rachael, as well as my sisters Muriel and Ann and my brothers Saul and Moishe were killed by you and your Nazi friends. I know that you were a part of the Einsatzgruppen as well as a key architect of Birkenau. Now take a long sip of your drink because you are about to receive a large shock."

Eli took a step back into the hallway and shouted, "Will the mystery guest please come out of the kitchen?"

Stark could not imagine who would appear. With that Micah walked into the living room. "Hello Gerhardt are you surprised to see me?"

Stark was dumbfounded. Micah said, "I have waited years for this day. Is there anything you want to say to me?"

Stark said nothing.

Micah continued, "I never knew that I could hate any human being but what you did to me and my parents has created a rage in me that torments my soul."

Stark finally spoke. "So, what do you want from me, an apology?"

Micah scornfully laughed. "An apology? For all the innocents that you directly and indirectly sent to their deaths? No Gerhardt, I want you to feel the terror that they felt in their last conscious moments of life."

"Do you honestly think you will get away with killing me?" Stark asked.

"Do you honestly think you will get away with killing my family?" Micah shouted.

Eli reached into his jacket pocket and pulled out a dart gun. He handed it to Micah and said, "Get up close and shoot for his arm. It will leave no real mark."

Before you die, you miserable bastard, it is good for you to know that we will not be caught," said Eli. "The dart in the gun will kill you but it is not traceable. It will appear that you died of a heart attack."

Micah took the gun in his hand and pointed it at Stark. "In the name of Isadore and Margret Goldstein, as well as Eli's loved ones and the countless souls you betrayed, I sentence you to death and eternal damnation."

Micha fired the gun and almost immediately Stark slumped over in the chair. Eli put his fingers on Stark's neck and said, "He is dead."

They lifted him out of the chair and carried him upstairs to his bedroom where they undressed him, put on his pajamas and placed him in his bed.

Micha said, "It will appear that he died of a heart attack in his sleep."

When they arrived back in Manhattan Eli brought Micah to his apartment. "Get some sleep. I will be back in two hours after I run an errand."

Eli parked the car in the local garage and took the bus to Beth Israel Hospital. He entered the Obstetrics floor and left a manila envelope for Dr. Esther Rosen at the nurse's station. After making her rounds she picked up the envelope and headed for her office. She opened it and there were two photographs of a will stating that the bulk of Georg Baum's estate was left to the Jewish Charity organization in New York and a separate sum for Beth Israel's new wing. The note said, "The gifts are now available because in the name of your parents and brothers, justice has been done. Shalom. Eli."

Esther took the photo of her parents and brothers on her desk into her hands. It was finally done and their deaths were avenged. She smiled, kissed the photo and uttered, "Now I know you will be at peace."

The End

The Architect of Auschwitz
Questions For Discussion

What did you like best about this book?

What scene did you find most difficult to read?

Should the author show Gerhardt's love for his wife and children?

Do you believe that Gerhardt would have become a Nazi if his father had lived?

Why didn't Gerhardt share with Frieda the reason for his meeting with Hitler?

Are there any valuable messages in the book worth sharing with others?

Are there any parallels to this story in the world today?

What other books did this remind you of?

Share a favorite quote from the book. Why did this quote stand out?

What feelings did this book evoke in you?

If you had the chance to ask the author of this book one question, what would it be?

Which character in the book would you most like to meet?

What do you think of the book's title? How does it relate to the book's contents?

What do you think the author's purpose was in writing this book? What ideas was he trying to get across?

Did this book seem realistic?

How well do you think the author built the world in the book?

Did the characters seem believable to you? Did they remind you of anyone?

> What did you already know about this book's subject before you read this book?
>
> What new things did you learn?

What questions do you still have?

What do you think about the author's research?

What aspects of the author's story could you most relate to?

Thank you for purchasing The Architect of Auschwitz.

I hope that it added at value and quality to your life. If so, I would appreciate it if you could share this book with your friends and family by posting a short review to Amazon, Facebook and Twitter.

I'd like to hear from you and hope that you could take some time to post.

Thank you,
S.J.Tagliareni

rovingleadership29@gmail.com